Sky

DATE			

WIND FROM AN ENEMY SKY

D'Arcy McNickle

Afterword by Louis Owens

University of New Mexico Press
Albuquerque

Library of Congress Cataloging-in-Publication Data

McNickle, D'Arcy, 1904-1977.
  Wind from an enemy sky/D'Arcy McNickle;
  afterword by Louis Owens.
       p.   cm.
  ISBN 0-8263-1100-8 (pbk.)
    1. Indians of North America—Fiction.   I. Title.
  PS3525.A2844W5   1988
  813'.52—dc 19   88-17575
                       CIP

1988 paperbound edition published by
University of New Mexico Press
by arrangement with Harper & Row.
Third printing, 1993

1

The Indian named Bull and his grandson took a walk into the mountains to look at a dam built in a cleft of rock, and what began as a walk became a journey into the world.

His relatives had been telling Bull that it would happen, the dam would be built and the water would be stopped.

Antoine, the grandson, a returned student, had read about it in the newspaper: "They are doing it, Grandfather. That's what it says."

"They can't stop water. Water just swallows everything and waits for more. That's the way with water."

Even so, the returned student said, "They been working a long time already. They got big machines up there."

"The big machines will just fall into the water and the water will still be hungry."

The returned student was letting his hair grow long again. It was long enough now to reach his mouth. Sometimes he chewed on the end of a braid, just to know it was there.

"They put big rocks in the water. Then they pour cement on top. The paper says that."

Bull was not so old that he had trouble seeing. Still, he squinted at the returned student and paused a moment. "Am I talking to you or to a piece of paper?"

When the dam had been finished at last and the local newspaper told about the great crowd that gathered to hear speeches, his relatives told Bull, "Go and see for yourself. They stopped the water."

Bull had let out a sound like a small rumble of thunder. "The water was there when the world began. What kind of fool would want to stop it!"

"Just go and see for yourself. We saw it and it made us sick."

He was named Bull—that was the English form of it. But the words men speak never pass from one language to another without some loss of flavor and ultimate meaning.

Bull, it was, the animal, but really something that was man and animal, and neither.

Everyone knew him thus, knew his massive, eroded face, his strongly jointed frame, his ponderous gaze when he considered a man and his words. He talked, though, in a lively, even lilting, voice, and that was an odd thing.

To the people who lived with him in his camp, and to others who encountered him, he had always been this man who "lives inside," as they said. Could such a man ever remember a time of smallness and softness, a time of being clasped to a woman's breast? Or led by the thin, warm hand of a grandfather? All this seemed not of his experience.

Men waited until he spoke, and spoke softly afterward. Children moved silently until they had passed his skin tepee. Women were here and there and never where they should be, so they moved quickly aside. He watched all this.

He looked large even when he walked in the woods, in a forest of ponderosa pine.

On this day he followed a trail that slanted upward on a mountainside. He passed from tree shadow into momentary sunlight and paused there. Looking down from the clearing, he could see the open valley far below, a white man's world. A world he sometimes passed through, but never visited. In a time not long ago, he would have seen a stream break clear from the foothill below him and swing in a slow curve westward to spill itself in a river—a river, they said, which pushed through the mountains until it opened itself to a great sea of water. He could see even from where he stood that the stream was dry. The gravels and sands of its course had the look of bleached bones. So it was true, what his kinsmen had been telling him. They had killed the water.

The silent man saw it all quickly, then turned again to the slanting trail up the mountainside.

It was not necessary to motion to the grandson who followed, a coming-man who walked under a large black hat. Like the man ahead he carried a rifle, an ancient .22 caliber single-shot, which he found excellent for picking a ruffled grouse off a high limb. The face that stared from under the hat was grave and watchful.

The boy was aware of his excitement, a deep thing that pulled at his breathing and charged his coltish legs with uncertain motion. The excitement had been growing inside ever since he returned from the government's boarding school and could throw away the government's uniform and not awaken to a bugle call and not march around a parade ground. It was good to eat at home, in one of the lodges that formed the cluster of his grandfather's camp. He could ride a horse, as before. He could go for fish, hunt with his one-shot rifle. It was almost as if the government school had never been— except for some hours in the night when he awakened himself by crying out. If others heard, they never shamed him by asking about it.

In the pleasure of being part of the camp, he joined the dancers in the midsummer ceremony. No one spoke to him about it. But when the people gathered at the dancing ground, he went to his uncle Jerome's lodge in the camp circle and said he would dance. The women thanked him elaborately and smiled and called him a man. They opened their rawhide bags and sorted out bits of beaded and feathered costume and strings of bells to make him ready. A small girl with fat cheeks and a dirty nose squinted at him through her fingers when he took off the government's underwear and tied his breechcloth in place.

His mother's brother, the tall, thin Jerome, made a place for him on the dancers' bench and moved into the dancing circle with measured, deliberate steps. Jerome never said "Watch me!" but he made it easy to follow his style. The first three nights the dancers stopped at midnight. It was an old order, handed down from government men of long ago, and no one questioned it anymore. The tribal police officer spent the first three nights on the dance ground, but on the fourth night he always received a message telling of serious trouble in another district. Then the dancing continued until dawn, as was proper.

The excitement, the deep excitement, began for Antoine on that last night. He went to the dancing circle after dark, as on other nights. He had already danced all afternoon, and for three days before that, and his legs were numbed beyond pain. Sometimes it was as if he had just an upper body, without legs, and he would look at himself with surprise. And when they rested between dances, he worried that he might not be able to rise. The legs no longer belonged to him.

When he reached the circle that night, he looked for his place at Jerome's side. But his uncle had moved and had not made a place for him. He stood there, lost and tired, and ashamed. His uncle did not want to be troubled with him any longer. And then a hand fell heavily on his shoulder and moved him to the bench. His grandfather, standing tall above him, had accepted him.

When the drumming started, the great Bull moved out carefully, giving the boy a chance to pick up his step and follow close behind.

Antoine danced into the dawn, feeling no numbness, no fatigue, a great excitement burning inside.

Now they were together every day, great man and small boy. Bull never said much on the trail or when they rested on a warm hillside. But even without words, to travel with a man like his grandfather was to learn much. You watched how his moccasins met the ground and you found it very tiring. The foot never struck the loose pebbles, always avoided the dry twig. You followed the example, but you lost your balance, crashed into a bush, scattered stones. After a while, from far ahead, the grandfather would stop and watch the floundering one.

"A good thing we aren't hunting today."

A big man like that could show a very small smile.

Antoine's face under the large black hat was grave and watchful. The shadowed eyes burned with a reverent excitement.

The mountain slope stiffened and narrowed to a vaulting ridge, and the canyon below deepened. The tops of the spruce trees growing up from the bottom just barely reached the sunlight.

There should have been a great roar of tumbling water and mist plumes rising from the chasm, but only the quieter sound of needled trees straining the wind rode the ascending air. Man and boy stood listening, as if they might yet hear the greater sound. It was truly lost, and they turned away.

Bull took the steeper climb as easily as he had walked on level ground. They were now among shattered boulders, stunted timber, and storm-blasted snags. They crossed a massive rock-slide, a place of perilous snow-slides in winter. The blackened rock mirrored the sun in hot flashes.

Above them, the bright green of aspen marked moisture-seepage from a glacier that hung in a cleft of high rocks. Soon they would be at the top of the climb. The boy's ribs pounded and his mouth had gone dry. His leg muscles were cramping with pain. When he looked ahead and saw that his grandfather was already disappearing in the aspen grove, he almost broke into sobs. The cherished excitement of the summer dance almost died right there. But then the ground leveled off and he caught his breath and was proud again.

Beyond the aspen grove the mountains opened to form a wide basin. Sharp crags and granite cliffs hung upon it on three sides, and in the far wall a ribbon of white water spouted from a perpetual snowfield.

It had been a holy place, this mountain-locked meadow. "Be careful what you do here," the boy had been told by his relatives. "This is a place of power. Be careful what you think. Keep your thoughts good." He was just old enough to walk by himself on that first visit, and it was important that he begin to understand the proper way to behave. "Don't have angry thoughts here," he was told.

When the boy caught up, Bull was standing spread-legged on a bare rock outcrop. His rifle hung loosely in his right hand. He was looking down into the canyon. Here it was narrow and rockbound. The only trees were stunted junipers, sprouting from the rock itself. The boy had to climb all the way up before he could see what his grandfather was staring at in such astonishment.

What they saw, man and boy, was beyond belief. They looked at it, just there below their feet, and could not believe what they saw.

Bull talked, more to himself than to the boy, and as he talked the boy watched the shadows grow deeper in his face. The boy began to tremble.

"I said my kinsmen were foolish, talking about stopping the water. I made them stop talking about it. Why didn't I come and see for myself, instead of trying to make them feel small?

"How can a man do this?" He raised his head and stared at the far-away ribbon of white water leaping down the high rock from its glacial bed. That had not disappeared. The water tumbled its way over stony passages to the head of the forested basin—but the basin was no more. The place where anger was to be left out of men's thoughts was drowned.

A concrete dam had been driven into the opening of the canyon leading out of the mountain meadow. What had been forest and grass where big-eared deer stared in wonder was now a body of purple black water.

When he looked back to the dam below him, Bull saw that a canal had been cut into the mountainside just below the dam. The water leaped and roared as it came from a dark hole, swirled wildly for a while, then calmly flowed away through the big ditch. That was how they killed the canyon stream.

The shadows were now deep in Bull's face, and burning lights seemed to dance in his eyes. The boy watched, knowing that something would happen.

Bull looked down at the gun in his right hand, as if

6

he had just become aware of the weight of it. He raised it slightly and stared at it. What could a gun do? What could a man do, against that thing down there? Then he worked the lever and pumped a cartridge into the chamber. No need to hurry it. What was down there was not going to run away. He raised the gun waist-high and fired into the concrete dam. Once. Twice. Nothing moved. It wasn't far down there—three hundred yards. Not even a flash of a splinter. If the lead-nosed bullet smacked against the structure, no one heard it. The sound of whining machinery and the thunder of water even smothered the bark of the gun.

The boy Antoine saw this happen in bright sunshine, and while he could not understand all of it, he knew how terrible it was. A man alone, with bare hands and a gun. And the man was his grandfather. He could not look at him. He kept his head down and heard his grandfather's breath come in bursts from his throat. What would happen? In this place, where one had been told not to have angry thoughts? Would he throw his gun at the white man's dam? Would he leap down there and tear it with his fists? Yes, it was a terrible thing to witness. If he had seen a hole, he would have crawled into it, just so his grandfather would not have to show himself before anyone.

Then the angry words came, almost shouted: "I am a man walking this earth! Who is this creature who built that thing of rock and stopped the water? Is he two-legged like other men? Or is he a monster first-man, who decides things in his own way? Why should he do this to me? I have not offended him. How could I, when I don't know his name?"

He stopped then. He had seen his grandson and saw his eyes bright with fear. And his own eyes no longer bulged.

"But he has done it just the same, Grandson. He has done it. Come, let's think about that."

That was all he said. He turned away from the unbelievable thing and started down the mountainside.

Antoine found himself running part of the time. He tried not to be left behind, but he was fearful of coming too close. His grandfather was certainly going to find the two-legged man, and when he did, who could stand against such great anger! Man or beast, he would be cut down in his tracks. The ground would be black with blood.

He slowed his pursuit. It might be better not to see it. His grandfather would not want anyone around. His knife would flash in the air! He would pound and slash! Such towering anger!

The man ahead disappeared in a wooded area, and the boy, alone, felt a different kind of terror, alone on the big mountain. It waited behind rocks, behind trees. It was in the sudden chatter of a pine squirrel. In the cry of a jay. He ran as hard as he could, scattering stones. A pine bough whipped his face and brought water to his eyes.

When he saw the big man again, he slowed to a walk. Boys were scolded for running when they should move quietly. On a mountain trail, one watched what was ahead and at each side. A hunter who ran noisily never saw anything.

Now they were down where the ridge broadened and the slope was more gentle. Familiar country again, where he often hunted for grouse and squirrels in the tall pines. Soon they would be back in camp.

Antoine walked quietly now, but rapidly, eyes to the trail. And because he was careful about his feet and forgot to look ahead, he almost collided with his grandfather, who waited at a turn. The old man put out his hand and caught the boy by the shoulder.

"Grandson, when a man goes anyplace, whether to hunt or to visit relatives, he should think about the things he sees, or maybe the words somebody speaks to him. He asks himself, What did I learn from this? What should I remember? Now, I will ask, What did you see today? We will sit here, and you tell me what you saw."

The boy sat in the trail with his legs tucked under. "What do you mean, Grandfather? I saw the mountains, rocks, big trees. I looked down the canyon where the trees looked small, because it was so far down there. I saw just one rabbit, but it was already jumping behind some bushes. What else, Grandfather?"

"I could tell you some things maybe you didn't see. The stray buck we followed on our way up—but I guess you want me to say what I mean. Maybe you think I don't want to talk about it. You heard me speak angrily, up there, in a sacred place. It frightened you."

"I thought you would throw your gun, and it might break on the rocks."

"That isn't what frightened you. I am a big man. I have always been called so. They gave me my name, Bull, because they said I was strong even as a boy, growing up. But when we saw how the white man built that place in the rocks and stopped our water, turned it away, I was not a big man. I fired my gun—a puff of smoke. You were frightened because I could do nothing. Is that what you learned today?"

"No-o. I was thinking, if you found that white man, he wouldn't be so big. You'd shoot him and cut off his head. The disciplinarian at the government's school tried to be a big man. He whipped us with a leather belt. But you could cut him to pieces. When I went to bed at night with a sore backside, I made pictures in my mind. I saw you take his whip away and knock him down. It made my hurt go away. His name was Mr. Monroe, but they called him the disciplinarian."

Of course, there was no such word in his language, but Antoine made it come out right by calling him "man with one long arm"—that is, man with a whip in his hand.

"Just the same, you will remember what happened today. After a while, you will understand it. The white man makes us forget our holy places. He makes us small."

His hand dropped from the boy's head, then he started down the trail again. Antoine hurried to catch up, scattering stones.

2

In Bull's camp, meals were eaten when anyone was hungry. Fires burned somewhere in camp and a hungry person went to the household where food was in a pot.

The camp was built just where a small but noisy stream emerged from the pine forest. The timber approached on three sides, opening on a rolling meadow where horses grazed. The tepees and a cabin were placed at the head of the meadow. A hill rose sharply behind the camp and ran upward toward the mountains. Here Bull lived with his two wives, his sons and daughters and their married partners and children, and other households of his own generation. The camp had been in the same general location since a time before the Little Elk Reservation was created, and there it would remain. The government men, coming in succession to superintend the affairs of the Little Elk Indians, used to visit his camp and try to persuade him to move where the soil was deeper and less rocky, away from the hills. His answers grew shorter and sharper, until they stopped coming. He had grazing for his horses and for a few head of cattle. Firewood for the women. Sweet water. Let others worry about lands suited to plowing.

The only eating time Bull cared about was the evening meal, which the women served in his tepee. He shared it with never fewer than a dozen men and older boys. In summer there was no fire inside the tepee, and light was given by a lantern hanging from a lodge pole. The canvas covering was rolled up several feet from the ground to allow the air to circulate. The camp dogs waited just beyond the circle of eating men.

Bull sat at the head of the circle, opposite the entrance, where recently he had made a place at his side for his grandson, home from school. He said nothing to the camp, but everybody talked about it and it pleased them. The boy would grow up to be a leader.

Meat was brought in, roasted or boiled, in a large basin. Each man reached forward with his knife and speared what he wanted. Fried bread was piled in the center, with a pot of coffee. Each man speared his own bread and filled his own cup. Nothing was passed unless it was called for. Sometimes the women would boil potatoes or even turnips with the meat, but the men pushed these aside or threw them to the dogs. A dog would catch a potato before it hit the ground, then drop it and wipe the taste away with its tongue.

For Antoine, it wasn't always a good thing to be sitting next to his grandfather. Sometimes the big man asked him a question, or directed attention to him by telling what he did. Antoine then tried to make himself small.

And his two great-uncles (in his language, they were also grandfathers), Basil and Louis, each in a different way, found ways to make him small.

Basil was tall and emaciated, but a prodigious eater. He had a pleasant, chattering voice, womanish in pitch, which he used in a teasing way to remark on how much his grandson could eat and what a big belly he would have one day.

Louis was small, dainty, and bitter-speaking. It seemed to be his duty to scold at everything. His grandson slept too late in the morning; he never went for the horses; he spent too much time in camp instead of running and building his strength, and someday he would regret it.

Yes, in some ways it was better when he sat in the shadows at the bottom of the circle, where the young men kept up a murmur of their own and played jokes on each other. When the food gave out in the main dish, they could slip away to the cooking pots and get their own. To sit at the top was to be among men.

Most often he was rescued from confusion by the oldest man in camp, Two Sleeps, who sat halfway down the north side of the circle. This old man was not related to Bull nor to anyone in the tribe—still, he was also called Grandfather. He had been a member of the camp for as long as anyone could remember. It was said that he appeared out of a stormy night, almost naked, a fierce light burning in his eyes that frightened the men of a hunting party which had just crossed the mountains on its way to the buffalo country. Some wanted to kill him right there, others wanted to chase him away. Before anyone could touch him, he fell down just next to the fire and they let him lie. After a while, somebody threw a blanket over him. He would rise up and talk, but they thought he was in a dream state, since they could not understand his words. Then he used signs, and they made out that he was telling them of a big buffalo herd beyond the next ridge. When they went there the next day, they found a very large herd sheltering from the storm. They killed all the meat they needed right there. They decided he was a diviner by dreams, a holy man, and they brought him back with them.

Antoine thought of this story many times as he watched the old man. The strands of his white hair were never braided or tied back, but hung about his shoulders like a tattered shawl. He was not at all blind, though his watery eyes floating in loose skin often looked sightless. He had a small, thin face and he always looked as if he would begin to smile at any minute.

"This boy," he said, and stabbed the air with a thin finger, "will have power. But he must be left to find it for himself. Don't scold him. Give him his head, like a young horse, and let him test things out. You'll see. We have made a good choice in this one."

Bull looked at the boy, chewing and considering. "Just now, his feet are too big," he said. "When he grows up to his feet he'll be all right on the trail."

"In good time," Two Sleeps insisted. "Everything has a young stage, but after a while you ask yourself, was this man, this powerful person, ever a child who had to learn things from the beginning?"

Louis, the scold, coughed sharply. "Just the same, a child is not a tree that will grow by itself. You can't stick him out in the sun and wait for it to happen. A little

12

scolding, a little pushing and pinching, a little hunger and thirst—these make a boy grow."

"Hunger and thirst—" Basil, the eater, caught at the words. "Starving a boy is no way to make him grow. Look at me. I starved all that winter when the big river froze over. We ate nothing but bark. Sometimes we boiled it, but it didn't help. It just made me go to the bushes oftener, when I already had nothing inside— nothing that could say, 'Look at me! I've been through a man!' Oh, I mourned for my insides all that winter! I was this boy's age. I never got over it. My advice is to fatten him while he's young. He'll run it off later."

"My brother has a long gut, but he can't make up for a winter that visited us fifty years ago," said Louis.

Bull looked at the boy. "Antoine, these old men can't make up their minds. Eat what you like, when you feel like it. Now, my brothers. Let's talk about other matters.

"I took my grandson up the canyon today. We climbed all the way up there, where the people used to gather for the summer dance. We stopped doing that dance, and then we stopped going there, unless somebody went to hunt or to gather huckleberries.

"Then we heard the white men were going to stop our stream. They were going to take the water away from there and give it to the farmers out on the flats. Somebody told me that, and I said it was foolish talk. Who would kill a stream? Dry it up? I said that. I remember it.

"But the word kept coming to us, every year, it seemed. And finally we were told they would really do it. A man was coming from east of the mountains, and he would do it. He would take a shovel and dig a hole in the ground.

"It seemed so foolish. I just laughed. You wanted me to go and stop that man. You wanted me to make speeches. I said, 'Very well, go and make your speeches. If you can stop a white man with a speech, make it a good one. You can come tell me about it afterward.' "

He was smiling as he talked, but the men knew it

was not a real smile. It was the look of a man who has his rope on a wild horse, or who rises from the concealment of his pit and grabs an eagle above the claws.

"I was the one who told you, and I was the one who went to talk." Louis looked pained to remember it. "And now I suppose you found out for yourself it wasn't foolish talk."

"That's what I found out today. I walked up there with my grandson, and we both saw it."

"We tried to tell you, but you wouldn't talk about it. Were you afraid?"

Bull held back for just a moment, then admitted the fault.

"Yes, I was afraid. How can a stream out of the mountains be killed? Will they open the earth and drop us in it? Will they take the sun out of the sky? It was bad for us when they came with guns. Now they will kill us in other ways.

"Old man, what can we do against these men who dry up a stream and make new rivers where none were meant to be?"

Two Sleeps was not sleeping, though he sat hunched forward and had not stirred for some time. He talked without lifting his head and his voice just managed to reach across the space.

"Something will come, like a shadow on the ground when a bird flies under the sun. I saw the shadow, but not the bird. It will come."

Louis interrupted. "That crazy old man! You can't get answers from him. Why do you listen?"

"My brother, I don't want your scolding tongue," Bull put up his hand. "He is telling us something. You don't have to listen, if you feel that way. Nobody is holding you here."

"I will stay and listen to his childish riddles." Louis poured tobacco from a little sack into a brown paper and rolled a neat cigarette. "If you want my advice after you hear his backward talk, I'll be here to give it."

"Go ahead, Grandfather. I want to hear about this bird. How will it help us?" He turned away from the bitter Louis.

14

The old man was packing his old long-stemmed pipe. He removed the stem and blew through it to clear it. He kept his head tilted all that time.

"Listen!" he called.

Every head turned toward the entrance, and only Antoine sitting at his grandfather's side watched Two Sleeps. With the long willow pipestem at the corner of his mouth, he blew a short, hard blast upward.

No one heard what he seemed to hear. But a strange thing happened. While everyone looked away, the lantern, lashed to a tepee pole by a buckskin thong, began to sway. The night air was still, yet the lantern moved and the light faltered and the shadowed faces in the circle seemed to move, though no man stirred.

Antoine had seen it and his heart leaped when Two Sleeps caught him looking. The boy glanced aside and pressed hard on his lips.

"Listen," the old man repeated, more insistently.

Then they heard it. A man's voice, singing. The voice was coming from below, from the trail that led to the camp.

It was an old way of telling a camp at night that a friend was approaching. An enemy came silently, but when a man came singing, everybody knew what to expect.

"This man..," Two Sleeps began to explain.

The men looked at each other, at the swinging lantern, then toward the tepee entrance, as if someone might appear at any moment.

"He's coming up the trail now. Now he's at the meadow. I want to tell you this: he is coming to talk about something that troubles us more deeply than the water in the canyon. It has troubled us for a long time, even when we don't talk about it. Be good to this man. He comes with a heavy heart. Hear him to the end."

The young men who sat near the entrance had already disappeared. The camp dogs had started an uproar down in the meadow. Then suddenly they were silent. Thudding sounds, sharp cries, and the dogs went padding into the timber. Bull looked at Two Sleeps, but held back his question.

The rider tied his horse to a little fir tree just beyond the glow of the burned-down cooking fires. He crossed behind the huddle of women. A sharp cry of surprise, hurried whispers. Then he stooped to the tepee entrance.

When they saw the tall, bent figure pausing there, the men inside, all but one, exploded in sounds of surprise verging on anger. They pulled themselves straight, knowing they had been tricked. No wonder Two Sleeps had asked them to be good to this man!

The voice at the entranceway was thin and high pitched. The face from which the voice came was drawn in the dim light.

"Peace in this camp. I ask to sit with you."

The proper response, "Peace to you," was a faint effort, just audible. Why should they be speaking of peace?

"I come to talk to my younger brother. But I don't hear him speak."

The others waited. It had been put to Bull to show them how to deal with this unwanted visitor out of the night. They began to realize that Two Sleeps had somehow managed this, but he only puffed at his pipe and gazed at the ground.

There were years to cover, years to live again, and the man at the top of the circle was going through it from the beginning. It was a long, harsh silence before he inclined his head upward.

"I haven't asked you to come, so I don't know why you are here, Elder Brother." The mocking tone gave his voice unusual sharpness. "Here is my grandson's seat. Perhaps he will make room for you."

None of the men was asked to make room—it was a suitable concession.

Antoine reached for the grasping hand, realizing that the thin old man was having trouble seeing his way. And when he touched the hand an unexpected flow of warmth and strength pulled at him. One learned to know a kinsman's hand. He looked down at the frail, high veins. After he had guided the visitor to the seat

16

he had occupied, he moved himself back against the tepee wall.

Then they waited, as custom would have it.

The newcomer pulled himself up at last. "You're not happy to see me here. Each of you says it in your silence. I would not be here either, except for certain things I will tell you. But I know well, Henry Jim has no place in this circle."

A man who speaks his own name is one who asks no favors for himself—he speaks out of weakness and shame and expects insults, if any should come. Under the wide-brimmed black hat, it was impossible to see the visitor's face, now that he was seated, but the voice came strong and calm. He talked without hurrying, as if he never doubted that he would be heard.

"Brother, it is thirty years since I sat in your camp, or you in mine. I thought many times before this that I should come here. Finally, it could not wait any longer, as you'll see before I finish.

"Our quarrel was a strong one when it started. Quarrels between brothers should not harden, as ours did, but I can say at last that I was at fault. It took this many years, but I can say it.

"Now, I come not to ask you to forget the quarrel. I leave that to you. My thoughts are more with our people, and what will happen in years to come. When we were boys in our father's camp, this was our country, the country of the Little Elk people. We traveled in any direction, without hindrance. Across the mountains to the buffalo country. West to the salmon fishing. North to the big camas country. South to take horses. It was our country.

"If we traveled out today as we did in those times, we'd be stopped by a fence, or a railroad, or a highway, all fenced. We'd find a white man's house, maybe a town of many houses, at the very places we camped, by a good stream. We couldn't get firewood or water, unless a white man opened his gate for us. That's how it is now."

When a man pauses in his talk, if he has talked well, the waiting circle will show encouragement by nodding heads, a confirming word. But no one responded while this old man gathered more words together. He meant to say what he came to say, and the others only waited.

"Why did we quarrel, Brother? Was it because you were chosen by the leaders to follow our father as principal chief, when I, the first son, had the first right? Many said so. Was it because I took from the grandmother's lodge the strongest of our medicine bundles, Feather Boy's own bundle, and gave it to the dog-faced man? Many said that was the beginning of our quarrel.

"These things happened, and we all know them. But they were not at the bottom. You and I know how it was. We were traveling on different trails and eating at different camps before these other things happened. I went to the white man, I spoke for him. I opened the gate and let him come in. I helped him build his own fences. You were younger, but you saw all this, and spoke against it.

"Because of your speaking out, they named you leader. That was when I tried to take away your power. It pleased me then. I moved away from our camp in the mountains and built a white man's house in the flats. They gave me a wagon, a team and harness, and a plow. I took our medicine bundle and gave it to the dog-faced man. All these years, I lived there in the flats.

"That's what we know together, Brother. Our quarrel went to early things and cut deeper every day.

"The fences are here, now, and our country is smaller —we have only what they left us. But that's not what I came to say, traveling in the night.

"My talk is this: Let's bring back our medicine, our power. Let's bring Feather Boy back to this country, to protect it for our children."

Here the words stopped. The speaker was again a shrunken, bent-over figure as he pushed himself back from the circle of light.

Antoine, the grandson, retreated farther against the canvas wall, into deeper shadow. He held in his breath. The young men had left their places near the entrance and disappeared into the night, and Antoine wanted to follow. It was not good to listen to "hard" talk, when

18

older men turned querulous. They might be shamed if they talked foolishly in the presence of their children. What was not heard was never said.

But he hesitated. Perhaps his grandfather wanted him there, to be among men. Terrifying things would yet be said, and it was meant that he should hear it all. Bull was only waiting to destroy with words, and Antoine was to be among the men who passed judgment. Was that the meaning?

The boy still felt in his fingers the warm hand that had reached for his. The gentle voice, the sorrowing face were held in his mind. No one talked about this night visitor—Antoine had known only his name until this encounter. Even a kinsman could be despised. But when such a man became a touch of warm flesh, a faltering voice, then you had to hold on to him. You could not throw him away. He did not want to be among those to pass judgment. He pulled back into the shadows and waited.

They all looked to Bull, who sat speechless, staring across the circle. His heavy, eroded face, framed by two thin side-braids, seemed to be all of one depth, with no deeper shadows. After some minutes, he looked at his hands, lying palms up across his knees.

"You gave our power to a white man. I guess you know how to get it back. I never learned how to talk to a white man. So why do you come to me and to my camp? Just bring it back here; then maybe we can talk."

The stirrings in the circle, the gutturals and deep exhalations, signaled approval. This man who made the trouble, let him show what he could do. It was a good answer. Not a destroying answer, but a man's voice speaking without hiding anything.

The old man pushed forward into the light.

"You speak from anger, as I expected. I came without warning, without consent. A man needs time to think over what he will say, what he will do. I gave you no time, because my time is going. That's how it is, Brother. The grass is speaking to me. The wind is pulling at my shadow. And I have little time left. That's why I came, without consent."

Breaths were caught sharply. Now they saw why this old man was willing to bow his head to their anger.

In his cave of shadow Antoine saw the faces lift and he felt his own throat close hard. Again he wanted to run, but again he stayed.

Bull stared, his lips parted for speech, but he could not yet bring himself to it. A hard center in his mind resisted. How could he push aside thirty years as if they had never troubled him or the people who stayed with him in their foothill camps and went hungry with him because he would not lead them down to the flats where they could have had government wagons and teams, flour and coffee, fence posts? Perhaps the thirty years had not been good to this man either. There was a sadness in his voice. An absence of anger. One could not say. . . .

Two Sleeps, the holy man, saw the trouble. He could speak and not shame anyone, since he came from the outside and no one was responsible for him. If they liked what he said and accepted it, he could not claim it later. And if they rejected his advice, he could not be offended. So he had liberty to speak in any council.

"We are like the children who sometimes got left behind when the camp moved too soon. Sometimes those children were stolen, and never found their way back. We are those children, in a strange camp. We have to live fenced in and pushed together. This man is telling us how to find our way back to our people, how to live with power in our thoughts. I knew he would speak of these things. We must listen. . ."

"How could you know what he would say, old know-it-all?" Louis demanded. "It's easy to say where the horses were, after somebody finds them."

"How did I know, bitter mouth? By listening to my grandfather, the badger. And to my aunt, the bluebird. When a light flickers, when a star falls, we know death will come for somebody. And we saw the lantern move tonight. But I have a simpler answer. People have been coming to me to tell me that this man was traveling everywhere and would come here, to make peace with this camp. That is how I know, bitter mouth."

Bull swung his arm forward to brush away such talk. In his own mind he had come to decision, and bad talk had no place in it.

"Grandson, we haven't offered food to my brother, and we sit here talking as if that didn't matter. Tell the women to bring meat and coffee."

A tightness went from the camp's breathing. A hardness went from watching eyes. . . .

Bull turned to the older man. "It is true, as you say, that the leaders of that time chose me to succeed our father. I didn't want it, because I thought it should go to you, the elder son. Also, I didn't know how one could be a leader in those days. They said we had to stay on the reservation, so what could a leader of the people do? I couldn't help anybody. A chief is expected to take care of the people. When someone is hungry, he shares what he has. He steps in between when they are quarreling. But there we were, with fences around us. We couldn't send out hunting parties, and I had nothing to share. We just sat there and quarreled among ourselves—and there were too many quarrels for me to settle. I myself quarreled, with the government people, with the white ranchers."

He looked away, bent his head to one side, thinking back. "The leaders made me chief, but the people went to you. For you had gone to the white man and you learned his ways. The people tried to keep it from me, but I knew when they slipped away to get grain and hay for their cattle, even food for their families. That was when it hurt, Brother. Word came back from the government men, saying you were leading the people on the new path. Every time I heard that, I went to the mountains to fast. But visions never come to an angry man.

"That's how it was. I never expected you to come to this camp. If that old man there hadn't played a trick on us tonight, I would have sent you away. He made us think a strange thing would happen—but what was strange was that you came, and before we knew what to say you were sitting here. And now I think I can see the rest of the trick: That old man told you to come. . . ."

Henry Jim had removed his hat when he started to

eat. Now they saw a quick smile brush his face, like a flashing wing.

Bull had not finished. "How many times have I promised to throw that old man out! He tricks us, shames us, and scolds us into doing his wishes!"

His kinsmen were all watching Bull now, not staring in an unseemly way, but with lifted heads and listening minds. He was speaking gently, even teasingly, as one might speak to a tender woman or to a child. It astonished them, knowing his anger of other years. And then they understood.

"You say you haven't many days left. I don't understand how you can know this. But I guess death talks to those he is ready to take. My mind will be heavy with this." He waved it away. "You didn't come to talk about this. You say, bring back the medicine bundle. How can we do that, when we don't know where it is or how to get it? Can we steal it? Pay money for it? Just tell me."

Henry Jim wiped his fingers tidily on his moccasin tops as he ate.

"I'll go to our new government man. He tells everybody he wants to be a good friend. I have already been there, not to talk about this. His door is always open, he says. So I will go and ask him to help. They will know from their books and papers, or this new man can talk to the dog-faced man and find out what happened."

When Bull's thoughts wandered, he would sing between his teeth, a far-away song, such as one might sing from a hilltop at daylight. He was doing this now as Louis began to speak.

"Brother, you have more hope than I have. You think this new man will tell you, if he knows? They laugh at those things. 'Big Indian,' they say, 'throw all that away! Cut your hair short! Put hard shoes on your feet!' For a while, when you talked, it sounded good. But when you say, 'talk to the government man,' it all falls down. Am I wrong?"

Louis, the hard talker, a small heap of yellow paper cigarette stubs on the ground before him, described in detail the faults of government men. Then he rolled a fresh cigarette, the crisp paper crackling in his dry hands.

"For my part, I won't have anything to do with men who despise my blood. If we have to go to this man and ask his help, we might as well relieve ourselves in the bushes and walk away."

Two Sleeps pushed this aside, answering Bull. "When a camp was short of food in winter and the hunters came back day after day, leg-tired and with pinched-in bellies, to listen to the crying of hungry children, whoever said, 'We'll just go squat in the bushes?' The men went out again, and they prayed along the way, and game came to them. A government man is no worse than a cold and hungry camp. But do we pray in the morning light? Do we keep going until we get our game?"

He looked across the circle to the calm old man, still slowly eating. "Our leader is not wrong. He speaks of what he knows and the bad times we have shared in this camp. We had no help from down there, so he speaks a truth of his own."

And to Bull he said: "But our elder brother also speaks of what he knows. Perhaps he has eaten food with this government man. If he talks for us, the man will listen. He may agree to help. Who knows? It is better than sitting in camp."

Henry wiped his hands for the last time and pushed the dish away. "I will ask this man, I will start it. But after that. . ." He raised his hand halfway, then dropped it.

"You can see why I had to come tonight. Maybe I won't come again. That old man," he pointed his lips toward Two Sleeps, "promised that his young nephews would drive the dogs away when I arrived. How many days—who knows? The voices are around me, as in a dream I had long ago. I was no older than this grandson, and the voices came from all sides. Each blade of grass was singing, and the pine needles, the leaves of the willow and cottonwood. And the song said I would have many days, but watch for the time when the voices came again. After that the days would be few. They are starting now. That is all I know.

"So, I will start the talk, but who knows if I will be here when it ends? I came tonight to ask my brother's help. You are our headman, our chief. It will be up to you. Our people will thank you. They'll remember the old leaders who chose you, and they'll be thankful that you were the one."

Again he pushed back into shadow. He had said finally what he came to say.

The others looked to Bull, and a question hung between them. Would he have to leave his camp, to talk and travel with white men? He would never do it before —would he do it now?

But Bull did not speak of this. "Strange things have happened," he said. "I climbed the mountain with my grandson, and we found what others already knew, how the white man has turned our water away. It is hard to believe that anyone would do this. How can a man know what a stream wants to do? How can he decide this by himself?

"A man and woman fit to each other after they live together a long time—that is the way a stream fits itself to the earth. They have no secrets from each other. A stream has its life. It starts from many small springs and from the snows, it brings them all together. It flows over rocks, washing them smooth and round. It feeds small bushes and large trees. It provides for the needs of fish, muskrat and beaver, the kingfisher, and the little bugs that skip on the surface. Were the animals and the trees asked to give their consent to this death?

"I was angry when I came down the mountain. I wanted to find the man who built that dam. I wanted to cut his guts out and throw them in his face. I wanted him to answer my question.

"It was foolish anger, Indian anger. I couldn't even find such a man, and if I found him, he would laugh at me. My grandson saw it. He saw my weakness. He was frightened. He's a brave boy, but this frightened him.

"And now my elder brother comes to my camp. Let's bring back our old Indian power, he says. But he tells me we have to go to a white man to have what was ours returned to us. I don't want to say what I will do. One likes to think over something like that and not be foolish. That's how it is.

"As for my brother coming here, after all these years —I see now that it was not a big thing that stood between us. It was at first, but something was eating it away all the time. I thought it was there, like a mountain, but when I looked, it was gone. My brother did this for me, and I am thankful.

"It is a long ride down to the flats from here. I ask my brother to sleep with us and we can talk again tomorrow."

The talk ended there, and those who had been listening beyond the tepee walls, in the shadow, as well as those who sat within, went to their beds, some to sleep, and some to burn with foolish anger.

When the camp dogs settled down and quiet was everywhere, Antoine, home from school, looked beyond the raised tepee covering at a forest of stars. He had removed the large black hat, his grandfather's gift after the midsummer dance, but it was not far away. He had only to reach for it.

Sleep crept upon him, but he tried to hold his thoughts together. What had he learned? What should he carry in his mind from this night's long talk?

Sleep came closer, pulling his head down. The stars were beginning to blur in his eyes.

For a flashing moment, he saw and understood. It stood out clearly, like a burst of morning sun. Then sleep caught up and buried him in the night.

3

How to translate from one man's life to another's—that
is difficult. It is more difficult than translating a man's
name into another man's language.

Bull would frown when white men smiled as they
spoke his English name. It made him small, the way they
smiled, but he never found out how to answer the smilers.
They were just men with bad manners and he turned his
back on them.

Henry Jim from the first had tried to discover what
white men were saying, and what they meant beyond
the words they used—and that had been the difference
between him and his brother. He had studied these strange
men from beyond the mountains and the words of their
discourse ever since they came among his people.

He rode down from Bull's camp that day, riding his
big bay gelding, and reined in at the hitching rack outside the gate opening into the compound of the Little Elk
Indian Agency, which had been built years before on a
site where the Little Elk Indians had once wintered with
smallpox and ever after had shunned. In his first years of
visiting government men at the agency, he had tried to
understand why they would choose such a site for a
common meeting ground. Even when he explained what
had happened there, the men paid no attention.

Henry Jim had his vantage point from which to watch
and wait. From under the brim of his wide black hat, if
he kept the edge just level with his eyes, he could watch
the hands of the man at the desk—thick, red-whiskered
hands, with blunt fingers moving among papers—and
try to decide what manner of man he was, this new government man, who talked quietly, smiled, and said he
wanted to be a friend. By tilting the black hat just slightly,
he could watch the round face, which was shaved, and

the red hair which came out only on top of his head and in little tufts out of his ears. When this man smiled hard, his eyes squeezed tight until the blue light disappeared. Henry Jim right away noticed one good sign in this man. He did not insist on talking at once, or all the time. He sat at his desk, moving papers around, writing on a piece of paper, and now and then he looked up, not impatiently. He was just waiting.

The Indian tilted his hat still higher, until his face was in full view of the man at the desk.

"You said your door was open. So I came to see you."

The old man said it every time he came to call, and Toby Rafferty, superintendent of Little Elk Indian Agency and Special Disbursing Agent—the regal title—always acknowledged the truth of it. It was developing into a formalized social gambit.

"Any time at all, Henry. My door is always open to the Indians. To you especially. All my people respect you." Then the squeezed-eye smile.

This man spoke always with friendliness. His voice never went cold.

"This time I have to ask for something. I have to ask for help. . . ."

"Fire away, my good friend. That's why I'm here. I came more than three years ago, and nobody asks for help, not real help. Nickels and dimes, not real help, you understand?"

Henry Jim nodded. He thought he did. Sometimes the picture wasn't sharp, but it was there. He could say quite well in English some of the things in his own mind, and that was what he came for. He talked a long time that afternoon.

The shadows of the young trees in front spread across the green lawn, taking the reach of full grown trees. A water sprinkler swished and sparkled on the green lawn. Beyond the compound, the sandhills rose hot and barren and made a shimmering atmosphere which blurred the far mountains. Toby Rafferty felt the passing time as he watched the progress of events beyond his window and heard the voices of people coming and going beyond his office door, but he was surprised later when he realized how much time had passed. Not that it mattered. If people would not come to discuss their problems, at least he could listen when they came to talk. It might amount to the same thing in the end.

Henry carried him far back to the beginnings of the Little Elk people, where they lived at different times, where they hunted and fought battles, and wintered out. Where sickness struck their camps. Where a child had been lost from a camp and never found. Where they first met a party of white men, and what was said and done on each side.

It was not just an old story intended for the passing of an afternoon. As he had announced, he had come to ask for something—and a white man, a government man, might not understand the importance of the thing he asked unless the story was carried back to the beginnings. Today talks in yesterday's voice, the old people said. The white man must hear yesterday's voice.

When he finished at last and was ready to go, the man at the desk rose up and said what a government man always must say: "Henry, my friend, I'll have to look into this. I don't want to tell you I will help you and find out later I can't do anything about it. I'll try to find out what happened to your sacred tribal object, but whether I can get it back for you, that remains to be seen. I'm glad you told me about it. Believe me."

He held out his hand, and his eyes smiled.

Henry Jim knew the talk. He had heard it many times. He stood in front of the agency building, in the fading sun, and tried to tell himself that it was all right. He could remember so many times when he had come to the agency building and heard such words, and thought he understood. So many times when the understanding fell apart afterward. And the people in the camps laughed at him or were angry. How would it be this time?

It was so important this time—so much depended on a good understanding.

The men who had been huddled in the shade of one of the young trees when he first arrived were still there, but the shade had passed them by. Their inward-leaning bodies all but obscured the blanket around which they sat, playing pitch.

The players, looking up, saw Henry Jim under his wide black hat. His moccasins whispered on the cement walk.

"Enjoy your play, my kinsmen," he said.

"Keep well, Grandfather," they answered. When the People spoke his English name it came out "Henly Tzim."

He walked on, an old man's walk: short strides, the knees scarcely flexing. His horse was by itself, tied to the hitching rack just outside the entrance.

It was a big bay horse, high at the withers, with a broad chest and arching neck. It whickered softly at the old man's approach, took a dancing step when the halter rope was unfastened, then quietened and seemed to sidle closer. The rider grasped horn and cantle and strained upward. The horse quivered but never moved its feet.

A card player said, "Better help the old man."

Before anyone moved, the rider was in the saddle and the horse stepped off smartly, its hoofs bouncing lightly from the ground. The fine small ears were sharply erect.

The card player said, in English, "Son of a gun!" And then, in his own language, "Look at that old man! I thought he couldn't make it!"

Another said, "You don't know that horse or that old man. Put a stranger up there, he wouldn't stay a minute. But when the old man gets on—look! Like sitting in a white man's rocking chair."

All the way home, five miles from the agency, the sun plunging into the heavy air of the west, the big horse danced and blew out its nostrils.

And Henry Jim, riding into the sun, saw nothing of the roadside or the sandhills or the mountains beyond. His eyes were closed, keeping out the sun, keeping a vision within.

The song he sang was no more than a murmur, scarcely audible, yet cadenced and melodious. The horse caught it, the sharp ears turning like vanes.

The song was old, telling of a time when a boy listened eagerly for voices, wherever they might be, the voices of men, of the wind, of stars moving through the night.

A time when a boy came to a campfire and men were talking in the shadows, their voices rising to laughter, falling away before a drumbeat, coming strong again.

A time when the dawn lay in dampness on the prairie grass, and cooking fires were starting up, the smoke a blessing power.

A time when a grandfather explained the tracks along the trail, pointed out where the eagle nested, and showed how to cleanse the body in the sweat bath.

A time when the plover cried and the song of meadowlarks wove the world together.

And bitter times! When the belly hungered and quaked. When winter sickness came and people tumbled dazed out of their tepees. When quarrels rose to sharp, hard tones and children ran to their mothers' skirts. A gun spoke in firs and there was blood on a gooseberry bush. And the soldiers dragged guns over the road and turned them toward the people.

The song was without end in the mind of the old man on the horse.

After bitterness came times of confusion, when many changes came, with young people going against the old ones, and old people waiting only to die.

Men from a far country, from somewhere east of the mountains, came and said: "You must build fences. Four strands of barbed wire, stretched and stapled to cedar posts set sixteen feet apart. That's a legal fence and you can prosecute for trespass if anybody lets his stock in on you, if you have such a fence." The words were a marvel of obscurity, but in the days of the telling they seemed important. One cut the cedar posts and dug holes sixteen feet apart, carrying a measuring stick. A strange man brought the wire, and one built the fence.

Another man said: "This is small grain country. Plow up your sod and plant wheat and oats and you will do well." The sod was ripped apart and planted with little seeds, but one had no machine for cutting when the grain turned golden like the prairie grass. The man said

30

nothing about a machine and went away before the cutting time. But cattle and horses liked the golden grass and the snow beat it to the ground. The next year the little seeds grew again and one did not have to rip the earth. After a few years the prairie grass came back, but thinner.

And after that another man came and said this is potato country. And later a man came and said this is hay country. The words always seemed important, and the strangers were happy to see these things done.

The sun was gone, but still a burning brightness was in the west and halfway up the sky. The song was not finished. The horse's sharp ears still pivoted forward and back to catch the rise and fall of the muted voice.

A man said: "Dig a hole, then build a little house, back of your living house, out of sight of the road. There you can be private and sit in comfort, instead of squatting in the bushes. And your family will have less sickness." One dug a hole of the right size, built the little house. Only the woman did not care for it. She was living then; today she was in the rock-slide on the mountain where they carried her. She complained: "Why should this be? In the brush where I have always gone, I know what is above me, what is around me, what is below me. How can I tell what will be in that hole?"

The time of confusion was the hardest time. Kinship lines were broken. Children went against their own relatives. The people, left to themselves, could have saved themselves, as they had against days of hunger and winter sickness. But the new men, coming from across the mountains, set family against family, telling them to build legal fences, tear up the sod, build little houses. They only scattered the people, like quail rising from the grass. In earlier days men with hair on their faces also came from across the mountains, but they only wanted to trade blankets and guns for beaver skins. They always went away and nothing was changed. The people remembered them and had no hard feelings.

The burning light was gone from the west. Shadows no longer stood out alone, but a moving shadow came up from the earth itself and gently pushed hills and trees from view.

The bay horse, ears pricked forward, shifted strides and cantered softly. The road was soon at an end, and the song with it. The horse knew.

In the barnyard, Henry Jim eased himself to the ground. His legs stiffened these days, even after a short ride. His hands went quickly over the animal, feeling the sleek hide for sweat.

"I will let you drink, Red Son. First I will take this iron from your mouth. Then drink, but only a little. That is good—enough, greedy one! Now to your bed. A handful of oats, yes. Some fresh hay."

The old man paused, holding fast to the flowing black mane.

"It can't be much longer, my strong one, my red one. The dream is here, around me. It is around you also, Red Son. And I can't tell how it will be. The new man will help us, I think. I said it many times, when a new man came. Until my kinsmen laughed at me, and one threw me away in anger. But this time, certainly, we will have help. I saw it in his face. That's what I saw today."

The bay horse waited, not chewing, until the man passed his hand over withers and back. A pat on the rump. It whickered softly, then plunged its nose into the oat box.

As Henry Jim moved out into the open, the song was again on his breath. Telling of a time when the plover cried.

4

Toby Rafferty was a new man in Indian affairs. A reform wave in Washington had enticed him away from city social work and, after what was termed an orientation tour with the Bureau in Washington, he was assigned to Little Elk.

He did not conceive of himself as a reformer, but as a professionally trained person he felt a certain responsibility—which he disparaged by calling it curiosity—in responding to an invitation to enter a field that had eschewed professionalism. His appointment, and others made at the same time by the new administration, was announced as a repudiation of the military-political-missionary tradition that had prevailed in the past. He represented what was described as "the new settlement-house humanism."

Rafferty was aware of the tag that had been attached to his name, and he found it awkward in his associations with veteran Bureau employees. He could sense their watching him, measuring his words and actions, as they tried to decide in what ways "humanist" might differ from plain "human." It forced him into telling jokes, at which he was not very good.

Also, he realized after three years that whatever was to happen at Little Elk would not happen in a hurry. It would not be revolutionary—it might not even attain the stature of a reform. Though there was room for both.

After three years, Bull had not come down from his mountain camp. From reports of his predecessors Rafferty gathered that this had been the goal over quite a number of years; each new man assured his superiors that this was about to be accomplished.

Also, after three years, Indians who previously had taken up farming had not improved their crop yields—or paid off government loans. The midsummer dances, which required a period of preparation and a period of recuperation, and were followed by mass movements to neighboring reservations where similar dances seemed to get scheduled in succession, made a big hole in the summer months, just when white ranchers sweated in the sun and were calling for extra hands as they ran from task to task.

Toby Rafferty was a patient man, the Indians said, as they watched him from under the shadow of a hat brim or when he sat in their homes and listened while they explained why they butchered the milk cow for which they still owed the government money. But after three years, he was having disquieting thoughts about the role he was expected to play. He had pitched hay in the hot sun in upper New York State without discovering particular virtue in the occupation. Powwow dancing was no less strenuous, he surmised, after watching all one hot afternoon, but the people looked contented. They poured soda pop down their dusty throats and laughed among themselves—perhaps talking about their sweat-drenched white neighbors.

Such mental ramblings came to him more and more often, and left him wondering how he was to apply the "humanist" tag.

He occupied the smallest of the cottages, at the very edge of the fenced-in compound. Mindful of his bachelorhood, he had refused the eight-room superintendent's residence and assigned it to the farm supervisor with his swarming family, thus creating a procedural and status crisis that propelled ripples all the way to Washington. He offered to pay rent at the large-house rate and charge the farm supervisor the small-house rate—and that made the ripples bigger. That had happened within the first weeks of his installation, and the time since then had been taken up with employee requests for sick leave, recommendations for promotions and transfers, annual supply estimates, and the periodic changing of desk blotters. No ripples reached Washington from these intramural struggles.

Of the thirty-odd employees who lived in the agency compound, he could talk comfortably with only one, and this at times was a strain.

Edwards, the agency physician, was the oldest employee, in age and years of service. He knew most of the Indian families—their ailments, marital complications, feuds, and credibility. He knew Little Elk history and tradition, of which little had been written, and he quarreled with the few books that had been published. All of which, at times, made him pompous and irritating.

Rafferty saw him as a small, graying, but quick-moving man, full of crotchets and opinions, and devoted to the Indian people. His office record showed that he had refused repeatedly to accept a transfer to a larger station at an increase in salary.

After the long visit with Henry Jim, Rafferty felt a need to know a great deal more about the things that Henry had talked about.

As he said, "Nobody in Washington tells you about medicine bundles or culture heroes or folk ways. The emphasis in the instructions we get is on the mechanics of the job we are expected to do—as if these other things don't exist and won't get in the way of doing the job."

Up until that afternoon, Rafferty explained, he had seemed to be a spectator, assuring himself that what he saw passing before his eyes was what he might see in Marietta, Ohio, except that the river was missing, and of course some of the male subjects in the passing parade wore their hair in long braids. You'd never find out anything different if you confined yourself to the instructions. Just carry on as you would in Marietta, give guidance and leadership, and the people will respond.

"Guidance and leadership! When that old man talked this afternoon, I felt like a boy scout offering to guide a professional woodsman.

"I watch them, or go among them, shake hands, let them know I'm here. Naturally, I don't tell them my job is to do away with their 'nonproductive' dances—an expression used in the field circulars. If I could get hold of the circular-writer, I'd like to ask him, Nonproductive of what? For I suppose the dancers produce something, if it's only sweat. They wouldn't go on repeating if something didn't come from it—that's a guess on my part.

"Anyhow, I leave that subject alone when I make my rounds. I talk on the positive side: 'My friend, let me help you get some cattle,' or 'How about fixing up your house?' or 'Let's get that young son of yours off to school.' They smile at these suggestions, whatever they may be thinking. Nobody tells me to mind my business. They don't even remind me that this agency used to be pretty damned nasty about taking their kids away with or without parental consent. They smile, but they don't do anything about my suggestions. Nothing happens, which I suppose is the most eloquent kind of rebuttal.

"Then, today, comes this wonderful old man, the only Indian on the reservation who lives in a modern house, farms like a white man—even better than some—and is all paid up on his government loans. And he asks me to help bring back this old bundle, whatever it is—this old symbol. It's been gone twenty-five or thirty years, but he thinks the people should have it.

"Nobody in Marietta, Ohio, would make such a request—in Marietta, if it's like towns I know, they're trying to get away from the past."

"Well," Edwards rasped, "what did you tell him?"

"You can't answer these things right off."

"Why not?"

"Well, lots of reasons. What it is? How important is it? What happens if it comes back? Do we scrap all our ideas about improving their way of living, let them do a flip-flop back to the past?"

"You just said this is not Marietta, Ohio."

"Yeh, but the instructions say it is. If I go it on my own, I want to know what I'm doing."

"That's sensible. Go on."

Rafferty shifted in his chair. He began to feel his red hair prickle.

"Look. I haven't got this thought out. Don't press me."

"Sometimes I think you fellows expect these people to apologize."

"Apologize? What for?"

"For being redskins."

"That's the most ridiculous thing I've heard you say. But go on."

"Old Henry asked you something he considers important. After all these years of doing what the white man said was important, you have to stop and try to figure out whether he knows what he's doing. Don't you suppose he's already done a lot of thinking about it?"

As they talked on, tilting their chairs back from the railing of his cottage porch, half obscured behind the trellis of vines, the night deepened, and Rafferty felt an increasing irritation. Their cigar ends glowed and moved through the shadow, sometimes in impatient streaks.

"I'm trying to keep a sense of direction. Are we going forward or backward? Who's getting reformed? Why is it, after three years, nobody has accepted my offers of help? Why doesn't someone take me up on my offer to get him started in cattle?"

"That's a good question. Suppose someone should come along and ask you that, get him into the cattle business. Would you go right out and buy the cattle?"

"That would depend, of course."

"Depend on what?"

"Well—could he manage them? What experience? Would it be a good thing? I couldn't just give them away. He'd have to borrow from us, and we'd want to get our money back."

"As far as I'm concerned, you've answered your own question. These folks know you'll ask all those questions. You're the government man and you have to do it that way. They know they aren't up to that—they haven't decided they want to be. Being Indian is enough just now. They understand that. That's where they live."

"You say it's important, what Henry talked about. I suppose it is. Let's say it is. But where does it fit in? I wasn't sent here to rescue bits and pieces of the past."

The doctor's agitation had been growing, and as it

mounted he chewed his cigar until it was too mangled to draw. He threw it into the shrubbery to emphasize a point and hauled out his pipe.

"Nobody thought to put it into the instructions!"

"Bother the instructions! I told you they're meant for Marietta. But I have a commitment—to somebody. Maybe it's to myself. Maybe it's to the twentieth century. Otherwise, what am I doing here? I drew better pay where I was before, where everybody was scrambling to get on the fast express. If these people don't need what a white man has to offer, then we should all get out."

The doctor modulated his tone, turning almost placatory. "Now, now! Don't jump over the moon. I give you credit for trying to think your way along."

Rafferty winced, but the doctor could not observe the spasm in the dark.

"You wouldn't feel flattered if you'd seen some of your predecessors. Why, one fellow—but never mind. The fact is, Henry Jim has been watching you. They all have, be sure. If you've never hunted wild horses, you've no idea what these people are like. I haven't done it myself, understand, but I rode out with a group once and watched the pursuit at a comfortable distance. Their bodies are alive with sensory ends, just like those horses —always alert, always telegraphing warning signals. One unexpected move, and they're over the hill.

"If you want to bring these people around to ranching and farming, I suggest you start by taking this request seriously. If you can bring that medicine bundle back to the Hanging Mountain mother lodge, the rightful custodians, these people will be walking in your moccasin tracks, as they say. They'll be dirt farmers, sheepherders, grocery clerks, anything you ask—or they'll give it a try, just to keep face with you. White men just don't take them seriously, and there the matter ends, most of the time. If you can persuade an Indian you aren't laughing at him, you've got a friend. But I guess that applies in Tibet or Timbuktu—I know it does in my house, where my wife tries to practice it."

He knocked the ashes out of his pipe, wished a good night, and disappeared along the walk leading to his own cottage, where his mending-and-darning wife would look up and ask, "Have you been visiting with that nice Mr. Rafferty and telling him how to run this place?"

But for Rafferty, left to the shadows, something had been said at last—a clue, an intimation. Or, as he said with inward words, "Maybe I wasn't listening before."

5

Bull told his grandson, "I'm going to the pasture to get my horse. You stay and look after the camp for me."

It was then early morning, just when the sun should climb above the meadow, but rolling clouds moved across the sky and held back the day.

Antoine knew it was a joke, to be told to take care of the camp, but he also knew that Bull could have asked to have his horse brought to him. It meant that he wanted to be alone, and since he left his gun behind, hanging in its scabbard from a lodge pole, probably he was going some place to pray. He might be gone all day. Maybe all night. And he would come walking back, the way he left, forgetting his excuse about the horse.

Antoine then had to decide what he would do all that day. He had been with his grandfather so much since the summer, it was now a problem to be alone. He could join the younger boys in trying to lasso the camp dogs, who ran with their tails between their legs. He could take his single-shot gun and go hunting. But he decided just to sit in his grandfather's lodge. Since he had been left in charge, he should not be playing with children. And maybe they would bring his meat to him, as a man could expect.

He was sitting there, cleaning and oiling his old gun, when he heard his uncle on one side, Theobold, and his uncle on the other side, Pock Face, talking just beyond the tepee wall. These were the young men in camp always in trouble with their gambling and drinking, always being scolded by someone because they slept too much or ate too much or failed to show respect for their elders. But they laughed and played jokes on people, and usually it was exciting to be with them, unless you became the victim of one of their jokes.

He put his gun aside, thinking to join the two uncles, but he remembered again that he was told to watch the camp, and if he sat with them he would be just a boy listening to their funny talk. Worse than that, they might tease him. They might say, "Little chief, why are you sitting in camp? You should be out doing something for your people. That's what they expect of you."

He crawled to the wall and lifted the skin covering, just so he could see what they were doing. There they were, side by side, their backs against a thick fir tree. They had nothing to do, so they just talked.

They had nothing to talk about either, it seemed, except to say how sleepy they were, how tired they were. They had been some place where they played the stick game all night, and somebody had a whiskey bottle, and somebody was fighting. And next they were saying they were hungry, and one said, "Just go to the fire and bring me a pot of coffee," and the other said, "My legs won't carry me. Go bring me a bowl of stew and then I'll be all right." So they continued to lean against the tree, their hats tipped over their faces, and neither one would move.

They were an unpredictable pair, however, and, as everyone in camp liked to say, no one knew what they would do next. Usually Pock Face, son of Louis, was the leader. He was older, but neither was yet twenty-five. He was a good rider and followed local race meets and rodeos, and he could talk about horses like a white man. Also, he had a quick temper and was frequently brawling with other young men, and the milder Theobold, Basil's son, got involved in these affairs before he could get away. They were both tall and stringy and they wore cowboy boots and high-crowned hats which elevated them even more.

So it was Pock Face who sat up and pushed his hat back from his face. "Me, I'm going up to that canyon where they built the dam. I went there once when they were building it. I never thought about it again. Somebody said the old-timers used to go there all the time. But I didn't know why that was. I want to see it full of water. I want to look at it. Maybe I'll get mad at it, like the old man the other day. Only white people go there now. They put fish in there, just for the white people."

Theobold roused up. "It's too far to walk. Let's eat something."

Pock Face was on his feet, stretching. "Who said walk? I'll ride my horse until I come to the rocks. After that it's a short climb. I'll take my gun. Maybe I'll meet the man who built the dam, then—" He extended his arms in the manner of aiming a gun. "Pow! Right in the belly!" He laughed. It was a good thought.

"Me, I'm going to eat something." Theobold started for the cooking fire at Veronica's lodge. It was by then late morning and no other fire showed life. Pock Face had not asked him to come, but that was the way it always started. Pock Face said what he would do, and Theobold found himself agreeing to go along. This time it would be different. It was too far. It might turn cold. He needed more sleep. He didn't like what Pock Face said about carrying a gun.

Theobold began to laugh and the drowsiness went from his eyes. He turned to Pock Face, just coming to the fire.

"Our guns are gone! Last night. You played the stick game and lost everything. Your gun, then my gun. You were going to put up your saddle, but I hid it from you, and I made you stop before you put up your horse. I brought you the whiskey and you forgot it."

Pock Face ignored this and set up an outcry. "Old woman! Some food! This pot is empty. I'm a starving man. Never mind. I'll take somebody's gun, and when I find the man who built the dam I'll shoot him in the belly. The old man will thank me."

Veronica, Bull's first wife, a small woman without fear, came to the opening of her tepee.

"Get away from my pot, you big noise! Go to that little thing you just married and get your food."

"Ah, Grandmother! I'm going up the canyon to shoot the man who built the dam. But first I must eat."

Veronica picked up a stick of firewood and advanced. "I'll give you this in your teeth and you can eat it. I don't like your talk, even if it is all noise. You, shoot a man!"

It started just like that.

Antoine was watching from Bull's tepee, just next to Veronica's lodge. He was sitting in the shadow opposite the entrance. The next thing he knew, Pock face was there, blocking out the light.

He stopped just in the entrance until he discovered the tepee was not empty. Then he pushed in.

"Hello, little chief. I have to borrow Bull's gun. It will be well used. Just tell him I have it and will return it."

Without using further words, he took the gun, scabbard and all, and started to leave.

Antoine grabbed for it, but Pock Face lifted it up out of reach.

"Don't be angry, little chief. The gun will come back."

Antoine grabbed again, but Pock Face put his hand out and gave a little push and the boy went spilling across the ground.

Theobold was waiting outside, and now he looked frightened. But Pock Face laughed, and when he went to the corral for his horse, Theobold knew he had to go.

Antoine watched it all, watched them go to saddle up, and he began to shake. His grandfather told him to watch the camp. He had watched all right, but he lost the gun just the same. He stood outside as his uncles were riding away. He decided then to go look for his grandfather, who would be somewhere on the mountain, a different part of the mountain.

That was how it started.

It was not yet midday, and the clouds were even thicker and darker than the dawn clouds. They were rolling and shredding against the high slopes.

The two on horseback rode up the trail. The higher they climbed, the colder it got. They pulled their shoulders toward their ears and rode with one hand in a pants pocket. Theobold didn't like it. Usually when they went out from camp, they dashed away in a cloud of dust and a clatter of stones. This was different. Something was wrong. When he spoke up, Pock Face didn't answer. So he rode along, listening to the chatter of his own teeth.

Pock Face had not thought it out in advance, but

from the moment he said he was going up to see that dam, the idea appealed to him. He said it first as kind of a teasing remark, then he turned serious. Even before they reached their horses, the fun left his eyes. A different look was there, and when Theobold saw the look he wanted to cry. It was an old man's look, a mixing of quietness and contempt. Crazy Dog soldiers looked that way when they went to battle.

He knew Pock Face, son of Louis of the bitter mouth, as they called the father. At times, meanness broke out right in the middle of fun-making, and his friends could never understand how it happened or how it would end. It often seemed that he paid no attention when the older men were talking in camp, but in fact he heard everything, and would talk about it afterward. On the night of Henry Jim's visit when the men talked almost until dawn, Pock Face sat just beyond the reach of the lantern glow and caught every word. And it burned in him afterward. Usually at such times, when his insides were burning, he would go off on a tear, drink a bottle of whiskey, fight anybody who happened to be near, drag a woman into the bushes—and come home singing a war song with everybody laughing with him.

It was different today. He rode in the lead, not even aware that Theobold was following along, feeling the cold wind, but feeling a deeper chill in his blood. The lowering sky and sharpening wind went unnoticed by Pock Face, except that the reflexes of his body caused him to huddle within the blue cowboy jacket he wore.

When they reached the place of rocks where they would dismount and Pock Face drew Bull's rifle from its scabbard, Theobold was shaking.

"It's a long climb up there, my friend," he said, almost inaudible. "It will be snowing soon. Our horses are not shod and it will be bad traveling in the snow. If we start back now, we'll be safe."

Pock Face looked at him for the first time. "You don't have to come. Better you don't come. Me, I'm going up there, where they built the dam and killed our water. Our leaders talk about this, and quarrel among themselves, but they do nothing. I'm going to look at it." He broke off and laughed. "Then I'll just come back and tell them what to do. You stay and watch the horses, or go home—as you wish." He turned away.

He started up the trail, while Theobold tied the horses and went to gather wood for a fire.

Pock Face climbed steadily in spite of his high-heeled boots. He crossed the rock-slide, went up through the aspen grove where the yellowed leaves were flying in the wind, crawled over and around the tumbled boulders, until at last the dam of purple dark water was just below him.

At the very moment that Pock Face gained his vantage point, a man on the opposite side was mounting the concrete stairway which led to the top of the dam. One hand glided along the iron railing bordering the steps. Pock Face crouched within a crevice in the rock and watched.

The man on the dam wore a sheepskin jacket and a cap with patches over his ears, as if midwinter had arrived. He walked along the railed catwalk on top of the dam. Approached the nearside. He peered at a white marker which came up out of the dark water near the shore. He drew a notebook from his jacket pocket.

He was standing on top of the dam, gloves off, making marks in the notebook, when Pock Face drew him in the sights of his rifle.

The bark of the rifle was muffled in the roar of wind and water. Even the smoke from the barrel's end blew away without a trace.

On the dam's catwalk, the man simply dropped and never moved. His notebook fell from his hand and the pages fluttered in the wind.

Pock Face watched, but when no one appeared from any of the buildings below the dam, he went quickly over the rocks.

It started to snow, a light, drifting ice powder.

6

The days of high molten skies moved into nights of withering frost, and presently the skies came down to the mountaintops and sharp winds lifted dead dust from the road.

Rafferty walked out from the agency just after the noon hour, saw the low sky and the mountains, and paused.

The hills of home of his childhood had been pleasant green mounds running in a flowing line across the horizon. It restored the mind and calmed the soul to look out upon a world in which ordered forests and nurtured meadows were all anticipated. Here, the horizon tilted violently, vaulted into perpetual cloud. Here was no repose. His mind raced to assemble the disarray of shattered rock and his soul grieved for the naked loneliness of timberline.

Then his reflecting mind brought up contradicting images of Indian faces, in timeless repose. As if to remind him that here he was an outsider, trying to find his way inside.

Little Elk valley ran roughly north and south. Northward and eastward was the high, rough country of the Continental Divide, with the glacial cap of Goat Mountain bedded in clouds at eleven thousand feet. Nearer at hand, approaching even to the agency, were the broken, twisting courses of the sandhills. A Tertiary lake bed eroded by glacial action, he read in a geological report— and that was as much as he knew about it. An outsider in this as well.

He crossed the wooden bridge which lay flat across a gullied stream bed, and just beyond, on rising ground, were the mission church and parish house. Quick strides brought him to the latched gate, where he paused to kick the dust from his shoes. And the thought intruded, just then, that when he pushed the gate open and went inside, some new event would require a decision, some strangeness would be waiting.

"I ask you to do this," Henry Jim had said. "I ask you to find out for us."

Maybe the request was the first tentative offering of confidence, maybe it was nothing. An old man trying to shift a burden from his soul. Or maybe the only trouble was in his own discipline of thinking. He was acting for an Indian, accepting a mission not required of him in his capacity as the government's representative. He had been cautioned to stay within channels, to request instructions when in doubt.

He kicked impatiently at the gatepost and passed through.

The house stood back behind a screen of poplar trees, an old planting now dying out at the top. He looked sharply about, at the vegetable garden to the right, of which nothing was left but late-growing weeds and withered potato tops; at a berry patch reverted into a tangle of brambles.

It was a mild day after the first frosts, really quite warm in the sun. And because it was pleasant in the open air, Rafferty came unexpectedly upon the Reverend Stephen Welles—the dog-faced man, as the older Indians and Doc Edwards called him.

Wearing a shawl about his shoulders, the missionary priest was preparing for his afternoon nap in a small arbor at the side of the house, where a flower bed had turned into a matted brown mass. An old man whose whited hair fell in scant wisps over a skull netted with pulsing veins.

Welles heard the footfall and raised his head slowly. He was a tall man, with thick shoulders that folded over a sunken chest.

"Awfully sorry," Rafferty apologized. "I won't disturb you."

"Not at all." Welles pulled in his long legs and pushed himself upright. He held out a hand to detain the unexpected guest.

"Do pull up that chair. A bit more this way where the sun won't get your eyes. That should do it."

The tone was genial, but Rafferty sensed a holding back. The superintendent of Little Elk had not made a practice of dropping in.

"Some of your trees seem to be giving out. A shame to lose them."

"Quite true. It's the dryness of these last years."

"I had a reason for dropping in on you," he said, pushing out. "It has to do with a bit of Little Elk history—a bit in which I am told you had a part to play."

The long, thin face raised up and the deep-set eyes met his gaze. Neither curiosity nor encouragement showed there.

"I heard the story just recently, and it may not be accurate. Your comments will be valuable."

Welles's long legs uncrossed and crossed again.

"It is said that on a certain day, back maybe thirty years ago, you set out for Elk City, driving a team and buckboard. You had something with you, a parcel stowed away under the seat. A storm broke as you were going over the mountain pass. A bad storm. Lightning struck a tree just as you were under it. The tree split and crashed upon you. Your team ran away, but you escaped, I believe without injury, you and the parcel. You found it intact in the demolished buckboard.

"From these details, it would almost seem as if somebody had been following you, watching, doesn't it? You picked up the bundle and walked to the railroad station at Elk City. Do you recognize the incident?"

Welles did not look up. His hands extended together and his index fingers pushed against his lips.

"Odd incident to be recalled after all these years. I remember it quite well. The horses got tangled up in their harness, and when we found them they were quite gaunt. Hadn't had any water and not much to eat."

Then he looked up. "Who, may I ask, told you this story? You said it seemed as if somebody had been following behind—"

"Most of it is told in an old report in our files." Rafferty offered no further information. "Would you mind telling me something about that bundle? You sent it away, I understand."

Welles straightened. "Yes, I sent it away. What else?"

"Did you know what it was?"

"But of course. It was one of those bundles they keep in a medicine lodge. An Indian brought it and said they were finished with all that—and would I send it away."

"I see. You sent it away. Would you tell me where it went?"

The question was pondered. "Why are you asking? It's ancient history."

"I've been asked to inquire. To find out if there's any chance of getting it back."

"And who made this inquiry?"

"Henry Jim."

Welles looked up quickly, then away. A moment passed before he expressed himself. "I'm surprised. Was that all he said—just about getting it back?"

"He said it was a mistake to give it up. It split the tribe, they quarreled. He thinks it will bring them together again. They won't feel so beaten down. He expressed it another way, but that's the sense of it. He talked all afternoon, with genuine concern, I thought, for the future of his people."

"What kind of future?" Welles seemed himself to stare ahead into years to come. His voice lost its sharp edge. "In those days, he was a young man, and also concerned for the future. He thought his people would not survive unless they gave up some things and accepted new ways. I remember clearly his saying the old leadership was trying to hold the people back. 'You take this,' he told me, 'and the old men won't be strong anymore. The people won't be afraid of them.' That's what he said: 'They won't be afraid.' "

"Well, after thirty years, it looks like he's changed his mind. Some men do. Where did you send it?"

For a moment Rafferty thought his question would be ignored again. Welles made a slight gesture with his hands.

"The object was a museum piece. I might have destroyed it—no conditions were attached when it was handed over. It appeared to be old, and I thought it might have historic value. So I corresponded with the Americana Institute, learned they were interested, and that's where I sent it. I believe they gave a small donation for our mission work, but that was quite voluntary."

"Would you be willing to ask for its return?"

"Certainly not!" The edge was back in his voice.

"Who's the director of the institute, by the way?"

"Adam Pell."

"Why should I remember that name? What else does he do?"

"What doesn't he do? You've lived in New York—did you never read the financial pages?"

"You mean *the* Adam Pell?"

"Then you know him, or know of him. He was out here a few years ago. I introduced myself, but he remembered nothing about the article I sent him. One of his companies was the contractor for the dam up in the canyon. He came for the ground-breaking ceremony. Some Indians were up there, voicing a protest. He was polite, but I believe he was annoyed. Some of us were standing with him on a little platform overlooking the canyon when the steam shovel took the first bite of earth. The Indians looked frightened, and they went away in a hurry.

"As I look back, I realize Henry Jim had a very clear view of the years ahead. He knew that there would be those among his people who would make such protests—would carry others with them if they could, to block their own advancement. Such an object as this so-called medicine bundle would have strengthened their negative influence. As it was, the protesters were only a small minority, without effectiveness. They just made speeches that day, then faded away when the steam engine began to snort."

Rafferty leaned back in his chair and felt heat at the back of his head, and realized it was not the sun.

He began quietly. "When the old gentleman talked to me about it, he was very tentative. He could not be sure how I would react, but it was plain that he was in trouble with himself. He wanted help."

His voice became brisker. "If this is your answer, I won't take up your time. It just struck me that an old fellow like that might be allowed the privilege of changing his mind. We all do, one time or another. Or some do."

Welles held up his hand in protest. "You are putting me down as an unbending old man. Well . . ." he paused, then came to decision. "In this affair, I am, and I'll tell you why. Our mission here is not new. We came into this general area some seventy years ago. Our work at Little Elk is more recent—and it has been a peaceful mission. Earlier, in our work among the Sioux, the Nez Percé, the Columbia River Indians, it was, at times, dangerous. You know of our post that was massacred—

"What I mean to say is, the act of savagery never colored our later relations with the Indians. We carried on, perhaps with greater dedication."

He looked away, as if responding to a distracting afterthought.

"I must admit, in spite of the long effort, the dedication, our accomplishment is meager. Perhaps that explains part of my, shall we say, intransigence. As you like. I say we have been too forbearing, too Christian, I could say. Our race, and the Indian race, will never come together so long as we continue to speak the language of love as we use it among ourselves. The Indian people start from origins about which we speculate but know next to nothing. We do know they are a people who are unlike us—in attitude, in outlook, and in destination, unless we change that destination. We have tried—the churches, I mean—since John Eliot's day, and the Spanish church tried it even before, to make that change. Regardless of what we white men have attempted, the Indian has always remained beyond our reach, just beyond our reach. He is always slipping away into the distance. The strategy of his fighting was no accidental discovery—the strike and retreat—the sudden assault, savage and swift, then over the hill and away. How many good people met that fate!"

The words had been tumbling forth, as if in blind disregard of what they were leading to, an explosion of unpremeditated sentiment. A trickle of saliva seeped from the corners of his mouth.

"The Indian is anti-civilization!" A climactic cry, after which his lips firmed. He drew a bunched handkerchief from his breast pocket and wiped his mouth. Then proceeded more quietly.

"Because of his beginnings, and the road he has traveled, he is not where we are now, nor where we have been—he's not even going our way. If there were two humanities, I'd say he is with the other party. He's in the human family, but I'd have to describe his relationship to the rest of us by saying that he is both opposed to us and trying to escape from us—as if he could escape! A curious way of speaking of the matter . . ."

There he paused, and suddenly smiled. A smile without warmth. "Of course, these are my personal views. My colleagues would be shocked, no doubt. I can only say for them that they are dedicated, but not realistic."

Another pause, and a quieter voice. "No. They will not abandon the old and the familiar, if left to themselves. They can only choose what they have always known, and that choice means extinction for them.

"You see now that I acted upon design when I sent the bundle beyond their reach. I would have to oppose any effort to bring it back."

Again he smiled, this time with effusive meaning.

"Indeed," Rafferty murmured, rising to go. "You have made it quite clear."

But it was not clear. He looked again at Stephen Welles, slumped back in his lounge chair, and he seemed to be out of focus, as if a mist from another age, of frankincense and chasubles, had come between. And again Rafferty realized that he was an outsider.

7

The big bay horse, Red Son, carried Henry Jim all the way to the end of the valley and back again, going up the dirt road that skirted the eastern foothills, winding in and out of the coulees and draws on the west side. The Indian families lived in the foothills, wherever water came from the ground in pools, and where timber gave them shelter. The white men who came to the valley at the government's invitation took their homesteads in the flats, where the silty soil ran deep and stoneless and thirsted for water. The summer sun blistered their pink faces and the shrill winter winds turned them blue.

Henry Jim had relatives in all the hidden meadows. Some he had not seen in many years, because of their bitter thoughts, and others he had seen only when they came to his camp for help. Now he must see them all, whatever their thoughts, and ask them to end the quarrel.

The words that he would say ran along with the softly cantering horse.

The wet snow that fell in the mountains that day, fell as cold rain in the valley and the ground was heavy with dampness. Balls of mud formed in the hollow of the bay horse's hooves and flew to the rear like a scattering of the old man's thoughts.

This was a thing he had to do—afterwards, a different time would come. *A different time will come,* declared the mud.

The first camp belonged to Jerome, the eldest son of his first sister, the same Jerome who led Antoine to the dance floor. He had not joined the open quarrel, but he had stayed away just so he wouldn't hurt anybody's feelings. He would be the first one.

The three weathered tepees and one old log cabin stood among trees, with a corral and small haystack in front, a broken plow, a broken hay rake, and a broken wagon in between.

Henry Jim spoke his greetings. Then after a while they smoked, then they ate, and after that it was time to talk.

"It has been healed over, this quarrel with my brother. I talked to him in his camp. At first he was still angry, as I expected. But I told him of the singing voices that are with me these days, and his anger fell down. We remembered how it happened and what we said to each other and to our kinsmen. It was like in the old days, as I have heard, when two camps met out on the hunting grounds and the people had not seen each other for maybe ten or twenty years because they had moved away to give each other more room, and then they found themselves together and a good feeling filled their hearts as they told what had happened to each one. It was like that in my brother's camp when we talked. Then I told him I would go to the new government man and ask his help. He will go to the dog-faced man and ask him what happened to our Feather Boy bundle. He will do this for us. He said so. I believe he is a good man, this new government man. We will have our sacred bundle again, and after that the people will be one, as they were before these troubles came."

Jerome and his relatives and the visitors who stopped by all said they believed this was true and they were glad to hear it.

"It will be up to my brother, since I will be called to the ground before I can do any more. He will take care of it for me.

"Now I must go and tell the others, so their minds can get ready for the thing that is to happen. It will seem strange to many of our people."

Jerome saddled his horse and said he would ride with the old man.

Up the valley to the next camp, and there Frank Charley saddled his horse and said he would ride along.

Sometimes they met riders coming from the opposite direction, and they would huddle their horses together in the middle of the road, each man leaning forward on the horn of his saddle, and Henry Jim would repeat the

54

story of the quarrel that was healed and the coming of the Feather Boy bundle to its proper home. It made everyone who heard it feel better and they offered to go on and tell others.

By nightfall, when they reached the head of the valley, five of his kinsmen were riding with Henry Jim. They stopped for the night at Iron Child's camp, a large one with many horses, many children, and many dogs. Iron Child was one of those who had taken Bull's side of the quarrel and in the past had spoken harshly against Henry Jim. He would not come out of his lodge at first. The men just sat their horses until Jerome got down and went inside.

Later, when it was all right and the group sat together inside, Iron Child, a rugged man like Bull, told them: "This quarrel lasted too long. It will please me if we can just settle this. Tomorrow I will ride with you myself and my kinsmen will see that we have healed it over."

That night, after they had all talked and Henry Jim lay down with his feet to the fire, the song from the grass came very loud and close. A spring morning flooded the tepee and he seemed to float just at the grass tops. It was new grass, freshly green, and new leaves shot glances at the sun. The singing came in wave after wave of soft sound, wordless, yet filled with sorrow and lamentation. He could see himself, his weeping eyes. Then the singing went shrill, and as suddenly it turned to bird song. First the plover was crying: *ke-ree, ke-ree, ke-ree.* Then the meadowlark fluted: *tu-lee, tu-lu, tu-lee, tu-lu-lee-ul.* The song came from above and below and from all sides. Then a speaking voice mingled with the song, and it too came from all sides. Henry Jim could see himself still floating, looking for a speaker, but the words came of their own accord: "Now you must sing the song you heard long ago. Don't stop. Keep singing. Otherwise I will not be able to help you. When you stop singing, you will float away and be one of us."

The words ended there, and Henry Jim sat up and found that his face was wet, but whether it was the wetness of tears or of sweat he could not tell. He found his dried bladder rattle and began to sing, there in the tepee.

The others wakened and knew at once that the old man was singing for his life.

One built up the fire, and they sang with Henry Jim until it was dawn and the birds freed their heads from their wings and ruffled their feathers.

He told the camp what he had seen and what had been told, and they cried "*Heu!Heu!* This is bad!"

They rode all that day, winding in and out of the coulees and draws on the west side of the valley, and now there were ten riders in the party. The singing never stopped. It never swelled to loudness, and it never stayed the same. A few riders would start the chant and carry it along, others would take it over, still another part of the group would pick it up, and then it would spread to all voices. And after a while only a few would be carrying it along.

The big bay horse carrying Henry Jim in the front row of riders flicked its pointed ears to the shifting sound.

Birds fell silent as the group rode by. Pine branches hung low and still. The water in a roadside pool was as stiff as glass. The earth itself listened as the men rode on.

It was evening, just at the setting of the sun, when the singing voices approached the Little Elk Agency. Henry Jim rode in the center of five riders, and five others came just behind. The sun and the shadows of the west were still farther behind.

"Who knows if I ever ride again," Henry Jim told his kinsmen. "I will talk once more with the new government man, tell him we look to him for help. Our quarrel is healed. It is up to him now."

A heavy-footed horse, then another just behind, pounded up the road in the deepening shadows, coming from the direction of the agency.

"Halt! Halt where you are!" A voice of seeming anger came at the singing riders out of those settling shadows.

In the commingling of riders, no one spoke out, but even in their surprise the singing never broke, it only went softer.

The heavy voice was at them again. "I warn you to stand back. The agency gates are closed. No one is to come in. And stop singing those damned war songs! Who is spokesman here?"

Out of great effort, pulling himself to the surface from a deep enchantment, Henry Jim remembered other faces and other voices. In a time that he could now scarcely remember, he had interpreted for this man.

"I am Henry Jim. These are my kinsmen. It is important to see the new man at the agency. We have been riding all day."

The man inched his horse closer. They could see he was a big man against the sky. "Well, so it is. Well, you know me. I am Sid Grant, United States marshal. Tell your boys you'll have to go back. No one gets in tonight. We want no trouble."

The words were slow to turn over in Henry Jim's mind. They had a sound of anger, and this he could not understand. The quarrel among his people had been healed over and that should have ended all trouble.

"Will the Mr. United States Marshal tell us what is wrong?"

"There's been a killing, that's what's wrong! Bull and his whole damned outfit are inside and we don't need nobody else, not tonight. So just tell your boys to go on home. Come back tomorrow and we'll see what's doing. Now git!"

Iron Child, the rugged one, gave heel to his horse and pulled up alongside the marshal.

"This man is ready to die." The English words came hard, because of the singing and the spell of their talking together, but Iron Child pulled his brow into wrinkles and made the words come.

"When a man is ready to die, you have to give in. You have to let him go. It's a shameful thing to stop him."

Sid Grant looked to see how close his deputy was behind, then turned to Henry Jim against the evening sky.

"He don't look that way to me. He's sitting his horse as good as anybody else. What you trying to hand me?"

"He wants to see the government man. You have to let him go."

"Tell it to Sweeney! Nobody gets in there tonight."

No one understood this, so they were silent.

At first they just sat their horses and tried to decide what to do and what the man meant.

"Let's jump him," Iron Child said, in his own language. "I think he's afraid."

The others held back. "It would be hard on the old man," Jerome pointed out. "We have to keep singing."

So they turned their horses finally, and the song started again.

And that was how the people in the valley learned that Bull and his kinsmen were in trouble.

8

After Pock Face and Theobold left the camp, the afternoon became very long. The men, all except Two Sleeps, had ridden away soon after Bull left in the morning. The women, alone, moved about in a worried way, but no one talked about it. They watched the sky and argued about the signs. It would rain. It would snow. The air smelled of change. Aching bones told just how it would be.

The wind came up sharp and cold just at midday, and deeper cloud masses poured in. A heavy dampness weighed upon the air, and smoke escaping from smoke holes blew crazily without rising. The horses in the meadow threw up their heads, their tails and manes whipping out. A nervous colt reacted by breaking into a wild run up the meadow and back.

It had been summer until only yesterday, and now all that was blowing away.

Two Sleeps was roused out of his cabin finally and asked to settle the matter. He startled everybody when he spoke.

"This is death you smell, you foolish women." His voice was dry and without vibration. He was a frail old man, leaning on a gnarled willow staff. His old eyes watered in the sharp wind.

The women jeered. "You smell your own stink."

"Who ever heard of snow before the geese fly over?"

"The geese don't make the snow, old mare. The snow comes of its own accord. I say there's death on this wind."

The elder wife, Veronica—they pronounced it Velonika—disliked squabbling. She settled the matter by sending Two Sleeps back to his cabin. Then she made her prediction without consulting the sky.

"This day will bring something. You heard those two crazy ones. They took the old man's gun. Maybe that Pock Face will blow a rabbit into little pieces and will be satisfied. Watch carefully. Keep your tongues between your teeth, if you can. We live here so close together, one man's behind is always in another's face. It is necessary to hold ourselves in. Watch yourselves today."

They were frightened then, since she touched on the subject that worried them all. They had heard the crazy words, but no one mentioned them, as they huddled, first at one fire, then at another. Now they fell silent, forgetting the weather. They respected the senior wife, not entirely out of fear of her sharp tongue. She alone dared to challenge the men, even her own man, and therefore every woman of sense kept mindful of her good will. There were times when women needed each other.

"She never talks out of idleness, so we can expect something."

They knew what was meant, and they looked at each other.

"Did he bring liquor to the camp? Was he drinking before he left?"

All turned upon Lucelle, the girl-wife of Pock Face. If trouble came, it would be her man who brought it. They were already accusing her.

The girl turned hot with embarrassment. "Oh, no! My man has done nothing. He brought no liquor." Lucelle was plain and thin and had a young girl's flatness.

"That may be, but we will look." It was Basil's wife who spoke. Basil, the emaciated one, the eater. His wife, called only by her people's name, Star Head, carried the fat for the two of them. For all that her face was round and placid, she was a meddling woman.

"Come, we'll just see what he's been up to. To me, he sounded full before he ever left here."

The tepee stood off by itself, only a few yards away. Before the other women realized that she would do it, she was already inside the flap. It was a disgraceful thing to do, but no one stopped her.

Lucelle rushed after the woman when no one else moved, but only stood fluttering at the entrance. She whimpered and dodged in and out of the entrance until finally she was brushed aside by other women.

"She must know there's something in there, the way she dances," was the way they excused themselves.

Star Head tossed blankets, clothing, boxes, bags, and all the household stuff away from the walls. Suddenly she began to scratch at the ground just under the canvas tarpaulin where the bed was laid. A sharp cry struck out at Lucelle.

"Just see! She whines, does she?"

Star Head raised high a full quart of whiskey. It had not been opened, but nobody mentioned that.

"Oh, leave it!" Lucelle shrieked. She hurled herself at the massive woman, and was brushed aside with one sweep of a ponderous arm. "He will say I took it!"

"Who knows? Maybe you would."

Star Head lowered her great weight to a box and examined the bottle. She turned it around in her hands as if it would tell her what to do now that she had come this far.

Marie Louise, the wife of Theobold, was suddenly excited. She was an older woman, years older than Theobold, and she had a knife scar running from the corner of her eye to her chin. The wound had pulled her mouth crooked, in a perpetual smile. She snatched the bottle.

"Why should they have this? They would only get drunk and fight. This will keep them sober."

Marie Louise twisted off the cork while she talked, and was the first to tip the bottle to her lips.

Star Head recovered the bottle and began to scold.

"Now you've done it, you greedy gut! Maybe I was going to break it. You spoiled it all. Our men will beat all of us. We better just get ourselves drunk before they come back." She washed the words away in one great gulp, which left her gasping for breath.

The next to drink was Evangelique, a tall woman visiting from another camp. She said little, but her thirst was obviously great. The bottle gurgled twice before she lowered it, and she didn't even breathe hard.

Marie Louise, grown spirited, was dragging Lucelle in from outside and insisting that she drink from the bottle.

The girl shrieked. "Oh, no! Let me run away! I'm afraid!"

"Listen to the chicken!" Star Head jeered. "That's just what your man would like. Then he could take another one as silly as you."

No one noticed that Veronica stood inside the entrance. She did not hesitate. In one stride she was at Star Head's side, just as the whiskey bottle was tipped up. In snatching it, the liquor spilled over the woman's face and down her front. The voices died all at once.

"Leave the girl alone," she said. Then she lashed at the women: "When your men are gone, you have no heads, only guts. You shame me and yourselves."

She took the whiskey to the creek and let it pour into the running water. Then she tossed the bottle into the middle of the stream and watched it bob away.

A light snow had begun to drift out of a darkened sky as she stood by the creek.

"The stupid ones!" she muttered as she climbed from the creek. Her moccasins left dark spots in the trail.

It was quite dark when Bull returned in the whirling snow. Antoine had found him and came trailing behind.

The big man went directly to Veronica's tepee, where he squatted at the fire and sipped carefully at the hot coffee she handed him. It was a wordless meeting. She had no warning of his coming, and only managed to get to her feet when he was already inside. Then she poured coffee and watched his face. She knew when he tried to keep trouble from showing there.

"Have those two come back yet?" Thus he showed where his thoughts were running.

"We have waited all afternoon."

He drank more coffee.

Antoine had come in just behind Bull. He was wearing only a cotton shirt, and the freezing air had drawn the skin tight over his cheekbones. He crowded upon the fire, shaking. Veronica threw a Pendleton shawl around him and made him sit down. In a few minutes his hand stopped shaking and he could hold a coffee cup.

Bull looked at Veronica over his grandson's head. "He's a strong one, this one. He keeps reminding me what it was like when I was that size."

Then he told the boy, "Watch for them. When they come, tell them I'm waiting." He got up then and went to his own lodge.

"Where did you find him?" Veronica asked. She was filling a bowl with boiled meat.

"Just up on the mountain. He saw me before I saw him, and after a while he was behind me, following along. He always fools me like that."

"Don't you walk with your eyes open? He's trying to teach you."

"I know. Just now I'm trying to watch my feet, like he said. That's why I don't look around very much."

"Some day you'll be like him. . . ." It was a pleasure to think that. The boy would not be like the wild one who fathered him. He would not be touched by the terror that struck his mother. He would be a strong one—his grandfather said it.

"What did you tell him?"

"I told him about the gun, and what my uncle said."

"That crazy—listen!"

It was nothing, or perhaps the wind. Everywhere in the camp it was the same. People were eating as if nothing had happened. But at each least noise, they stopped chewing.

After a while, the snow stopped. About three inches covered the ground and hung wet and heavy on low shrubs and pine boughs.

The horses came after that, heaving and snorting in the cold air. Pock Face and Theobold were not singing, as the custom was with them. They just pulled up at the corral where they unsaddled and threw in some hay from the low mound lying near. A darker shadow was left where they lifted the hay out of the snow. They picked up their saddles to carry them to their tepees.

Antoine was waiting for Pock Face.

"Bull says come to his tent—and bring his gun."

"I am coming, little chief. But I have another thing to do first."

Lucelle, the girl-wife, who dreaded this coming, looked at her man. In the lantern light, she saw the little smile. Something had pleased him. He would not scold her. That was what she saw.

"I came, just to say I'm all right." That was all he said, but it was what she wanted to hear.

He went out again.

Bull sat there looking up as Pock Face filled the opening and stepped inside. Theobold came just behind and replaced the covering. He always stayed with Pock Face, even when it might mean trouble.

For the first time that day, Pock Face hesitated. Starting in the morning and all through the afternoon, nothing had stopped him—not the words spoken by Theobold, or by Antoine. Not the cold wind or the snow. Not the man standing in the line of his rifle sights. But now he hesitated. All his life until now he had looked to Bull, his mother's brother, as the man to follow, the man who took him on his first hunting trips and showed him the way of managing a horse. It was good to follow such a man, to watch his way of speaking, to have his understanding of what passed. Others might say of him that he was a hard man, that his anger destroyed. But to grow up under such a man was to learn gentleness toward children, to care for one's kinsmen, to speak strongly and fairly in public meetings, and to speak always for others, not for himself or his camp alone.

And now Pock Face hesitated. He looked at his action up there on the mountain, and it looked strange. He handed the gun over and sat down.

Bull looked at it for a moment, then worked the lever and threw out the unfired cartridges. One was missing. He looked up at Pock Face, his own face showing no feeling.

"So. You fired it?"

"Yes. I fired once."

"At game, maybe?"

"No, Uncle. I shot a man. He was the one who takes

care of the dam up there. He came out to measure the water, I think, and I shot him."

The big man's face tightened. He did not look up and he did not speak at once.

"He just came out and looked at the water, like it was his water, not our water—and I shot him." Pock Face explained no further. Words could not follow the thoughts he had, and the thoughts themselves were slipping away.

Bull sat with the rifle across his knee. He would have to say what was hard to say.

"Maybe I should put this gun to your head now, Nephew. Because the white man will do it before he is through with us. That's what I am telling myself. I try to see it all, but only so much of it is clear. I don't know what you have done to us. We have lived here a long time. They tried to make me go below and tear up the ground. I stayed here and kept all of you with me. But I had to be quiet. One bad move, and they would come up here and drive us out. I knew this long ago, so I stayed quiet and watched all of you. You were the one who troubled me, because you were the lively one. But I never tried to hold you down. I waited for you to find your own way. . . . I think you have killed us. When they finish, we'll be gone from here. I don't know where.

"You better go to your wife now—you may not have many more days with her."

Bull finished by spitting into the fire the bad taste that was in his mouth.

9
■

The man on the dam was not discovered until after dark.

Bartlett, the station engineer, whose name was scarcely known to Rafferty, called on the telephone, his voice so nearly incoherent that Rafferty first thought the man was drunk. He insisted on talking about a Jimmie, Jimmie Cooke, a name that meant nothing at all.

"Tell me again—I don't follow you—"

The voice rambled on. "He was supposed to leave. Tomorrow, in fact, he was going to leave. Yes, sir. Tomorrow. I can't get over it. He was leaving tomorrow. And to get married. I keep thinking about it. And he didn't have to go up there. That hits me too. He was off duty, really. I was fixing to go, but he said, 'Never mind, Pop'; he always called me Pop. He was just like a son to me. 'Never mind, Pop,' he says. 'I already got my jacket on.' And it was true. He had his jacket on and went out to read the stream gauge. And there was no need of it. That's what I can't get over. It's in your hands now . . . but anything I can do—"

In such a matter, the book was clear on what to do; a white man killed within the reservation was a federal matter. That meant a call to the United States marshal, Sid Grant, at Elk City. Then he called Doc Edwards to do the medical report. Next he called the hospital to provide an ambulance. Then he composed a carefully worded telegram for Washington to be transmitted first thing in the morning, remembering to include a request for further instructions.

He gave no thought to the event itself until he had taken care of these details. The young man, from what he could find out—hardly anyone at the agency knew him—minded his own business, which was engineering.

He had not become part of the community—either at the agency or at Elk City—and most certainly not part of the Indian community. He had no enemies, no jealous rivals, and obviously he had not been robbed. The snow around the body had not been disturbed. That much detail he had managed to extract from Bartlett.

After he thought about it for a while, Rafferty decided it was not his affair. He went along, but he meant to let the federal attorney and the marshal make what they could of it.

Rafferty had only a speaking acquaintanceship with Sid Grant at that time. They had been introduced, and the talk seemed to turn on the marshal's long experience with Indians. The man looked competent, and what he had to say for himself seemed creditable. His grizzled hair, face stubble, and general leathery look were of a nameless age, anywhere from fifty to seventy. His dress, speech, and actions all suggested the range, the open country, and the mountains, which he knew, he said, as ranch hand, brand inspector, game warden, sheriff's deputy, and now U.S. marshal for fifteen years.

It was not difficult to reconstruct the event at the dam, as the group huddled in the fog of their separate breaths. A heavy frost had followed on the wet snow, and in the dampness at streamside a scale of ice covered everything.

The body had been left in place, at the marshal's insistence, covered with a blanket and a tarpaulin.

The doctor explained how the bullet took a downward course, burned the right side of the neck, entered the chest cavity behind the breastbone, and lodged in the left pelvis, where it showed up just under the skin and was easily extracted. The men looked upward from the catwalk and scanned the abutting cliff.

"Just like I figured," the marshal announced. "The killer was waiting up there."

Doc Edwards seemed almost to sneer. "I didn't say the shot came from above the man. It took a downward course through the body. Maybe he dropped something and was on his hands and knees, or just bending over. The gunman could have been at the other end of the catwalk or the bottom of the cliff. On the same level, anyhow."

Sid Grant towered above the little doctor, who was bundled in layers of sweaters and coats, and he looked at him steadily, but made no reply. Instead, and to prove his point, he and his deputy, Ambrose Whiteside, began to scramble over icy ledges up to the top of the cliff. It was not too difficult a climb, except for the ice, since the walls consisted mostly of shattered rock left over from construction.

As he watched the two men maneuver around the rocks, Rafferty expressed his mild surprise.

"You jumped him pretty fast, didn't you?"

"Listen! That bag of wind couldn't find his socks with his boots pulled on over 'em. You just watch."

Farther down the catwalk the two men from the ambulance were talking with the engineer, Bartlett, who was hatless in the frosty air and recounting in detail the fatal, and unnecessary, trip to the stream gauge. He was taking on himself full responsibility for the young man's death and, hair blowing in the fresh morning wind, looked quite distracted.

The marshal had his triumph. He scrambled down the rocks in a matter of minutes, it seemed, bearing a brass cartridge shell from a .30/30 rifle.

"Just like I figured," he repeated. "And I could make out the prints of a pair of cowboy boots plain as anything."

"Under the snow?" the doctor inquired crisply.

Again the marshal held Edwards in his gaze.

"There's at least one good print under a bush where the snow didn't reach." He looked at the cliff again and spoke to his deputy. "We cain't get our hosses acrost here—we'll have to go downstream, then come up the other side to pick up the trail."

They all left the catwalk, descending the concrete steps to the roadway below the dam, where the marshal and his deputy had left their horses and Rafferty had left the agency automobile. In the quiet, away from the rush of water and the whine of the turbines, Sid Grant spoke what he intended as a final comment.

"I tell you fellows how it's gonna be. Ain't nobody

but In'ians lives on the other side of the canyon. When we get to the end of this trail, we'll find us an In'ian, like as not. I got a hunch—"

At first Rafferty misjudged the statement, taking it as a continuation of the crossplay between the doctor and the marshal. He matched the marshal's steady gaze for a moment.

"You're not serious?" he asked, still tentative.

The marshal peered down—he had the advantage of standing half a head above Rafferty—then looked away.

"I could just about tell you who it'll be, but you might think I was playing my hunch too hard."

"Unless you know something you haven't told us, that sounds like a conclusion."

Sid Grant chewed it over, and came back. "Might be I know something, maybe not. We'll see."

"You're a law officer, Mr. Grant."

"That's my job." The marshal was now standing with his feet slightly apart, with his coarse woolen jacket thrown open and his thumbs hooked into his belt.

"Judge and jury make those decisions."

Grant pulled his feet together and straightened his shoulders. "I know what I'm supposed to do. But I want you to know something. Take a look." He handed over the brass shell. "Take a good look."

Rafferty turned it over in his hands. He noticed nothing out of the ordinary—a cartridge that had been fired and still smelled faintly of gunpowder.

Grant reached for it. "This cartridge was fired in an old gun. The firing pin is slightly off center, and worn. Yes sir, an old gun, such as an In'ian is like to have. I'm goin' out and find me that gun. That's as far as I got my mind made up."

Rafferty steadied his voice. "There must be any number of old guns in a country like this. No reason I can think of why they should all belong to Indians. While you're looking for that gun, why not ask around about the man who was shot? Who knew him?"

The marshal hesitated, but only momentarily, then continued to move away.

"Come on, Amby," he said to his wordless deputy.

"We got ground to cover. See you later in the day, Mr. Rafferty."

Rafferty watched the pair walk stiff-legged to their horses, and then exploded. "I'll be damned! I'll be double-damned!"

He turned just then and found the little doctor standing spread-legged, hands buried in the pockets of a thick tweed overcoat, and smirking.

Rafferty didn't see the humor. "Does he always talk like that?"

"That was mild."

Rafferty eyed the little doctor. "That old boy's no fool, in spite of what you said about him. He sees things pretty fast."

Edwards was serious again. "Just a piece of luck, finding that empty shell. Anybody who knows guns could make that little deduction about the firing mechanism. But it's given him what he wants—a chance to prowl around those Indian camps. As he said, they're all Indians on that side, and the marshal doesn't waste any love on the redskins."

"Just what I surmised."

"You know who lives on that side of the canyon, don't you?"

"I suppose so—I'd have to look it up."

"Well, I'll tell you. Bull and his relatives, for starters. It would be an eagle feather in his Stetson if he could pin it on Bull or one of his men. Every lawman who's ever been in here has been after him. So, you see—"

Bartlett, the plant engineer, had come down the catwalk. He had just helped place the frozen body in the ambulance and was wide-eyed and sightless. He was an aging man, and the cast of old age had come on in a matter of hours. His red hair was graying to a sorrel color and his freckles had a greenish hue in the weak sunlight.

"You know, he was leaving to get married. Worked here just over a year. His uncle was very proud of that boy. His first job, just out of engineering school. A wonderful lad. The folks come from Ohio. How the uncle will take it, I don't know. Adam Pell was the uncle. I worked for him all over the country, when I was a young man myself. Said he wanted me to start the boy off right. Wasn't that a fine thing for him to say? But I don't know how he'll take it, since it was my fault, in a way. The boy didn't have to go up there—I shouldn't have let him—"

Rafferty and the doctor helped Bartlett to his quarters, a white stucco cottage built against the canyon, and they fixed coffee.

It was just after midday when the marshal and his deputy rode into Bull's camp, and they were at once surrounded by the camp dogs, all howling disapproval. No one tried to quiet the dogs, no one even appeared.

Antoine was hunting rabbits when the two men appeared on the trail below him. He watched them for some time, moving behind a low ridge and coming up for a view at intervals, his tall hat in his hand. He only wanted to be sure which fork they took where the trail divided, and when they chose the trail to his grandfather's camp, he dropped low and ran for home.

So Bull, who was sitting at a burned-down fire in his tepee, cutting and greasing rawhide strips to plait into a bridle, knew he would have visitors.

Sid Grant and his deputy reined in their horses. The camp dogs had tired of their own voices and walked back and forth and around, expecting somebody to drive them away.

Sid Grant sat his horse, waiting for somebody to act.

Down in the valley, a score of miles away, Henry Jim and his kinsmen were riding to the camps hidden away in foothill meadows, to tell how the quarrel had been healed and how the new government man would help them.

Away to the east, in an unimaginable place called Ohio, a man and woman, one wearing a black armband and the other a black veil, were mounting a railroad coach which would carry them to what was for them an utterly unimaginable place called the Little Elk Indian Reservation, where their son had been murdered.

In his tepee, Bull worked with his hands on a width of dehaired cowhide.

After a while he said to his grandson: "I guess those white men are just going to stay there. Go ask them what they want."

Outside, Sid Grant was saying to Ambrose: "Just watch. He'll send some kid out to speak for him. These old-timers like to play it that way. And they'll all act like they don't know a word of English. They'll stall around for everything to be translated. Most times, if you speak yourself plain enough, they understand all right. Just watch."

Ambrose, a small man with a large nose, had been with Sid Grant for a long time and had heard these views before. But he was not given to comment.

Antoine came out, standing under his black hat. "My grandfather says you can come to his tent."

"Who are you, boy?"

"Antoine, they call me."

"Antoine who? Never mind. Is your grandfather the one they call Bull? Tell him we want to see him. Tell him to come out here."

The boy just stood.

"Go on. Tell him what I said."

"I think you better come to his tent."

"You hear what I said, boy? Go tell your grandfather I want to talk to him out here."

Sid Grant increased the volume of his voice until it roared through the camp. Some of the dogs jumped up and looked around. Bull came from his tepee. Presently the old man, Two Sleeps, stumbled from his cabin. And only a moment later Louis and Basil, the uncles, came blinking into the bright sun. Why should a young boy be scolded by a white man?

"What did I tell you?" Sid Grant remarked. "They understood me that time. But just watch. They won't understand anything else I say."

He turned upon Bull. "So you decided to come out. Is this all of your camp? I want everybody out here. In case you don't know me, which ain't likely, I'm the United States marshal for this district. The name's Sid Grant. This is my deputy. Got that, all of you?"

They only stared at the ground.

"To go back to my question: Is this everybody?" His voice rose: "Is everybody here?"

Now the women and small children were staring from tepee openings.

But nobody spoke up.

"All right, boy. You tell me. Is this everybody?"

"I'll talk to my grandfather."

Antoine explained what the loud voice was saying, but with a surprising difference. "I think this man knows my two uncles have not come out. He keeps asking if all are here. He's got that big star on his shirt and that gun on his belt. It would be better to tell my uncles to come out."

"Yes, Grandson. Tell your uncles to join us here. Then maybe this loudmouth will leave us alone."

Antoine told the marshal: "I asked my grandfather if my two uncles came back from visiting our relatives in the valley. He thinks they are sleeping. So I will go to their tents, the last ones down there."

"Go after them, boy. I knew there should be more of you from counting your tepees. I ain't got all day, so shake a leg."

Antoine hoped his uncles had already slipped away. He walked slowly, as if a few additional seconds might help them out.

But Pock Face and Theobold had not run off. Theobold's wife, Marie Louise, with her two children, had gone to join other women, and Theobold was with Pock Face and the girl-wife, Lucelle.

"What does he know, that one with the star?" Pock Face asked.

"He doesn't say. He wants everybody over there where he is. My grandfather thinks it will be best not to try to run. I thought you would be gone as soon as you saw who they were."

All Pock Face said was, "I wanted to stay."

Lucelle held her man in her eyes. "He's been up there, that man. He's been in the canyon. He'll take you away!" A cry from deep inside.

Pock Face pulled himself up straight and walked out ahead of Theobold. Somehow they seemed not so tall as they walked easily toward Bull's tepee. They were both wearing moccasins. Antoine noticed it.

Sid Grant was leaning on his saddle horn, seeming to stare at the ground, as Pock Face and Theobold approached.

Then he looked up at the young men. "Do either of you boys own cowboy boots?" he asked.

The young men stared blankly and said nothing.

"I asked a question. Do you own a pair of cowboy boots?" He thrust a finger at Pock Face.

It brought no response.

"Don't tell me you boys never been to school and can't speak English! I won't go for it. Come on, speak up! Where are the boots you were wearing yesterday? You might as well tell me, because I'll find 'em."

Antoine moved his feet. "These two are my uncles. They never went to school. They jumped off the train when it was taking them away and they never got caught. I'm the only one been to school. Do you want me to speak for you?"

"I don't believe a damned word of it, but all right. You heard what I asked—go ahead."

Antoine translated: "This one has sharp eyes. Watch yourself, or he'll find out you can talk his language."

And to Bull he explained: "Grandfather, this man is looking for boots with high heels. He has been tracking my uncle, I think."

"Tell the big mouth we're all Indians here. What do we know about white man's shoes? Just tell him to go look some other place. I'm going back to my fire."

Bull turned to leave and Sid Grant shouted and slapped his pistol.

"Stop that old man! Nobody's to leave until I get some questions answered." Through the corner of his mouth he cautioned his deputy: "Keep your hand near your gun, Amby, and watch those tepees. Some hostile squaw is like to poke a gun through one a them openings."

Antoine grabbed Bull's arm. "Grandfather! He is angry. He might shoot!"

Bull looked at Sid Grant for the first time. He looked big, sitting on his big sorrel horse. And he was big because he had his hand on a gun. Bull had seen men when they were just on the point of using a gun or a knife. Sometimes it happened when anger came to the flaming point, and sometimes it happened when fear was about to turn a man into a fool. He decided that this man had no reason to be angry, but he might shoot just the same.

He turned his back on Sid Grant and put a question to Two Sleeps, who was standing watching through his faded eyes.

"Old man, what do you see now? Is this the way we are going to get help from the white man?"

Bull's voice reminded them of old days. He had hardly lifted his voice, but the lilt they heard cut the air like a whiplash. The older ones felt a stirring in their veins, and a song came up in their throats. But they held back.

Two Sleeps knew the tone. "My son. This man is a cloud that comes from nowhere. A nothing cloud. He wasn't even in the sky when we looked together a few nights ago. Nothing clouds blow away. He is not the new government man. Just let this one talk until he blows himself out."

Bull told his grandson: "Tell that big mouth if he wants to talk he should get down and sit with us by the cooking fire. I don't like a man looking down my throat."

Antoine translated: "My grandfather says he doesn't understand why you are angry. You hurt his feelings and he wants you to sit with him and drink some coffee."

Pock Face objected, speaking for the first time. "Don't be so easy on the white man. Your grandfather doesn't want to shake his hand. And now, listen. I'm going to run if he stays much longer. That's the best way to get him out of camp. Just be watching . . ."

Louis moved forward then, speaking with unusual mildness. "My son. I ask you not to do this. He is feeling us out. If you run now, he'll shoot you like a rabbit. That's what he wants. I think the old man is right—he'll just blow away."

Sid Grant stopped it there. "All right. All right. Whatever you're saying, drop it. Tell your grandpa I'm here on the law's business, not to visit. A man was shot and killed yesterday. We tracked the killer to this camp.

Got that? One of you shot that man." He stared at each of the men, starting with Bull and coming back to him, but no one even looked up.

"Now. I'm going to sit here, and my deputy is going into each one of your lodges. All of you will stay right where you are, got that? No one makes a move—and no one will get hurt." He slapped his sidearm. "He's going into each one of these lodges, and he'll be looking for a pair of cowboy boots. Also he is going to take your guns and bring them to me. That's what he's gonna do.

"All right, boy. Tell them what I said. Tell it exactly, so they'll understand. And nobody's to make a move. Make that clear."

When Antoine had translated, getting in every word, nobody moved or said a word. Sid Grant had expected an explosion, and when nothing happened, he was puzzled. He looked everybody over, watching for some sign of a break.

He asked his deputy, "You see anything fishy, Amby?"

"Nope. Guess you stunned 'em, Marshal."

He turned back to Antoine. "You sure you told 'em just what I said? They understand me?"

"I said it just like you said."

"Well, why the hell don't they say something? I'm going to search the camp! I'm taking their guns away!"

"You told them what you gonna do, so they wait for you to do it. You got a gun. Your other man got a gun. Nobody else here got a gun."

"Oh, ———!" Antoine did not translate the obscene word he used to see written on the walls at school.

"Go ahead, Amby. But watch it!. Watch the squaws. If a tepee is empty, search it, but watch the entrance. If you find a squaw in the tepee, make her get out. I think most of 'em are standing outside.

"The rest of you, you men, you can go over by the fire and sit down. This might take a while. Tell 'em, boy!"

It did, indeed, take a while. The sun moved across the sky. Veronica boiled up the coffee. She brought out cold fried bread. Other women, seeing her, came to the fire and helped. They talked among themselves, ignoring the man on the horse and what was happening in the lodges.

No one spoke harshly about Pock Face for causing the trouble. Louis grumbled, making his yellow paper cigarettes. Were they children, to let themselves be treated this way? Why didn't somebody put a hot coal under that horse's tail? No one answered. Everyone knew he was troubled. He stayed close to Pock Face, and they knew he was keeping watch on his son.

For Bull, it was a long afternoon. He sat with Two Sleeps, who told a long story of a forgotten hunting trip, but Bull heard only the speaking voice, not the words.

Finally, it was finished. The sun had moved toward the horizon and the air was turning cold again. The camp dogs drifted toward the fire, moving warily.

Ambrose had been in every lodge. He had searched everything. And all he had in his hand was one old single-shot .22 caliber rifle.

Sid Grant stared at this, and all he could think of saying was "Son of a bitch!"

10

The tribal police chief, called The Boy, reported for duty according to schedule, at 8 A.M., walking from his house at the edge of the compound. But when he arrived, Rafferty's door was closed and voices behind it were fast and angry. The Boy recognized the voices and the subject in dispute, but he did not stay to listen. It was not pleasant to listen to white men when their voices turned loud.

Some early lounging tribesmen had seen The Boy enter the office, so they waited just outside. One said, "He's a policeman, but he may tell us what is happening."

And when The Boy came out again almost immediately, the waiting Indians were surprised, but not too surprised to speak. One led the way, and he was the one who remembered the questions he wanted to ask.

"My relative," he began, using the courtesy term, "we hear tales that we think can't be true. That one," he pointed to a meek-looking half-breed with short hair who wore overalls of the kind worn by farmers, with a bib up the front, into which he stuck his hands, "tells us that Bull and all his relatives were brought down here from his camp and that he is going to be hanged. We went to the jail but found nobody. Is it possible that such a thing could be?"

The speaker was a tall man with braids down the front and a knitted wool cap on his head. His thin face had deep hollows and his eyes were sad and watery.

"He is too great a man," he added.

The official name given The Boy at school was Richard Marks, but everybody still called him The Boy, which was the translation for Son Child, his Indian name. He was over six feet tall and the agency roster showed him to be fifty-four years of age—still, he was The Boy. His hair was heavy and black and he moved easily on his feet, so the name was not entirely incongruous.

He looked carefully at the three men waiting at the bottom of the steps: at the hollow-cheeked man, the half-breed in farmer's overalls, and a third who wore a fur cap and a surplus army overcoat held together with horse blanket pins. He was one of the few who grew a moustache—Coffee Lip, they called him, because he sucked his moustache. The Boy knew these three, and knew that his words would be carried far before the day had passed.

"Who knows what will come out of what white men do? The marshall from Elk City brought Bull and his kinsmen here to ask them some questions. You wonder why these questions could not be asked up there in Bull's camp? I can't tell you why, except that is the way these people act. The new government man had nothing to do with it. When you tell this to others, just say that Bull asked the people to be quiet until we know what is going to happen. Maybe the questions are all asked and there will be no more to it."

The tall one asked: "Bull said that—to be quiet?"

Coffee Lip asked: "He didn't get mad?"

The inside voices had stopped; The Boy heard steps behind him, and hurried to answer: "That is so. Bull asked the people to wait and see how it would be—but I didn't tell you he wasn't mad."

He had said that much when Sid Grant, his deputy trailing, burst through the door and scattered the Indians at the bottom of the steps. They watched, saying nothing, until the two impatient ones reached their horses at the hitching rack.

"I guess that one is mad as well," Coffee Lip remarked.

When they turned back to ask more questions, The Boy had gone inside.

Rafferty was sitting at his desk, thumping rapidly with the eraser end of a pencil. He had a darker skin than most white men, and The Boy saw that his coloring was even darker than usual. He said nothing at first, just sat and thumped.

When he talked finally, he didn't look up, but stared in the direction of the door.

"Mr. Grant thinks whoever killed the man at the dam came from Bull's camp. He followed some tracks right to the camp."

The Boy stood in front of the desk, just looking at it.

"He said the man was killed with a .30/30 slug, which Doc Edwards dug out near the hip. But he couldn't find a .30/30 rifle in camp. Isn't that the kind of gun most hunters around here use? Do you know whether Bull has such a gun?"

The Boy shifted his feet. "I guess most people got that kind of gun."

"Also, he's looking for some cowboy boots. Just about everybody wears those boots around here." The statement seemed to be directed at himself.

The Boy transferred his hat from his right hand to his left and he stared at the wall back of the desk, where portraits of George Washington and Abraham Lincoln were together in one frame. The wall was a smooth white plaster and the window and door frames, the door as well, were stained and varnished. it was a big desk, with papers scattered all over.

"He wanted me to hold Bull for a grand jury, but I said nothing doing." Rafferty was still talking to himself but his voice slowed to his more usual way of speaking. The pencil thumping stopped.

"Not without something to go on. Just now, he has nothing, only some tracks, and that hunch of his. He's gone back up there, and he'll tear that camp apart. Fishing, we call it."

Finally he turned to The Boy, really looked at him. "Sit down! You're not on the carpet, if you know what that means."

He knew that, and many harsher expressions as well. For half of his fifty-four years, The Boy had served the government men who came to Little Elk—as janitor, teamster, interpreter, night watchman, and now, chief of the tribal police force, which consisted of two men, himself and Crooked Leg, an Indian from a neighboring tribe married to a Little Elk woman. As an adolescent sent off to school for the first time, he waited for the dead of winter to run away from Genoa, Nebraska, a government boarding school, and traveled almost a thousand miles, most of the time on foot, to reach home in the spring. He didn't like to talk about it, how he sheltered, what he ate. By the time he reappeared as part of the Little Elk population he was a grown man, and nobody threatened to send him back to school.

"I liked to hear it talked," he once explained to Rafferty about learning English. "I liked to hear the old people talk too. The kids my age didn't care much about that, and they got to talking a kind of lingo. They were scolded by their people, but they didn't care. I tried to say things just the way the older people talked, and after a while they would ask me to go with them when they wanted to talk to the agent. So they gave me a job here and forgot about my running away that time."

Rafferty pursued his thought.

"I doubt if Bull or anyone in his camp knew that young fellow, so why would they be out after him? It doesn't make sense. Of course, we have to find out what happened. If somebody in Bull's camp is guilty, we have to get him, we have to cooperate. I told the marshal we would—but I also told him I don't like to see people pushed around, anybody, but especially I don't like to see it happen to Indians. I wouldn't make a special case for Indians, but if they don't understand the language or our legal procedure they might act foolishly and get hurt. I agreed that Bull could stay here while the camp is searched, but I hope some relative doesn't stand out in the woods and take a potshot at the marshal."

He leaned back and studied his folded, stub-fingered hands.

"I haven't talked to Bull yet. When they brought him in, it seemed best to let everybody simmer down for a while. My first thought was that we would go over together, but now I'm thinking it would be better if you talked to him by yourself. I want him to understand how the white man's law works. He's not charged with anything at the moment, and for all I know he won't be, but we have to ask these questions.

"Another thing. He doesn't have to make any kind of a statement. Get him to understand that, if you can. Or if he wants to talk through a lawyer, we'll arrange it —but I guess that would really scare him. Forget it. My main concern is that he understand what we're doing, what we have to do. We're not against him—we're not accusing him—"

"If he did it, he will tell me," The Boy said with shattering simplicity.

"What? He would?"

"Sure. If he killed that man he won't say no. He'll say it right out. Why should he lie? If he killed that man, he had a reason, and he will tell me why it was. He won't talk to a lawyer."

It was an upsetting idea. Rafferty straightened in his chair and stared. "Now wait a minute. If he tells you that, if it should turn out that way, keep it to yourself. I don't want to hear it. If he wants to tell me of his own accord, that's different. But he should understand in that case I'd be obliged to put it in writing—"

Then he saw what must be the answer.

"If he shot that man, and intended to tell the truth as soon as somebody asked him, why did he hide his rifle, assuming he owns that kind of rifle? There wasn't a rifle in camp, and that seems odd."

The Boy shrugged off the logic. "Maybe he didn't do it. Maybe he didn't hide the rifle. Maybe Sid Grant couldn't find it."

"Yeh. Yeh. Three maybes in a row." he relaxed again.

He had been hearing the sound for some time. And now it came louder and could not be ignored. He turned to the window, looking out toward the sandhills. What he saw caused him to leave his chair and walk to the window, his perplexity increasing.

Outside, Henry Jim's kinsmen were at the gate leading into the compound. There were really two gates. The woven wire fence terminated at sturdy posts on each side of a deep pit which was bridged over by spaced rails to discourage stray stock from coming in to forage on the agency grass and shrubbery. Horses and wagons coming on legitimate business used a closed gate next to

82

the cattle guard. Most riders tied their horses at the hitching rack outside rather than trouble themselves with opening and closing the gate. But when these riders came to the gate, one dismounted while the others rode through. Then they waited for him. They had been singing as they came up the road—catching Rafferty's ear—and they continued to sing as they rode through the compound to the office building.

Rafferty turned to The Boy for an explanation, and the casual manner of The Boy's speaking was as unsettling as the singing men.

"Henry Jim's people. For two days they've been singing for him. His dream told him to sing. He will stay alive until the singing stops."

His gaze went from The Boy to the window and back again. Something was happening, he could not tell what, like the first toll of a bell. He would be listening for the following strokes and never be sure when or where it tolled.

"I don't understand," he said, his voice flat. "When he came here, only a few days ago, he wasn't talking of death. What has happened?"

The men came in, one at a time, lifting off their big hats as they crossed the threshold, and The Boy moved them into chairs around the desk: Jerome, Frank Charley, Iron Child, Baptiste, Tom John, Little Man, Old Charles, Quis-Quis, and Antoine Beauchamp, called Tony. These were the men who had ridden with Henry Jim. The fragrance of many campfires, of smoked buckskin, of sage winds filled the room.

Their faces turned to Rafferty, mildly and pleasantly looking up and beyond him. And Rafferty looked for The Boy.

"Tell them, they don't have to stop singing!"

"They will sing in their minds," The Boy offered, dryly. "They want to talk for Henry Jim. First this one, Iron Child."

The one designated placed his hat carefully on the floor—a tan hat, wide and high crowned, with a downy eagle feather attached to the narrow band. When he stood he was not tall, but the thickness of his chest and shoulders gave him the bearing of a big man. His clothing was old, but it had just come clean from an old suitcase. The side and back hair were carefully gathered in two even braids and wrapped in strips of mink. The top hair and forelock were brushed upward and fell to one side. It was clear to anyone that such a man had a good wife, one who knew how to take care of a man. His earlobes, slightly elongated, were pierced and threaded with fine silver wire, from which disks of irridescent shell were pendent.

"I talk here for Henry Jim," he explained through The Boy. "He asked us to come, since he was too weak this morning to make it to his horse. We are his kinsmen and have come to speak for him, to ask this government man to come to his house for a talk. We tried to come here last night, but a big man put his horse across the road and said we had to go home. He said Bull had some kind of trouble, but we couldn't understand what kind of trouble. The man was angry so we didn't stay there.

"People say this new man is all right, he has made no trouble for us. They say we can talk to him and not hold back. Tell him we want him to understand about our people. We had a bad quarrel among ourselves. It started many years ago. Some say Henry Jim was at fault for starting this quarrel. I think it just started because we were losing out, we were weak. White men were coming in to our country, taking our land, killing the game, and sending our children away. We knew the white man was too strong for us, we couldn't fight him, so we began to fight among ourselves and we blamed Henry Jim. I myself was among those who put the blame on him. All that time, when the quarrel was going strong, I wouldn't go to his house. That was wrong, since we are kinsmen.

"What made it worse, we lost the Feather Boy bundle. Maybe this white man won't understand what I mean. Just tell him we lost our Indian flag, our Indian Lord Jesus, maybe he'll understand it better. They say Henry Jim, my kinsman, threw it away and that was what started the trouble. I don't know if that is true or not. I won't cry about it any more.

"I'm talking for Henry Jim, my kinsman. He went to Bull and took his hand. He said, 'Brother, let us fight no more.' Then he said this new government man will help us. He said he would come and talk to this man and ask him to bring back our Indian flag, which we call Feather Boy medicine bundle. Henry Jim said that to Bull, his younger brother. Then he came down from Bull's camp and rode up through the valley. He visited each one of these men. He visited my camp. And everywhere he said, 'Brothers, we will fight no more.' That is how the quarrel ended.

"But now, tell this man, just see where we are. Our old-time leader, the one chosen by the old men years ago, my kinsman, Bull, is here. Somebody said he is in jail. And Henry Jim, who brought the quarrel to an end, is listening to his voices and will soon leave us behind. Just when we all agreed to put aside this quarrel, we seem to be falling down again. We ask this man to help us. That is what I have to say."

Each man then rose in turn, placed his hat carefully on the floor, gave the same account of things that had happened, and asked for help.

While Rafferty thought carefully of what he could say, they rose together and filed through the door, still carrying their hats. He stood at the window while they mounted their horses and rode to the gate. One dismounted while the others rode through. Then they took their places, four riders in front, five in the rear, and the singing began again.

The fragrance of the many campfires lingered in the room.

Rafferty was at his desk again and heard himself say, "Do they really think they can keep him alive by singing—?" And then, "Never mind. I shouldn't have asked."

The Boy seemed to speak from a great distance. "I guess they'll try."

85

11

Bull and the men had been placed in a basement storage room of the schoolhouse, next to the furnace room, where they were warm and dry and could be served food from the school kitchen.

Sid Grant had protested when he realized the men were not going into the agency jail.

He had come riding in, in the early evening, the men riding behind his lead, Ambrose the wordless deputy bringing up the rear.

"I want them locked up," he had insisted.

Rafferty had calmly stated his reasons. The jail could not be heated properly. It had only a woodburning stove, and that was in the jailer's office. It had but a single cell, with two double-decker beds—not enough room. It was vermin infested and was scheduled to be torn down.

"At least nail those windows shut. I want those men in custody!"

Rafferty had reminded him: "This is not a committing court, even if you were prepared to place a charge against them. Take them to Elk City if you insist on detention."

"They object to feeding Indian prisoners over there, as you damn well know." It was a sore point. The county would not feed Indian prisoners at its own expense, and the agency said it had no authority to pay the county.

"Then let them stay here, as guests of the agency."

"This is murder, not a social affair."

"My instructions are to offer full cooperation—which is what I am offering. We'll feed the men, and have them on hand any time you want to question them."

The marshal glared, but it was getting late. It had been a long day.

The men were sitting on iron bedsteads when The Boy went to talk with them that morning. The room had been only partly cleared to make space for the beds. Behind them was a jumble of discarded student desks, three-legged chairs, collapsed blackboards, boxes of tattered books. The windows placed high in the wall subdued the daylight to a dusty pallor.

The Boy had learned long ago that an Indian who worked for the government never found it easy to be alone with his people. He came into a room as a stranger, and conversation stopped.

"I greet my uncles," he said.

"We greet this younger brother." Courtesy could always carry that far.

The Boy found a chair with four legs and moved it into the circle of beds. Then they waited. No one stirred. No one looked in his direction.

Two Sleeps sat with closed eyes. His yellowed hair framed his face and clung to his woolen white man's coat in whorls and shreds. Basil had eaten a large breakfast and looked comfortable. Louis stared and smoked, and yellow cigarette stubs accumulated at his feet. Pock Face and Theobold sat together on one bed, part of the group and yet separate.

Bull's bed was near the center of the arrangement. He sat on the edge, elbows on knees. It was an uncomfortable position for sitting. But they had found the concrete floor cold and hard, so they all sat on the soft mattresses and sagging springs, and their backs ached.

"What's he like, this new government man?" Bull asked without shifting position or looking up.

"I guess he's all right. He talks good."

"He wants Indian for his friend—is that what he says?"

"This man says that."

"He wants to be good to Indians—he says that?"

"That's how it is. He says that."

"Looks like a good man. Is that what you think?"

"I find it is so, my Uncle."

Bull reared back, clapping his hands to his knees.

"Then why am I sitting here in this hole in the ground? I can't even see where the sun is. What has happened to my camp? I left my grandson to take care of it for me. Have they stuck him in a hole also? Where are my horses?"

"I came to talk about these things."

"Then talk about it. You only tell us what a good man this government man is. Tell ine about my camp."

"You asked, and I answered. I will go to your camp, if that is your wish."

"I don't ask it. I know before you could tell me. The man-with-a-star is up there pulling everything apart and my women are running around with their shawls pulled over their heads. Your good government man is letting them do that to my camp."

"They are looking for a gun."

"Every time a white man is killed they look for an Indian."

"The man-with-a-star followed tracks to your camp."

"How should I know whose tracks he followed? We have three camps near us, and others farther down. People go from camp to camp, or they go past our place when they are traveling to the mountains. Sometimes they ride horses, sometimes they walk. Is this man-with-a-star such a good trail man? Did the horses wear iron shoes? Was one of them pigeon-toed, like the horse I ride? Were they big or small? Were they loose horses going for water or did they have riders? If that man can answer my questions, I will respect him. He told us nothing. Just poked his gun at us and told us to saddle our horses. Are they watering and feeding our horses down here?"

"It is taken care of. The government man did not ask that other one to bring you here."

"Why didn't he tell us to go home, where we belong?"

"The man-with-a-star made a piece of paper. He said somebody in your camp killed a man and we have to hold you until they tell us to let you go. That's the way it is in the white man's law."

It was Louis who exploded over the cigarette he was fashioning. "This is a trick. They will squeeze us until we can't stand any more. Maybe somebody will speak just to get out of here. We can't trust even our own relatives at a time like this."

Bull ignored his kinsman. "If somebody in my camp killed that man, let them tell us who did it. How many bullets hit that man? One? Here we are six. Were we all holding that gun? Or maybe six bullets hit him. That white man is crazy."

"That is the law they follow."

"What kind of law is that? Did we have such a law? When a man hurt somebody in camp, we went to that man and asked him what he was going to do about it. If he did nothing, after we gave him a chance, we threw him away. He never came back. But only a mean man would refuse to do something for the family he hurt. That was a good law, and we still have it. We never threw it away. Who is this white man who comes here and tells us what the law is? Did he make the world? Does the sun come up just to look at him? I want no such law if it tells you to hurt everybody because one person is at fault."

Bull looked around, realizing all over again where he was. "I am tired of sitting here—I am tired of a man who puts a gun in my face. I came here yesterday, I said nothing, because I was thinking all the time about my elder brother. He put our quarrel behind him. He said this government man would help us. But I can't stand much more. You better ask your questions and go back to your government man."

"No, my Uncle. I am not working for the man-with-a-star. He can ask his own questions. I came to talk for the government man. He was against that other one for bringing you down here. He would not put you in the jail. Also, he would not let them lock this door or nail up the windows. Just the same, he can't tell you to go home until they work it out. He sent me here to tell you how it is, not to make you feel bad by asking questions."

An unexpected thing happened then. Pock Face rose up to speak. His hands were nervous. He hooked his thumbs in his belt, then crossed his arms over his chest, even clasped both hands behind his head. His eyes were bright with rushing thought.

"My leaders," he said—as if to say "my captains"— "a young man is not asked to speak. So I don't have much practice and you will have to go easy on me. I want to say what is in my mind. It is wrong to keep these men here away from their homes. That man who brought us was rough in his speech, so no one tried to talk to him. This old man here, we call him Two Sleeps, he should be home in his own bed. It confuses him to be dragged away like this. The others have women and children, grandchildren, who worry about them. I just want to say there is no reason for it. I shot that man at the dam. I was looking down on the water when he came out and walked toward me on top of the dam. I thought, maybe he isn't the man who built the dam and killed our water, but he works for that man. He keeps the water from running through and the trees will die and the earth itself will not be watered. So I shot him. Tell this to the government man and maybe he will let the others go home."

He sat down abruptly, as if pulled from behind.

The silence lasted a long time.

Louis's mouth trembled before he spoke, yet his words were like a bark. "This boy who spoke is my son. His mother was killed when her horse ran away with her. She was dragged I don't know how many miles, but she threw the boy clear and he was not hurt. He is trying to make it easy for the rest of us. He knows nothing about that killing."

The room fell into another silence. Then Bull breathed deeply, pulling all the air in his direction. "I listened, but I heard nothing. I think, my kinsmen, that our troubles are enough for us. We don't need to look for more. The man up there was not one of us. He has people to mourn for him. Let his own people be troubled. It was that way when we were a free people and had to hunt in country where others came to hunt. Sometimes we had to fight, and somebody would get hurt, maybe killed. We learned to bear our losses by ourselves. No one else would be troubled by what happened to us.

"I am willing to wait here. The man-with-a-star can follow a trail, he says. Let him point his finger at the right one. If somebody will feed my camp and my horses, I can sit here all winter."

No one looked at him, but now they all waited for The Boy to speak. And he waited, scanning the floor near his feet.

"When I started to work for the government, I was a young man, like the young man who spoke to us. My own father turned his face away. It was the same with all my relatives. They thought I would never be one of them again. Sometimes I have to go to a man's house and take him away. His relatives spit at me and say I am on the white man's side. They say how can I be so mean? And if I wait half a day while the man talks to his family, he isn't even polite to me. If I didn't do it, a white man would do it. It would be different if a white man took him away. You saw for yourselves how this man acted in your camp. White men are like that, always angry, always shouting. Have I become like that, when I carry a piece of paper and have to take a man to jail?

"My friends, I never left my people. What happened in the canyon is not my affair. Since a white man was killed, it is not my affair. I heard nothing in this room."

He waited for his words to settle in their minds before he spoke again.

"I came here for a different reason. I came to tell you that your elder brother was here, riding his big horse. And just today his relatives from the valley came to speak for him. They say he is too weak to rise from his bed. The grass is singing for him. It troubles my mind. I think the government man is ready to help. I think that is in his mind. But everybody will be saying, 'An Indian killed a white man! Find the killer!' And Henry Jim will die before we can do the thing he asked. That is how I am troubled."

Louis rattled dry tobacco in a cigarette paper. Basil scratched his belly.

Two Sleeps opened his eyes, pushed forward from his sagging bed. It became clear that he had been awake all the time.

"This boy is one of us and speaks as one of us. He says the new government man will help us, and I believe him. I watched him last night, the government man. He had angry eyes when he talked to that other one, but he acted right. He kept his words soft. He was polite. He came back after we went to bed to see if we had enough blankets. Such a man, I say, is to be trusted. But maybe his hands will be tied because of what happened. In a little while you may begin to think this young nephew should stand before the government man, the way he did here a while ago, and take the blame. Just to clear up everything. But my kinsmen, that would be a mistake. He is young. He has a young wife to lie with. I was dreaming in one eye while you talked, and I saw how it would be. I am the one who will stand up and tell how I shot the man on the dam. I will even show them where I hid my old gun between some logs in my cabin. What can they do to an old man that hasn't already happened?"

When he said, "Even if they decide to cut off the things that make a man, mine are all dried up anyhow and no use to me," the room exploded with laughter. They all looked at the old man.

Bull sobered quickly and his face was heavy again. "I agree that Son Child, although he is our tribal policeman, talks like one of us. For the first time I know it, and I am glad to have it that way. We are one people here together. How much longer will it be?

"My kinsmen, it is too much to pay. What if we give up this boy, or this old man—or what if I show them where my gun is hiding? One of us will be taken, and we will be one less. True, a white man was taken by somebody's bullet. But are the white people so small that the loss of one lessens them? I think not.

"Our policeman tells us the new man is ready to help us. He has it in his mind. My elder brother came to my camp and talked in the same way about the new man. This old grandfather here—we thought he was asleep, but he looked at the new man and it satisfied him. I will accept what all of you say. I have nothing against this man. He is young. His face is clear. He talks quietly. Still, I have to sniff the air. Somewhere here there is a trap. The ground is well covered, but there is a hole down there. I am like a bear coming down from the mountains in the spring. I am cranky. I look all around me. I stand up and put my nose in the wind. It is like that. We older ones can remember when we would be in camp, maybe on a hunting trip. And some one would say, 'Listen!' Everybody would stop. But there would be nothing. Just the same, the man who called out would go to look around. Maybe a young man. And he wouldn't come back. Later, we would go to look, and we would find him, lying under a bush or behind a rock. Somebody had waited there. People who grow up with such stories never forget. Death always waited beyond the camp circle.

"I say, if we give up one of ours, the good feeling we buy will be the trap that finishes us. Just hear me out. The government man will be pleased if we do that. He will open his arms to us. He will even help to bring back our medicine bundle. But maybe the power will be gone from it.

"My mind travels ahead and sees that far. Then it stops. Something else is out there, but I can't see it. Maybe our grandfather here can go to the mountains and learn the rest of it—if he doesn't show them that old buffalo gun he hid somewhere and go to jail instead.

"How can a white man help us? When he looks at us, the way we live, the way we pray, what can he see? If his heart is good, maybe he will smile, put his hand on my head. I put my hand on my grandson's head when I see him as a child and I want to tell him to grow up and be a strong man—a man like one of us, a man with brown skin, speaking our language. But the white man means, 'You'll be a strong man when you become a white man.' It's his way of offering me friendship. He looks, but doesn't see me. I'm not a grown man in his eyes, a man full of hunger, who has traveled here and there, who has known what it's like to need a woman. How can he help me?

"It's a hard thing to say, my kinsmen, but I'm afraid of this friendship. Don't push me into it.

"I grieve for my brother because even now, when the

grass is singing for him, he looks to the white man for help, as he always did. And the white man has only destroyed us.

"Son Child, go to the government man and say we want to leave here and join those who are singing for my brother. We want him to see that we are one people."

After that, no one wanted to speak. Not right away.

12

The women moved about in the misty dawn, catching the firelight on their brown faces and throwing vague shadows against tepee coverings.

Horses brought up the night before made a dark huddle in the corral. They blew frost from their nostrils and nuzzled at a mound of hay.

The camp dogs sniffed their way around and quickly discovered that food was being prepared at only one cooking place. All the women and their children had come to Veronica's lodge. They drank coffee between tasks, but the children settled near the fire where bread and meat were frying. Talk was brief and scattered.

They watched the girl-wife, Lucelle. She walked distractedly from place to place, never finishing a task. The women took turns scolding her. Her dark, troubled eyes filled with moisture after each chiding and her hands fell to her sides.

Veronica said: "That child thinks she is miserable because her man isn't with her. Who of us wouldn't think it a pleasure to feel that kind of misery again? Tell her to come eat."

Bull's second wife, Catherine, slipped away from the fire. She was yet a young woman; her round face was still smooth, and she moved with a light step. Among all the women in camp, she was the quietest in speech, and she kept to her own lodge. No one could equal her in preparing fine buckskins, which came from her hands as white and soft as the white man's linen.

She neither scolded nor teased when she went to Lucelle, and the girl became silent and watchful.

"We'll take just what we need and leave the rest. We can tie things in a shawl. I'll help you. The men will come back in a few days and the camp will be the same as always. Our relatives in the valley will take care of us, so don't carry more than you need. It is a lonely thing, to be a woman alone, but your man will think well of you if you do your part in the camp. . . ."

She talked thus, gently, while her hands moved here and there, selecting things to be tied in the shawl.

And then the girl talked. "These women think my man did a bad thing and brought this trouble. They don't say it, but their eyes are like whips. If they would just beat me, so that look would go away! He did it to win his place with the men. Everybody thinks he is no good. They don't know him. I know he is like a small boy, who plays too hard sometimes, and he gets hurt, or he hurts somebody. Then he is sad, just like a small boy when you scold. He knows I never scold; that is good for him. I don't know what will happen now—and I'm afraid. If they take him away, I think, it will kill him."

Catherine sat on the ground, rocking back and forth. The bright scarf tied at the back of her head held the hair back and softened her face.

"When I came here to live, I was about your age. My husband was already old, but very strong, in the way men are. He was quarrelsome, maybe like your man, a bitterness was in his mouth. Sometimes his anger was so great the people in his own camp feared him—then when it got beyond his control he would walk out of camp and be gone for days. And we never knew what would happen, what trouble he would make for himself or for others. He always carried his gun. It was not my place to say anything or do anything. Veronica would pull her shawl over her head and refuse to talk to any of us."

She hugged her knees and rocked. "I was never afraid of him. People said he was mean and that he would hurt somebody. They said that because they didn't know him. When he came to my lodge, he left his anger outside. I think it is always the same with men. Even after they are leaders, they have to keep pushing, even when it means trouble for themselves. But when they are out of sight and nobody is watching, you see how different they are. You are a lucky one, as I was—I can tell. I would have it no other way.

"Come, now. We are finished here. The food is waiting. Bull will bring your man back."

Lucelle went quietly to the fire, and the women made room for her and put food in her hands. She smiled her gratitude, and this started a chattering, as if a nest of magpies had settled there.

Antoine came up from the corral to say that all was ready. The horses were saddled and waiting.

Veronica gave him his food. "Our man," she said. "Feed him well."

The meddlesome Star Head ran her hand up Antoine's narrow back. "He's got to be strong back here if he is going to take care of all of us. Feed him up!"

The boy kept to his eating as if nothing had been said.

Veronica did not like the woman and turned her head aside.

Marie Louise, the scarred one, was still grumbling as she walked from the fire to her lodge and back again, repeatedly. Earlier, she had pulled out a heap of bags, bundles, and old suitcases tied with bits of cotton rope. She insisted on taking everything.

It had been agreed they would take only what they needed. They would be away from camp just a few days. They had enough horses to ride, but no extras for pack animals. As it was, the mothers would have to manage their small children and their possessions all on one horse.

Everyone knew that Marie Louise had quantities of beaded finery. She wanted nothing left behind. Every time she went to her tepee, she came out with another dress pulled on over what she already wore and another beaded belt around her middle.

The women watched her without seeming to. They heard her grumble about people who "stick their noses in" and people who "should mind their own business," but no one answered her.

Finally she had put together in one very large bundle what she insisted she would take.

"Some of this was my grandfather's, who was a chief before any of you were born. Some was my mother's. Some was my first husband's. But most I made myself, and my beadwork is as good as anybody's. I'm not going to leave any of this behind for some lazy person to come along and think it was left for him to take home."

The others stared, but no one wanted to speak out. They knew she had two small children to manage, as well as the bundle.

Veronica said, "All right. We'll just see. Bring up her horse."

Antoine had already learned that women sometimes accomplish what a man knows to be impossible, and he thought maybe this was one of those times. He went for the horse.

Catherine, the second wife, and Lucelle offered to help. Each would take a child on her horse.

"You won't have to worry," Catherine said. "We'll take good care of the children."

Then they had to decide how to do it. If Marie Louise rode in the saddle, she could not very well hold the bundle in back. Neither could she ride on top of the bundle, which was at least three feet high after it was tied down tight. She decided to put the bundle in the saddle and tie it down, and she would ride in back and hold on to the bundle.

It was not a big horse, and it stood waiting with drooping head. It had blotches of roan and blotches of white, and one pink eye.

The women talked while the horse waited, and after a while they reached agreement. They would try it with the bundle in the saddle and Marie Louise in back.

Antoine listened and watched and held on to the bridle reins. He was not sure what would happen.

The bundle was heaved up—beaded buckskin is heavy—and dumped into place. The horse's eyes were suddenly wide open. It sidestepped, almost stepping out from under the bundle. But Marie Louise and Veronica stayed with it and kept the bundle from tumbling to the ground. The horse continued to fidget, but they got the bundle tied securely to the saddle.

The problem then was to get Marie Louise, in all her skirts, up on the horse. Antoine led the blotchy roan down the short slope to the corral, where Marie Louise could climb the rail fence. The animal went downhill smartly. Once the load was in place, it didn't mind.

Marie Louise climbed to the top rail, above the horse's back. Antoine handed her the bridle reins and stepped aside. She slipped her right leg over, pushed with the other, and was squarely over the croup, just back of the burdened saddle.

The horse snorted, then reared. But instead of leaping ahead, it merely sat on its haunches. Marie Louise rolled to the ground, a bundle of skirts. Relieved of that burden, the beast reared again, then vaulted high into the air, came down on stiff legs and was off. After three jumps the frayed old cinch burst, and saddle and bundle arched a low flight through the air before settling in some brush.

Marie Louise would not get up to see if anything was broken or hurt. She rocked back and forth, with one hand to her face.

By now it was getting late, and Veronica would have no more.

"Your bundle is too big. It was agreed what we would take. We'll carry your bundle up to your lodge and you can take out the things you need and leave the rest. The boy will go for your horse."

Antoine was already mounted and on his way. The talk of women worried him.

Marie Louise made her decision as she was getting to her feet. Instead of rising first on one knee, then pulling herself up, she rose like a cow—first putting both hands on the ground, then pushing up her rump, and straightening up afterward. This was a slow process, and gave her time to think.

"Me, I'm not going no place. I'm staying right here," she said.

"We don't want to leave you and the children. It's best to stay together."

"If I can't take my things, I'll just stay here. If somebody wants to rob this camp, I'll just watch them carry it away. But my grandfather's battle shirt and shield and my grandmother's elk-tooth dress will be right in my lodge and I'll be sitting on them."

None of the others wanted it that way, but it was getting late. They carried the bundle up to the lodge and made sure she had flour and coffee. Then the two children, boy and girl, did not want to be left behind, since the other children were going. Marie Louise did not soften even then. She just said, "Go on! Go on! Only don't make trouble for your relatives!"

Antoine returned with the blotchy roan, still flying its tail high, only to be told to put the horse in the corral. It was puzzling, but it just seemed that everybody was mixed up.

And when they set out at last, the sun was already above the horizon trees.

Sid Grant and his deputy, Ambrose, arrived soon after that and saw the trail of many horses leading off to the west. The marshal stared at the tracks, and cursed steadily for several minutes. The trail of the two horsemen he had followed the previous day was completely obliterated. To satisfy himself, he followed the fresh tracks all the way to where, on the previous day, he had found the ashes of a small fire. The ashes had been trampled and scattered. Then the fresh tracks led northward, toward the crossing in the canyon.

"It do beat hell!" he remarked.

13

While Bull and his kinsmen were riding at a soft canter toward Henry Jim's ranch in the flats, a train stopped at Elk City and people descended: the porter in his blue station jacket, then a stiff-legged man leaning on a cane, then a veiled woman. Each day at Elk City a train from the east and a train from the west brought the world to the incurious Little Elk Indians. This was the morning train arriving from the east, and the two passengers left standing on the platform with bags and wraps as the train whistled its departure brought that outer world. Their dress and manner and their air of uncertainty were foreign to the landscape.

The man stared down the tracks at the water tank, painted red but weathering to sooty black, then northward across the tracks to pine-shadowed hills moving away into the unknown. After some minutes of turning and appraising his surroundings, the man began to thump with his knobbed walking stick. The drumming was not very loud and the sound was immediately consumed by the silence.

"Must be somebody around to come for our things."

His wife began to organize matters. She was a small woman, encased formlessly in a black duster. A black veil was gathered back from a round, pale face.

"Leave the things there, Thomas. I'll go to the station. Somebody should be there to take care of business." As she walked, she felt the grit of the platform bruising her fine leather shoes.

The station agent, Bert Smiley, pushed his green eyeshade high on his forehead to emphasize his embarrassment. "Sorry I couldn't get to you folks sooner. Messages been coming in a mile a minute . . ." He jabbed his thumb backward in the direction of the clacking telegraph key.

"Lot's been happening around here, messages flying around like unsettled blackbirds. Ain't no message come for you, though. Say the name's Thomas H. Cooke, C-double-O-K-E? No, ma'am."

They faced each other across the waist-high counter separating the public waiting room from the station-master's domain, and Albert Smiley was already taking side steps in retreat. Mrs. Cooke brought a bit of cologne-scented lace to her mouth and nose to exclude the stale odor of mingled cigar and coal smoke.

"My brother, Mr. Pell, is to meet us here. He is coming from New York. I expected a message . . ."

Mr. Smiley's station-agent bearing vanished and he returned to the customer's counter with a certain eagerness.

"Mr. Pell, you say? Mr. Adam Pell? Well, now, that's something else. Half the messages coming in or going out of here are from him, or for him. Yes, ma'am."

"You've heard from him, then, Mr.—?"

"Smiley, ma'am. Yes, indeed. About him, at least. That's what all the noise is about. Say!" He pushed his green eyeshade still higher on his forehead, seeming to consider whether to remove it entirely, like a hat. "You must be the mother of that boy the coroner's sitting on just now! Jimmie Cooke, they say, was his name—same spelling."

There was a thumping just outside the door; the door opened and Thomas Cooke was there, balancing on his good leg. Closing the door against the crisp mountain air involved a clumsy pivoting on his right leg, the good one, and a kind of sculling motion with his thick walking stick.

"Seems not to be a hack or any kind of rig in this town." The voice expressed more exasperation than anger, a controlled voice not given to expletive. His striped trousers, black broadcloth coat, and hard hat accented the voice. Mr. Cooke was actually rather tall, but his thin features and sparse body seemed to diminish his stature.

His wife stepped forward at once, taking his arm. "Mr. Smiley, here, tells me that Adam has been sending messages. Does he say when he'll arrive?"

"I was just about to tell you that part." The station agent paused, struck perhaps by the enormity of what he had to say. "The last word over the wire was from the traffic manager himself, right in Chicago. He'll be here, all right. Yes, ma'am. They're attaching Mr. Pell's private car to the fast mail due to roar through here at 2:04 this P.M. Yes, ma'am, he'll sure be here. They'll shunt the private car to the siding, then roar out again. They'll put a switch engine on the siding and run water and steam lines to Mr. Pell's car. He must pretty durn near own this railroad to get treated like that."

His voice thinned out, then stopped, when he realized that the Cookes were not registering excitement. Their faces, he was astonished to discover, did not change color, or twitch, or frown—just stayed blank.

"Very good," Thomas Cooke remarked. "Now, can you get some kind of rig to come for our things? I suppose you have a hotel here?"

Mr. Smiley, feeling stepped on, resumed his station-agent bearing. "I'll get somebody over here right away. The whole town usually comes down to the depot to see the trains go through. But today they're all at the coroner's for the inquest. The boy—the body, excuse—that's at Doc Powell's funeral parlor, getting ready to be shipped." As he moved toward the door he added, "Thought you might want to know. Just excuse me. I'll go get a rig."

He might have used the telephone on the wall, but this was something he had to go tell somebody, just to get it out of his craw.

The emotion which had not surfaced for the station agent's gaze now brought deep color to Mrs. Cooke's round, pale face. "Oh! That Adam! There was no need for this! Private car! Our own arrangements were proper and fitting. No need to make a show of it."

"Now, Geneva. He's putting himself to great expense, and inconvenience, I'm sure, just to be here. He was fond of our boy."

"Expense means nothing. It's just his way of showing his importance. It's been that way since our childhood. He had other ways of putting on airs those days. Wouldn't go out with any of the girls our family knew. Said they were ninnies. The boys were clodhoppers, so he wouldn't go with them either. All he wanted to do during the summer—when Dad worked and scraped to get us to the lake—all Adam wanted to do was dig around in old earth heaps for arrowheads and skulls and—he used to make me so mad!"

Mr. Cooke tried a lighter note. "At least that way he didn't have to wear white pants and play the banjo summer evenings at the lake."

Both had taken seats, facing each other, on slatted benches in the waiting room.

Mrs. Cooke had come to a resolution. "Thomas, I want you to make a point of not referring to that private car. He won't mention it himself, but he'll be waiting for you to show deference. I won't have it. You have your own standing."

Mr. Cooke's naturally florid complexion deepened. "I find your remark unnecessary, my dear Gen. He is doing this for our boy, not for either of us. Certainly not for the local cowboys—and Indians. He never married, and treated Jimmie like his own son. I am grateful, and expect to tell him so."

Her retreat was slight. "Do as you like, but stand your ground with him. He'll try to take matters in his own hands. He always does. He may even be planning to talk to those Indians—he always talks to Indians—and he'll expect us to go along. But I'll not do it. I just want to take Jimmie home in a decent way."

The suggestion was startling and Mr. Cooke asked her why Adam would want to visit the Indians.

"Because he's made a hobby of Indians. Ever since he dug up arrowheads. You'll see."

"You mean, even at a time like this—"

At that moment the telegraph sounder began ripping off a string of code, and Mr. Cooke saw the station agent racing across the street, wiping his mouth with the back of his hand. Elk City was just outside the reservation boundary, and saloons flourished.

14

At the foothills camp of his uncle Jerome, where he brought the women from Bull's camp, Antoine saddled his buckskin pony and led her from the corral, where the other horses had their noses buried in a mound of hay. The morning was just coming light and was heavy with frost.

The little mare was his grandfather's gift, to celebrate his coming home from school. She was a trim animal, with black tail and mane, and a forelock that fell forward across the white blaze between her eyes. Her winter coat was coming on and the thickening hair was soft and warm where he ran his hand over her neck and shoulder.

He said aloud, but in English, in the manner of a returned student: "Those Indians don't know what's going on, so it's up to us to find out so I can tell them what to do."

He was standing at the pony's shoulder as he spoke, and realized suddenly that Veronica had come from the women's lodge and was standing behind him.

In his own language he added, "I'll just ride down the road, maybe to the government's house, and listen to what they are saying. Maybe I'll find my grandfather and he can tell me what happened."

Veronica knew he would go. She only said, "If a man keeps to himself, people will pass him by. Stay quiet and it will be all right. Tell your grandfather we are well here."

The pony preferred not to leave the other horses and she started off at a stiff-legged trot, but Antoine coaxed her, kicked at her ribs and pulled up her head, until at last she blew the frost out of her nostrils and settled into an easy loping stride.

It was a time of pleasure, to be riding in the early morning air, to feel the drumming earth come upward through the pony's legs and enter his own flesh. Yes, the earth power coming into him as he moved over it. And a thing of the air, like a bird. He breathed deeply of the bird-air, and that was power too. He held his head high, a being in flight. And he sang, as his people sang, of the gray rising sun and the shadows that were only emerging from the night.

To be one among his people, to grow up in their respect, to be his grandfather's kinsman—this was a power in itself, the power that flows between people and makes them one. He could feel it now, a healing warmth that flowed into his center from many-reaching body parts.

Still, he had no shell of hardness around him. He was going into a country where danger would be waiting. He knew what was behind Veronica's words. She was afraid of the questions they might ask: Who killed that man? What did you do with your guns? Who went to the mountains from your camp?

It was uncertain territory, this country of government buildings and government kind of people. They had loud voices. They pointed at you. They held your head and made you look them in the face. They could lock you up in a room and leave you by yourself.

He had already lived among such people and knew the fear that could snatch the breath away. Would it be the same today as it was when he went alone to the government school? Would he be a small body swept into a corner?

The Long-Armed-Man told them as soon as they arrived at the school: "You students, now, you listen to me. I want you to appreciate what we're doing for you. We're taking you out of that filth and ignorance, lice in your heads, all that, the way you lived before you came here, and we're going to fix you up clean and polite so no man will be ashamed to have you in his home. Forget where you came from, what you were before; let all of that go out of your minds and listen only to what your teachers tell you."

He couldn't remember all the words, but that was

the meaning of it. The students came from many miles away and from many tribes, all snatched up the way coyote pups are grabbed and stuffed into a sack while mother coyote sits on her haunches and licks her black nose.

They stayed together as much as they could when they first arrived, the students from each region or tribe favoring each other. When the strangeness wore off and they learned they were all Indians, wherever they came from, they found ways to work together against the common enemy. In spite of what Long-Armed-Man said, they had no desire to forget where they came from.

Within the hour of his arrival he was shoved into a small room where a matron and an older boy—called the Marching Captain by the other boys—awaited him. He was stripped to his brown skin and his clothing was taken away, to be burned, he was told. He wanted to cry. While he was still looking at the little pile of discarded garments, the Marching Captain began to clip his hair. When that was finished, kerosene was rubbed into his scalp.

"We don't like lousy Indians here," the matron said. She had dark spots on her face, and whiskers grew from the spots. Her hair was pulled up tight and made into a hard ring on top of her head.

"Your name will be Antoine Brown," she announced, and made a mark on a sheet of paper. "Just keep yourself clean," she continued, "so we won't have to do this again." Then she handed him stiff underwear that scratched and outer garments cut for a larger boy.

Before he could get into any of these garments, she put her hand on his shoulder and spun him around so she could look him over in front. "Take your hands away," she demanded, when he tried to cover up. Then she spun him further and looked at his backside.

"No scabs," she noted, and pushed him away.

Students who came from the southwestern deserts and from the treeless high plains were wonderstruck by the Oregon climate, where the grass stayed green, roses bloomed, and oak, maple, and walnut trees spread long arms across the sky. Neat white frame houses and brick dormitories were spaced among the trees, with wide lawns and hedged walks running between. Antoine and his mates moved among these splendors and knew only that they could not walk on the grass or disturb the flowers. And especially they were not to stray into the girls' section of the campus.

These were not warm memories, yet they crowded in on his mind and his morning song faded. The buckskin mare slowed to a walk, but Antoine never noticed. The sun was now out of the earth mist, making a warm place in the sky, but even this went unnoticed, so compelling were the crowding images.

He saw himself marching in line, the Marching Captain off to one side. "Hup, two, three—keep in step!" They marched like soldiers everywhere they went, and on Sunday afternoons they marched in dress parade. In between they practiced drill formations, shined their Sunday shoes, and polished the brass buttons on their dress uniforms. On weekdays they wore corduroy pants and jackets, but on Sundays they wore blue uniforms with black braid and stiff collars that hooked under the chin and made a red mark around the neck.

Mealtime was one of the few occasions when boys and girls could be together, and this sometimes brought disaster. They marched in from their opposite ends of the campus, and each had a place assigned, four boys and four girls to a table. Nobody could sit down until the dining room matron, a woman with white hair and blue-white skin, mounted a platform and led them in singing a song to Jesus, and even then they had to stand until she announced, "You may be seated." If somebody moved too soon, she held back the words and waited. The anxious ones who scraped a chair while grace was sung or before they were told to sit were called to the "praying platform" and made to stand there while the others ate.

The girls were supposed to be seated first, a boy standing behind each, ready to push her chair forward. Sometimes a girl locked her knees against the chair to keep it from moving, just to be mean, and if the boy left her and went to his own place, he could get into trouble, if the girl still wanted to be mean. She could complain loudly, and the matron might call the boy to the praying platform. This happened to the boy who slept next to Antoine in the dormitory. The girl raised her voice, and the boy gave her chair such a push that she was thrown against the table, upsetting the milk and water pitchers. The girl shrieked, and the boy had to go to the praying platform after all.

The blue-skinned matron moved hawk-eyed among the tables and terrorized the eaters with sharp commands about table manners. Antoine sat next to an Eskimo girl, an orphan who had come to the school as an infant and was still frightened after ten years. Others told her story —Antoine never heard her speak a word. She never looked up from her plate, but when the matron would pass their table, he'd see sweat on the girl's face. Usually she stopped eating and watched when she saw the blue-skinned woman approach. But one day the matron came up from behind and barked at the girl just as she overloaded her mouth with potatoes and gravy. The girl choked, her round, pasty face turning purple, and she fell to the floor, with gravy flowing from her nostrils and mouth. Antoine looked down at the stricken girl whose name he didn't even know, then ran from the room to lose his own meal on the concrete steps outside. The Marching Captain came right after him and sent him to the praying platform, where he almost turned sick again.

In spite of their seeming endlessness, the days at school did come to an end.

The Long-Armed-Man sent for him at Easter, when the school was in recess for a week. The message was brought to the play yard by the Marching Captain, whose small eyes had a hard shine.

"Now you'll catch it! They want you in the office. You got a dirty face, but don't stop to wash. When you get through bawling in there, it'll be all washed off. March!"

Antoine was so stricken that he seemed to crawl over the ground, and stood at last in the disciplinarian's office.

The man rose up from behind the desk until he

towered like a tree, a darkness against the light, and a moment later one arm of the big man was around the boy's shoulders and he was talking like a loving father: "My boy, it grieves me to tell you the news—don't pull away. I want you to realize that I'm your friend today, not just a school official. Look at me! There! I want you to be brave, like the good soldier we have been training you to be. My boy, your mother has died. We just received the word. We have been asked to send you home, and while we are reluctant to do this—you have been with us just over four years—maybe your superintendent will send you back in the fall."

Antoine heard none of it, only that he was going home—and that his mother would not be there.

The crying only started after he was outside again, standing dazed in the yard.

The Marching Captain came up slowly. He had been called to the office as well and had received his orders. And now he looked all dangling arms and stumble-footed.

"Chee! I didn't know you lost your mudder. He just told me now, told me to get you ready for the train tomorrow. I never been home—I guess I got no home. They made me the marching captain, and I have to be mean to you little guys. 'Show them you're boss' that's what they tell me." The Marching Captain began to wipe his eyes. And for the first time, Antoine saw the brown skin and black hair. The Marching Captain was Indian, like the others.

So he came home. Celeste, his mother, was Bull's first girl child, as he, Antoine, was her first child, and everyone told him she had never gotten over his going away. When the government men came to the camp and took him, without even saying where he would go, she told everybody, "He is dead," and soon she was dead. All this he learned when he returned.

And now, on this morning, riding his buckskin, the song came again, in snatches at first, then in a quiet flow. He pulled up on the reins, and the little mare moved into an easy trot, then into a loping gait. By the time he came in sight of the government's white buildings, his head was high.

He tied the buckskin mare among other horses at the hitching rack just outside the agency gate and walked into the compound, where the young trees stood in pools of yellow leaves. His hands were in his pants pockets and he held himself straight. Perhaps it would not be noticed that he was a boy walking under a big black hat. He moved toward a group of men sunning themselves in the crisp air.

Before he had gone far the one that was called Son Child, a big man, appeared on the sidewalk, blocking his way. Antoine didn't even notice where he came from, and just as he was about to pass, the big man spoke.

"You must be looking for somebody."

Antoine's eyes were bright with alarm. He said nothing, only looked for a place to run.

"It's all right. I just want to say, your grandfather isn't here. He and his kinsmen went to Henry Jim's ranch. I'm going there myself in a little while, with the government man."

Antoine watched the big man go on his way, then he turned. His feet seemed to go faster than he directed. It would not be necessary, after all, to get too close or stay too long in the country of the strangers. He could be with his own people again.

15

The boy rode through the low-lying sandhills that sloped down to the agency compound from the east and the north—hills of sagebrush, sparse grass, and scraggly jack pine. He followed the road, which had only a short distance to climb until the near hill was surmounted and the whole sweep of Little Elk valley was before him with the high mountains beyond. The road divided at the crest of the hill, one branch going eastward toward the higher country where Bull had his camp. Antoine turned into the north fork, which stayed in the valley and would bring him to Henry Jim's house.

The scolding of a magpie was the only sound heard. The sun was now high and warm, and earth creatures paused at their burrows, on leafless branches, or in brown thickets to stretch and dress their bodies. In the roadside dust were precisely made trails of night-visiting neighbors. A coyote loped up a hillside, going home late to a pine grove.

Antoine felt and saw all this, and felt the swinging motion of the little mare as she trotted steadily up the valley road—but these sights and sounds moved in the front part of his mind. He felt again the surprising hand warmth and the clasping fingers of the grandfather who had come out of the night and talked until the world stood still and his kinsmen all fell silent. Nothing had ever so filled his mind, and he would be part of it again, up ahead there, at Henry Jim's place.

It was a strange place to which he was going—not an enemy place though, and so he was not afraid. He remembered traveling the road before, when someone had said that the "runaway" kinsman lived in the house that looked like a white man's house. He had never stopped there—no one from Bull's camp ever stopped there. He could not remember seeing "that old one," as his mind thought of him, before the night he came and asked to sit in the circle. This in itself was so unnatural, a kinsman asking for the privilege of entering a camp, that one could not think about it. Sometimes it was best that way, not to think about a happening that frightened the mind or brought shame or anger. These were things he knew, and they were not taught him by the Long-Armed-Man or anyone else at that school.

Up the valley, riding steadily, he heard the scolding magpie as she dipped her tail on a fence post, then went on ahead to scold from another spot. He saw round heads popping up at prairie dog mounds. But ears and eyes were not for them. He was watching for the strange house that was an Indian house but did not look like an Indian house.

He had observed at the government school how a white man builds a fence—four strands of tight wire stapled to posts, with wire spreaders at intervals between the posts for extra tightness—and that was how he knew when he reached the boundary of Henry Jim's land. The house was not yet in sight, as it lay behind a slight rise of ground. But the fence was there, all posts firm, all wires in place. Beyond the fence, fields had been harvested and fat cattle gleaned the stubble. Antoine could not understand all that he saw, but he knew it was something strange, like the farms around the government's school in Oregon.

He pulled the little mare to a walk, then when they came to the height of land, they stopped. The house was just below and north of the road, wind-sheltered within a grove of planted cottonwood trees.

The house was two stories high and painted white, and the roof was different, even for a white man's kind of house. Instead of rising from two sides to a sharp ridge, it sloped upward from all four sides and had little windows with caps in the sloping sides and a flat place on top, surrounded by a kind of fence. The house sat within its own corral of white fencing, separate from the barns and pastures which sloped away from the house.

Antoine stared hard, studying these disturbing details and trying to accept them, trying to remember that his own kinsman, an old man, an Indian, had built all this and lived in it. He leaned forward, his arms at rest on the saddle horn. The buckskin mare pulled at the bit to get her head free to graze the roadside grass. He saw how the little stream that flowed out of a willow thicket from a hidden spring had been piped into a horse trough, then flowed away to water a hay meadow. He saw machinery backed into an open shed; stacks of baled hay ready for winter feeding.

All this he looked upon, and suddenly the vision before him changed and he was looking at a scene as familiar as his grandfather's camp: People were camped in the hay meadow beside the stream. Tepees were pitched, cooking fires were burning, children and dogs darted here and there, and hobbled horses grazed beyond the tepees and fires.

Even as he looked, recognition deepened. He heard low drumming, a rumbling of earth itself, and singing voices.

He pulled at the mare's head. "Greedy gut! Pull up!"

The strangeness of Henry Jim's house had not diminished—he could not turn his head from the planted trees and the curtained windows as he rode by—but Antoine was not uneasy now. His own people were here; they would have a place for him.

He knew this as a boy's hope, and then he knew it as a certainty when he stopped at the tepee of the singing voices and asked for his grandfather. Six men sat around a large, flat drum, while others sitting in the larger circle, including some women, passed the song around. The drumbeat was soft, the singing subdued. Jerome, the leader, started each phrase, then others picked it up, carried it along.

When the drumming stopped, as it did just after Antoine found a place inside the entrance, a young girl brought a coffee pot and a single enameled cup. They made smokes and passed the tobacco sack.

It was Jerome who answered. "Your grandfather is over there"—he pointed by pushing out his lips—"in the next tepee, with the old man. They say the old man was asking to see you."

Then the stick passed to another hand and the drum came back to life. As Antoine stepped through the entrance the singers started a song he knew from his own camp and he went out singing softly.

114

At first it did not seem strange that "the old one"—the elder brother—should be lying on a buffalo robe in the tepee—only later, after he had been there awhile, did Antoine wonder why he had left his big house to make a bed on the ground. The beds must be soft in such a big house. But he asked no questions.

It was enough just then to be greeted in the way that is proper between adult male relatives.

Bull motioned. "Come sit with us. Tell us how it is at our camp and how you traveled. We'll have food brought. Just sit."

Each in turn called greeting words or maybe smiled.

Henry Jim, on his buffalo robe, was opposite the entrance, which opened to the east. On each side, Bull at his right and Iron Child at his left, were the two men who had refused to visit or even to mention the "elder brother" during those years. On Bull's side were Louis of the dainty habits and neat yellow paper cigarettes, and Basil the emaciated, an empty food plate pushed aside. Next to Iron Child was the diviner, Two Sleeps, observing the world behind his closed eyes; his lips moved but no sounds came, which was how they knew that he traveled in a far country. And next to Two Sleeps were the young uncles, Theobold and Pock Face, who smiled gravely and had no secret laughs between them.

Antoine moved to the left of the entrance and took the place next to Basil.

"Sit right here, and I'll see that you're well fed," the emaciated one told him.

The singing voices beyond the tepee walls carried along, rising and falling away, then starting fresh, spinning a thread of song to hold an old man fast. And over and through the song the sound of playing children and barking dogs told how the world would be in all the years to come.

Henry Jim moved, pulling himself higher against the bundles at his back, and pulling away from the voices of his dreaming mind. He had put his black hat to one side, but otherwise was fully dressed and wrapped in a woolen blanket of Hudson Bay stripes.

"Is it the grandson who has come? They said you would come." He reached out his hand.

Antoine moved carefully around the central fireplace where wood had gone to warm embers. Antoine took the old man's offered hand, felt the knotted bones and the sinuous clasp, the dry warmth, and as on that other night he was filled with wonder.

"You will be a strong man," the old one said. "It is here in your hand. Even now your strength passes to me, as it will pass to your people when the time comes. Sit here with us."

What did you see? What did you learn? What will you remember? The words were with him as he heard them on the trail. Learn something from everything that happens and soon you will be a man.

And Bull, the speaker on the trail, was speaking again.

"When we came here, your kinsmen and I, we found this old man had already moved out of his big house and was in this tepee. He has not talked about it. Perhaps it is best not to talk about it; it is enough to be here, where we can help the others hold on to him."

Antoine, the coming-man, saw it clearly in the eye of his mind, but words swarmed about and he caught them poorly, trying to say how it had been that morning when Veronica came wrapped in her shawl and stood with him at the corral, telling him, "Say we are all well here"; and trying to tell about the ride in the frost mist, his memories of the days at school, of the Marching Captain who was an Indian like the rest and could cry like the others as well. And then to say how it was to come home from all that and find his own people. To say it was all beyond him, but he wanted his grandfather to know.

Bull was smiling—perhaps grandfathers knew of the difficulty with words. The talk between them broke there, as Henry Jim stirred again and all the waiting circle turned to him.

"It is true, as my brother says, I haven't talked about the big house and why I moved to my old lodge. My son, the one we call Victor, is up there now, with his wife and their children. It was best for me not to die in their house . . ."

A different thought seemed to catch up with him, and he paused, then started again:

"I built that big house in the days we were talking about. The government man said it would be a good thing. He wanted the Indians to see what it is like to have a nice house like that. In those days I had the foolish thought that a man stands by himself, that his kinsmen are no part of him. I did not go first to my uncles and my brothers and talk it over with them. The government man said how it should be, and I listened to him. I went to the woods and cut timber, and he gave me finished lumber in its place. I cut more timber, and he gave me nails and windows and doors, all those things that go in a white man's house. He sent a carpenter with saws and hammers, and a man with pipes and tools, and he sent a man to make a chimney out of square rocks. He would come himself to look at the work and he would say, 'You will have a wonderful house. Your people will be proud of you.' When men wearing stiff collars came from Washington, they visited my house and shook my hand. They said they would make a report. Maybe they did, because a man came after that with a machine and plowed my fields and they built a wire fence around everything. They said my wheat was so good the machinery was all paid for and they gave me a paper and said I could keep the machines. My son Victor was a man by then and he learned how to make the machinery go." The words faltered and for a while the old man listened to the singing voices and the children calling, until he was smiling.

"It went that way for a long time. I didn't notice it at first, but one day I could see that I was alone. That first government man had said my people would be proud of me, but my relatives didn't like to come inside the big house. When they visited me, they waited outside, sitting on a horse or in a wagon. They said the house was cold, or they didn't want to get it dirty. My son married a girl who was at school with him, from some tribe south of us. I never visited that tribe, but it is said they live in houses like white people. She covered the floors with thick stuff and the windows with thin stuff, and that troubled people even more. They said they couldn't see out because of the thin stuff at the windows—and an Indian likes to see what is coming.

"Brothers, I was lonesome, sitting in my big house. I wanted to put my tepee up in the yard, so people would come to see me, but my son and his wife said it would be foolish, that people would only laugh. I listened to them. Also, the government man—a new one all the time—would bring stiff-collars from Washington and they would come to my house to shake hands and sit in my big chairs and knock on the walls to see if they would fall down. Then they would ask me to sign a piece of paper and after a while a big bull and some breeding cows would be unloaded in my pasture and I would sign another paper. And my son would say, 'If you put up a tepee in your yard, the people from Washington won't come any more. You'll be just another Indian and they won't help.' He's a good son, he works like a white man, but he couldn't understand that I was lonesome. My old woman was gone and I was alone."

By then he was tired and slumped low against the backrest of bags; the bright lights had gone from his sunken eyes.

"He will sleep," Bull said. "Build up the fire. Perhaps he turned cold while he talked."

Pock Face moved forward and was stirring the embers to add fresh wood when the old one remembered what he had started out to say:

"Two days ago I told my son to put up this tepee; it is the old one from my father's time. 'Put up the tepee,' I said, 'the stiff-collars can stay away. I want to die in my own house.' "

Every voice in the circle murmured. Antoine looked up, stealthily scanning each face, and he could feel what was there among them. It shamed them that they had stayed away and had been hard against this old man. It shamed them, and they were in grief.

No one else talked, for then they heard a new and disturbing sound. An automobile had turned off the valley road and was rolling and roaring past the big house, coming toward the camp.

A little girl thrust her head in the tepee. "The government man is coming in his noise-wagon, the policeman is with him. We are going to hide." And she disappeared.

16

When Rafferty on the telphone asked the little doctor to go with him to visit Henry Jim, he wanted to suggest a medical examination, but stopped short of saying so. Doc Edwards had a way of ignoring suggestions.

"Nobody mentions any symptoms—they just say the old fellow is on his back, waiting to die."

Later, when they stood in clouded sunlight in front of the agency's office building, Rafferty tried in a different way to say what was bothering him.

"I've heard of such cases, where a fellow decides he's going to die, and goes ahead and does it. But I always assumed he was fatally sick, and maybe the psychic state hurried things along. Has Henry Jim ever been sick in your time here?"

Edwards was casual, almost exasperating, staring straight ahead as he talked. "For a man in his seventies, he is perfectly sound. I looked him over in the spring, when he came to see me for a stiff knee. He could be good for ten years. On the other hand, if he's decided the time has come, he could go out like a light. These people live close to their intuitions."

Rafferty looked his annoyance, feeling that his question was evaded. He almost decided to ask the little doctor not to come along, but yielded to courtesy.

"At least you'll ask him how he's feeling, I hope."

Edwards finally turned, and his little laugh sounded like a whinny. "Not an examination, if that's what you're getting at. He'd be offended if I suggested that, if I doubted those voices he hears. But I'll put some questions to his son and daughter-in-law. They watch him pretty closely."

"He's my first client, the first to ask for help," Rafferty

said, and at once recognized the crudity of the remark. "I'd like to keep him alive as long as we can—and I mean for his own sake."

"Yes," the doctor said, and sarcasm was fitted to the words like a saw-edge: "He has served us well. He's our masterpiece."

It deserved a retort, but Rafferty held it. And just then they heard the roar of the agency car. The Boy was bringing it up from the garage.

The old horse barn had been converted into a garage by removing the stalls and grain bins, but the hay mow still made it a barn, and one always expected the car to come out smelling of horse sweat and manure.

The Boy and his big hat seemed to fill the entire windshield space, but Rafferty climbed in beside him, accommodating himself as best he could to The Boy's bulk. This left the little doctor alone in the rear seat, wrapped in a thick overcoat and muffler, which his wife, he said, had insisted that he wear.

As they rolled away from the neat white building, the sun, which had started out strong in the morning, was slicing into sheets of icy clouds.

Rafferty pulled himself away from the others, into his own silence. He was looking ahead, thinking of the things that would have to be said. He was aware of areas of worry which at the moment he would not explore with any other mind than his own.

Opposing the marshal did not trouble him; the man's attitudes and methods were obnoxious, and he was determined not to let them prevail. But that left open the question of whether he nevertheless had a sound case and was therefore entitled to full faith and credit. That was one troubled area to wander in, as they jounced over the road. When The Boy drove a car he concentrated everything into it—his eyes sharp ahead, his elbows jutting out like wings from either side of the wheel—but in spite of the concentration he seemed to slide into and out of ruts, plunging into every hole within the roadway.

Part of the worrying area was the result of his decision to let Bull and his mates leave the agency. True, he knew where they were going; it was not far off, and the circumstances were extenuating. Still, if it should turn out that somebody in that camp was guilty of murder, his action would be difficult to defend. He veered away from that thought.

And then there was the more delicate question of how much his chief of police had learned from his visit with Bull's group in the school basement. He had offered no information, had not even discussed the visit, but Rafferty had a vibrating nerve end that kept insisting something had been said, something had happened in that basement room, and it made Rafferty watchful, like a man in a lookout post observing all that passed before him. And in this too the situation could arise in which he would have to answer for his judgment, at least to himself. He had excused his police officer in advance of any responsibility for reporting back.

The doctor, rolling around in the back seat like a loose marble, must have sensed some of the troubles which "that nice young man," as his wife persisted in calling Rafferty, was toiling with. He spoke out, without a preface:

"I hope you realize that Bull is one Indian this country would like to put behind bars, guilty or not. All these years he stood out against fellows like this Henry Jim, his own brother. If it hadn't been for him, more of this Indian land would be in white ownership. I don't take anything away from Henry Jim for what he accomplished —although he had an extraordinary amount of help. He was the display case all these years. But if the others had followed him, if they had tried, that is, they would have been suckered out of everything. That is strictly my medical opinion.

"To come back to Bull: he has been a hothead, he's been cantankerous, but he's no fool. Whoever shot that man up there was a nut, or a prankster, or it may have been an accident—"

He turned suddenly upon The Boy and asked, "What do you think?" and used the Indian name for "Son Child."

The Boy seemed to grip the steering wheel tighter

and to pay particular attention to the road.

"I think they better forget about the man who got shot. Nobody ever find out anything."

The doctor muttered a word that suggested agreement, relaxed, and was immediately tossed into a corner of the back seat.

Rafferty shot a questioning glance sideways and wondered whether this was a conviction or a fervent wish.

He did not pursue the matter, and even if he had intended to, the moment would have evaded him. For just then they dropped down from the low-lying ridge and came in sight of Henry Jim's ranch.

"Holy Judas! Look at the tepees!" Rafferty lunged toward the windshield.

The Boy brought the car almost to a full stop and, in the habit of his people, pointed with his lips, both hands on the steering wheel.

"See the big tepee, with the pointed things on it— that's a real old-timer. Henry Jim is in there. He moved out of his big house two days ago."

He said it with a kind of wonder in his voice.

"They have been singing now for four days. People are coming from everywhere to help, even those who quarreled with him. They go around shaking hands . . ."

He was aware again of his companions and his mission and his role, and he let the car go forward.

Rafferty said, a flatness in his voice, "I have to say this now, before we go in there. Henry Jim sent for me, so I am here. But I still have to find out what I can about who killed that man in the mountains. Just to make sure the wrong man is not put in jail. I want Bull to understand that, if he asks."

"He understand all right," The Boy said quickly, and Rafferty watched him.

By then the car had rolled past the big house "with the fence on the roof," and had entered the pasture where the tepees were put up. It was immediately surrounded by leaping and howling dogs which managed somehow to avoid the rolling wheels.

When the car finally stopped, only the dogs were in sight. The meadow was empty of people. But sounds of *shh, shh* betrayed invisible bodies trying to control the yelping dogs. The singing broke off, but only briefly, and then resumed more quietly, as one sings who also listens.

The men from Bull's camp were not accustomed to sitting down with government men. Their backs stiffened and their faces went flat. When Rafferty and Doc Edwards edged into the "old-timer" tepee, Pock Face and Theobold slipped outside. The Boy saw them go but said nothing. He had squatted on his heels at the foot of the circle.

Rafferty had learned the etiquette of waiting before starting to speak. Henry Jim would probably speak first, since this was his house. He and the doctor took the places just vacated, and Rafferty offered his cigarettes to be passed around.

The old one pulled himself up again and a delicate smile greeted the government man and Doc Edwards, "the cranky one." But Henry was not the one who spoke. Two Sleeps, stirred out of his dream world by the commotion, addressed himself to The Boy, surprising everyone. But it was said of him that he saw more behind his closed eyes than others saw with wide-open eyes.

"Our people are surprised by the coming of these men. We had no warning, as the old one here forgot to tell us. So I want you to talk to this government man for us, while the others think over what they want to say.

"Tell this man: We are camped here at the old man's place so he will feel our power and not be discouraged. It got so we forgot to do these things, or it didn't seem worthwhile. Maybe this man will think we are childish to believe we can do this. He comes from a big world where his power is in a machine. Or maybe he carries it in his pocket and he can take it out and tell you where the sun is. We live here in this small world and we have only ourselves, the ground where we walk, the big and small animals. But the part that is man is not less because our world is small. When I look out in the coming day and see a bluebird—we call it our mother's sister—I see the whole bluebird, the part that is blue and the part that is yellow, just as this man does. I don't have half an eye because I live in this small world.

"We began to forget such things after those men came here from beyond the mountains. They thought we were men with half-eyes, or maybe they thought we were children born out of our mothers before we were fully made. They brought their big machines to cut down our trees and tear up our earth and they told us they would make a big world for us, like theirs, and our power would be greater than ever. Some people stopped praying in the morning. Our shrines were too far away, or they were on top of a mountain, and people wouldn't go to them anymore. When a man got sick, we left him alone. Until today it has been that way.

"Tell all that to the government man, and to the cranky one, who sometimes understands what we are talking about. And then I am going back to sleep and the rest of you can talk."

Laughter broke from the group like a splatter of sudden rain, and the air was easier. All this was interpreted by The Boy, in snatches, as Two Sleeps talked, and none of it was held back.

Louis-the-bitter then said: "I don't understand why these men are here. They broke our circle and it is difficult not to have angry thoughts while they are here—and that is wrong."

Bull said simply: "Perhaps these men will tell us why they are here, and we can listen."

Henry Jim took the talk to himself, speaking first in his own language.

"I asked the government man to come because I have to tell him something, and I guess the cranky one came to listen to me through his earpiece. He will slap me on the back to see what he can shake loose, then he will give me a pill. These two are puzzled, I think. They are looking at me hard, even when they look at the ground, or at the air. They don't understand why I am lying here waiting to be called by the grass. I will talk to them and make it seem right in their understanding."

He had started to speak in English, as he could do around white men, but he kept slipping back into his own language, then into English, like a man following a vanishing trail.

124

"I guess you want to know why I asked you to come. I will tell you, but first I have to tell you a story. An Indian can't tell what's on his mind until he tells a story. My story is like this: When I was a young man I started on a journey . . ."

The Boy moved forward to stir the fire and add fresh wood. The singing in the near tepee had grown louder, and now children's playing voices were heard again.

Rafferty watched The Boy's deft movements as he worked on the fire—the delicate touch of the large hands, the ease of his crouch—and he could see the fitness of the man in his situation. What a man learned, and it was all he learned in a lifetime, was a degree of fitness for the things he had to do. A woodchopper had to learn the tools of the woods. A fisherman, the sea. A priest had to learn the practice of humility. Some men learned to perform with grace and competence, while others stumbled through tasks they never mastered. And in making judgments on a man, we have to forget the language he speaks, the beliefs he lives by. Here in a tepee world, the parts fitted together. The people had grace and understanding; their acts were competent. The tepee was snug. A small fire gave the needed heat and the wood smoke rose untroubled to escape through the opening among the crossed poles. Here was all that was needed of a house; only the customs of other men made a house of stone and mortar seem more desirable. The problem is communication, he said with inward words, as Henry Jim told his story of trying to travel on the white man's road. These people find it difficult to believe that a white man, any white man, will give them respect, as it is difficult for me to understand why they push me away and keep me from coming into their confidence. The answer, obviously, is that we do not speak to each other—and language is only a part of it. Perhaps it is intention, or purpose, the map of the mind we follow. And again inwardly he said, I am glad I left this man free to make his own decision, this deft man at the fire. He will know how to decide. Not only for me and my way, but for all these people.

And then it seemed that Henry Jim was answering

the very questions Rafferty was raising with himself.

"That is how it went, my friends. As that old man said before he want back to sleep, like the badger who is always falling asleep in our stories, we can feel how it used to be when our people were close to each other.

"Somewhere it went wrong, somewhere along the road I traveled. When I was that young man, they told me: 'Do these things. We will show you how. Your people will follow you, and in your lifetime a great change will come. Your children will be stronger, your food will be better, you will have boys in college—all good things will come.'

"That's how it should have been. That's what I wanted. But the people didn't follow; they stayed just the way they were. Maybe in your minds you are saying they were foolish not to follow after me—and for a long time that's how I felt.

"But how would you have it? In the old days, when camp had to be moved quickly, because enemy soldiers were coming, or because a scout rode hard into camp to tell us of a buffalo herd moving in another valley, sometimes we had to leave behind an old man or old woman too sick to travel. It tore our hearts to do it, but the whole camp would suffer if we stayed behind. So we left the old people with food and water and rode away.

"When you have no choice you can do it—the enemy is coming or your winter's food is getting away. So you leave some of your people behind and tell yourself it's all right.

"I didn't understand that at first; I thought the people were just spiteful because they would not follow. Now I see why they were afraid and why they held back. They knew it would split us up; some could do it and some could not, and those that refused to go would be left behind with nothing—no game, no wheat. In their hearts they were saying, 'We'll just all starve together.' Today, I'm glad it went that way. The people stayed together—I was the only one who left the camp.

"Brothers," he said, slumping back against the storage bags, "I'm tired. I can't hear the singing. Has it gone far away?"

They looked at him, then at each other, and each saw his own alarm. The singing was actually loud and clear, as if a number of fresh voices had joined the singing group.

Doc Edwards seemed to dive forward; he had removed his overcoat and muffler soon after they entered the warm tepee, and so moved unencumbered. He pushed the bags aside so the old man could stretch out flat, and felt for a pulse.

In his dismay Rafferty rose halfway to his feet, then settled back on one knee. Scattered talk went around the circle as they all watched the doctor.

And then a strange thing happened. Henry Jim's eyes opened, turned inward at first. Soon they focused. But he did not recognize the man bending over him and only stared.

After a moment, he talked in his own language. His first words were all run together and had no meaning. Then he stopped and started over. And he could be understood. The Boy moved up beside him, across from the doctor, and translated.

" 'I know this man,' he says. 'He is the cranky one.' That's what he says. 'Tell him to listen through his earpiece. Maybe he can hear the singing inside. Where is the government man? Is he here?'

"Yes, grandfather. He is there at your feet."

"Ask him, did he find out where the dog-faced man sent our medicine bundle? And will he bring it back?"

Rafferty expected the question, and still he was not ready to give a clear answer. "I know what happened, where it went," he said. And there he had to stop.

Henry Jim's interest wandered away from his own question to another matter.

"Tell him I want my horse to go with me to the rockslide, the big red horse. Tell him not to be angry when my people do what they have to do. It was in my dream." The voice disappeared.

The doctor had been listening with his stethoscope, flashing a light in the fading eyes.

He sat back. "Just a spasm, I think. He seems to be getting stronger. Hello, my friend! Can you hear the singing now?"

Henry Jim looked at the doctor, then turned to The Boy.

"What does he say?"

That was when they knew he had forgotten the English language entirely—as they said, turned his back on it.

Bull moved now. He had been watching his elder brother, watching the strong color drain from his face. He knew that he had crossed beyond a certain point and would not come back.

He spoke to The Boy: "The people will want to pray for this old man and carry him to the mountains. They expect me to go with them. But I think the government man wants me to go with *him*. I think he came to tell me that."

Others in the circle looked up, as if just now aware of Rafferty, a stranger among them. No one spoke, but their faces were heavy.

Rafferty questioned Doc Edwards: "Will he last much longer?"

"Can't tell. His breathing is shallow. He might last the night, maybe longer."

Rafferty made a decision. He turned to The Boy. "Tell Bull to wait through the night. If the old man is still with us in the morning, he can come to the agency for some talk. I want to answer as best I can the question Henry Jim asked me, but I don't want to take him away from his people at this time."

He did not say that he suspected the United States marshal was already at the agency and might insist on coming to the camp to make an arrest.

"Tell him to come tomorrow, if he can get away."

The Boy did not translate Bull's soft reply: "Maybe this one is different, as you said. He doesn't push."

17

They rode together, the big man on his pigeon-toed horse, the boy on his buckskin mare. The animals matched strides as best they could, the big one keeping to a fidgeting walk, the small one going in and out of a trot, her ears turned back. Sometimes a kick in the ribs was needed to bring her even, and then her ears came back flat.

Journeys can be long and difficult, and Bull was finding it so, although they had only five miles to travel to reach Little Elk Agency. But he was traveling through time and over mountains and prairies of thought and feeling. Until his brother had come to his camp on a certain night, he had lived in a waiting world. It wasn't clear what he had waited for, but the habit of it had been there, whether he sat in camp, herded his few cattle, or walked a mountainside.

Or maybe in all that time he did know that he waited, not just to grow old and finally to die. Maybe in all those years he had waited for the very thing that happened, for his brother to come to his camp and speak of the trouble that separated them. But if that was the way of it, it was a troublesome thought to carry. People of long ago would have said he played poorly his part of the younger brother. It was not intended that the elder brother should shame himself by coming first to admit a fault; what was expected, rather, was that he would provide the feast to show that all was forgiven—after his younger kinsman took the fault to himself. A proper world was so ordered.

A journey could be difficult beyond endurance, when a man had to travel with himself and bring into his thoughts the bad actions of a lifetime.

Because he had waited and had not taken the first step, it fell on him all at once. He could remember times when, if he had acted differently, the trouble might have ended. Times when he might have sent word. When he might have talked in council. When he might have gone himself, taking his kinsmen, and stayed to visit. Two Sleeps had come from a vigil in the mountains on many occasions to tell how he had dreamed and how peace would be restored: Bull remembered those times, how he accused the old holy man of meddling, and how afterward in anger he went himself to the mountains and had no vision of his own.

Bull looked across the valley as they rode forward. He saw the far, clear mountains, the dark forest coming down to the edge of the valley, the fields of brown grass, the road running between fence lines of four strands stretched tight, as a white man builds a fence. But what he saw more clearly, without turning his head, was the grandson who rode most of the time at his side. His grandson's little mare had small feet and short legs, and she would fall behind until he kicked her and she shot ahead. Bull knew that a hurt had come to the boy, because his own elders had quarreled. The very kinsmen who were to guide him and make him into a strong man. He would find a way to take away the hurt.

The distance was not far, but the journey was long.

And he could see, though it was not yet visible, what he would come to at the end of the journey: the government houses, the government man, all waiting. An old feeling boiled up. He shuddered in the morning sun.

The burning fire of those first days was in him, and he could see clearly for a moment how it had been. It was not his elder brother on whom at first he had cast his anger—that came later. That was when the anger settled and turned into rock. It had come first when these men from across the world, from he knew not where, had told him that he could not have his own country, that he no longer belonged in it. They would make it into a better country and let him have just a small piece of it. He wouldn't need a big piece because it would be easier to live in the new country. These mountains, trees, streams, the earth and the grass, from which his people learned the language of respect—all of it would pass into the hands of strangers, who would dig into it, chop it down, burn it up. They came with great beards on their faces, smelling of sweat, but smiling all the time and talking without pausing. They left big scars in the mountains where they went digging for gold. They cut down the biggest trees and hauled them away to make houses—or sometimes they just let them rot in the forest. They scared away the game with their heavy tramping feet. They plowed up the prairie grass and spoke out in anger when stones broke their plows. They were a people without respect, but they managed to get what they wanted. The older people thought they would just give up, because their awkwardness got them into so much trouble. "They're just like young bears, poking their noses into everything. Leave them alone and they'll go away." That is what the people said.

How could one tell this to a boy, not to raise him up in anger, not to feed him thoughts that would eat out the guts, but to give him understanding of what it was like in those first days?

It was vague even in his own thinking, but at first nobody had been angry at the stranger-people with the big feet who squirted brown juice from their mouths. The old people told stories about them, about what they saw, and the stories went from camp to camp, and laughter rolled through the hills. Yes, that was how it was at first. When a stranger's tent blew down in the wind because he didn't have it braced properly, and his food was scattered—that was told all over and the people laughed about it. When one of them became lost in the hills and had to be led out by an Indian, every detail was reported: how the stranger was followed, how his actions were watched, how the rescuer had grown weary of following in a circle and had taken the man just over a ridge and showed him the valley below —but didn't tell him that a deep canyon lay between. Such a story was good for many tellings, and each telling became funnier.

Bull's father, Enemy Horse—called Vincent in the white man's language—enjoyed playing jokes on people, even though he was the headman and everybody respected him. And when he played what he thought was a great joke on the first schoolteacher it almost turned into a joke on Bull, who was no older than the grandson at his side.

The man had come to his father's camp, not far from where in later years Bull built his own camp. He was a small man and he had a small woman with him. They drove together behind a pair of fine gray horses, and the harness had flashing bright spots. The small man wore a gold chain across his chest, and his face was covered with hair. The woman crowded very close against him, holding his arm, and even a young boy watching from inside the tepee entrance could tell that she was frightened.

The interpreter, who came riding behind on a slow horse, explained that the small man wanted to start a school down there where the government was building a house. He wanted the chief's son to come and live with him and be the first pupil in the school. Other families would see it was all right and they would send their children as well.

The interpreter, sitting cross-armed on his drooping horse, pointed his lips in the direction of the smiling man and his pale wife, and expressed his private thoughts on the subject. "I think this man and woman, I think they're too small to make a baby of their own, so they want your son. He better go down there and make them happy."

Bull saw his father laugh and he felt good. People liked to visit his father's camp and tell stories, because he laughed and fed them well and everybody was happy. It was a good camp when people laughed.

Enemy Horse told the interpreter: "I will send one young boy, just so this teacher won't think I'm a hard man. But tell him he will have to get up early, long before the sun, and see to it that my boy gets up to run. Don't let him get lazy. He is to take him on the trail and show him where the deer cross to water, where the grouse nest, and where the beaver build their houses. My boy will have to live in this country when he is a man, and I don't want people to think he is a fool. Tell that to the small man, and say I will be down there before the new moon, and if my boy hasn't learned more than I can teach him I will burn this man's schoolhouse to the ground and run him across the mountains where he came from."

Enemy Horse's speech ended in a burst of laughter, then he called for his three boys. But two of them had already crawled under the tepee wall and were off in the woods, and because Bull liked to hear his father laugh he was the only one left. He kept thinking his father was playing a joke, and he waited for everybody to laugh and the small man and his woman to go away. Instead, he found himself standing in the little box behind the buggy seat and the gray team was flying down the road. The interpreter, riding his horse alongside, was the only one laughing. He laughed all the way to the schoolhouse.

Bull could see very clearly now, riding his pigeon-toed horse on a journey that would end at almost the very spot where the other journey ended, that nowadays there was less laughter and fewer joke-makers in the camp. It seemed to be a time when people waited and did nothing. Maybe the boy they called Pock Face, his sister's son, had some of the same mischief running in his blood that young men used to have. For surely it was mischief that sent him up to that dam, and mischief in his heart that fired a gun. But one could not laugh about it or even tell a white man how it happened to go that way.

He would tell his grandson at some campfire, when they were all back in his mountain camp, how that other journey ended.

First, there was the meal, the only meal he ever ate in the schoolteacher's house. He sat at a table with the man and his little woman. They showed him how to put his hands together and bend his head toward the white cloth, and the man talked fast and low. Then the woman took his bowl and filled it from a larger bowl with something that wasn't a stew. It stayed all together and was colored like a kind of clay. She sprinkled white stuff on it which he knew was sugar and was supposed to go in coffee. Finally, she poured milk into the bowl and handed it to him. She pointed at the dish and repeated the word "mush." He understood that she was trying to

teach him her language, and to satisfy her he said, "moosh."
She clapped her hands and laughed and said more words.

It was a strange substance in the mouth. It just went
to pieces and left nothing to chew. The sugar made it all
right and he finished right away. He waited for the meat
to come, but nothing followed. And there was no coffee,
either. He kept looking, but there was nothing more to
eat, just "moosh." And a cup with nothing but milk.
That was all the man and woman ate.

Then it was night. The woman made music come
from a box by pushing with her feet and singing at the
same time. Afterward the man signaled to follow him
outside and they went to a little square house in the back.
The man opened the door and pushed him inside, where
it was dark and the smell was bad. He just stood in the
dark, not moving, until the man opened the door and
said something. Then the man went inside, and when
Bull heard his water running, he went under a tree and
made his own water, after which he sang a little song,
such as men sing when they stand alone and look at
the stars.

The teacher came out of the little house very fast and
spoke many excited words.

Enemy Horse told the next part for years afterward,
until he died suddenly of a cramp in the belly, and he
would laugh until the tears came to his eyes. It was the
best part of his joke:

The teacher and his little wife showed Bull the room
where he was to sleep. The woman even turned down
the bedcovers so he could get in, but when he started to
lie down in his clothes, she grabbed him right away. She
started to undress him then, which was easy to do, since
all he wore was a shirt, a kind of sack with sleeves;
trousers held up by a braided sash; and a breechcloth
between his legs. The woman turned her head away
when she got that far, and carried his shirt and trousers
to a chair. She held them away from her.

Then she brought a garment from the bed. It was
folded together and he couldn't tell what it was until she
unrolled it and began to pull it over his head. When he
saw what looked like a woman's dress, and realized that

he would have to wear it, he stayed no longer. It was bad enough to be given nothing but "moosh" to eat, but they were not going to turn him into a woman on the first night.

He slipped from under the woman's reaching arms, grabbed shirt and trousers, and was gone from the room. On the way out, he knocked over the little man teacher who stood in the way. He forgot about wooden doors in white men's houses and ran straight into the door to the outside. It was fastened only by a wooden bar which dropped into a slot. The bar splintered, the door flew open, and Bull didn't even pause. He still wore his moccasins when he left the house, and he didn't stop to put on his other clothes until he had run halfway home.

When he reached camp, breathing hard, the men in Enemy Horse's tepee were sitting around a low fire, still talking. Nobody had gone to sleep.

Enemy Horse didn't even look surprised when Bull, his second older boy, stumbled through the entrance and sat down. Enemy Horse just acted as if he didn't know what happened.

"My boy, we expected you sooner. We had to eat without you. Did you go some place?"

Then he threw back his head and laughed like a coyote. But he fed his son meat and fried bread and coffee when he heard about the awful "moosh."

How would all this be explained to the grandson riding at his side? Nobody had been angry at first, he would have to say that. Because nobody had been afraid of them; they were awkward, they made mistakes, they knew nothing about the country and didn't try to learn —nobody expected them to last very long. Wait until a hard winter comes. Then, wait until a dry summer comes. Then, wait until their food runs short. Everybody seemed to know just when the strangers would get tired of running around and falling over their own feet. Then they would go away and the world would be as it had been from the beginning, when Feather Boy visited the people and showed them how to live.

But the strangers did not go away—and that was why anger took hold. The strangers not only stayed, but new ones came in larger numbers every year. They fenced in the land for themselves, fencing the Indians out. They made a railroad, down there at the end of the valley, so more of their own kind could come in. They put wires on tall poles so they could talk to their own kind across the mountains and tell them about the nice country they had picked out for themselves. They still had big feet, but they got around just the same; and they built roads into the mountains, so nobody got lost anymore.

All this he would tell his grandson, and more.

He could hear in his mind how he would finish his talk, how he would tell the final sorrow: "Now they have power. They can put a rope around an Indian's neck and let him hang. We never fired our guns at these people and that was our mistake. We laughed at them when we should have been angry, right there at the start. Then, when we became angry, it was too late. If we had only killed a few, they would have come with their big guns and killed us all. They would be walking over our heads today, but we wouldn't have to care anymore."

And so in his thinking, Bull came to Little Elk Agency. He looked to his grandson and saw that his eyes were bright with an inner hurt. No doubt the boy had a fear of what might happen in the government's house.

18

It was a time for confrontations, the first of which fired up an old antagonism.

The antagonists were Adam Pell—engineer, indus-trialist, museum owner—and his sister Geneva, Gen in the family, now Mrs. Thomas Hendricks Cooke. Adam Pell had taken rooms in the one hotel that flourished in Elk City, a parlor suite furnished with horsehair uphol-stered chairs, a print of some Rosa Bonheur horses, a cretonne-covered sofa, a porcelain cuspidor, a library table standing lonely and naked in the center of the room, and hissing steam radiators.

Mrs. Cooke had removed her long traveling cloak and her round hat and black veil, and sat stiffly on the edge of a thick chair, the toes of her shoes just reaching the floor.

Adam knew her pout, the frozen look in her small blue eyes, the toneless face. These he would encounter, as he did now, when he came home after an afternoon of walking in the fields and would start to tell her of the flowers he saw on a spring hillside. And she would inter-rupt with, "You never take me on your old walks." He would remind her then that she didn't care for walking— they always ended up at somebody's house making fudge and never walked at all.

In the growing-up years he took his role of elder brother, his six-year seniority, with proper seriousness. He fetched and carried, got her through algebra, squired her when she was all legs and going to her first parties, never forgot her birthdays, and learned the right things to say about her dresses and hair.

And it often happened that when he expected her to be pleased, or at least appreciative, when he went out of his way to be helpful or provide for her comfort, she wasn't at all pleased. Her face froze and she waited for him to make amends.

Adam Pell watched his sister, sitting straight and silent on one of the hotel's elegant chairs, then looked at his brother-in-law—and decided that Cooke had shared some of his own experiences. He was standing at the tall window, leaning forward on his knob-headed stick and gazing through the lace curtains at the mixed traffic of horse vehicles and automobiles moving in the street—and having no part in the conversation.

Adam repeated what he had already said: "We could leave tonight—the coroner's jury has finished its where-fores and whereases—if you really insist." And when it still brought no response—she had already expressed herself—he continued. "Something happened here, Gen. I want to find out what it was, and why. I understand your unwillingness at the moment to think about it or take part. There is no need of that, though I do think you might prefer traveling out there in the morning in-stead of spending the day in this hotel. You wouldn't have to stay in the hotel, of course. My car is quite com-fortable—I've just had it redecorated, and steam and water lines are attached. I have a small library on board . . ."

She unfroze then, momentarily. "That interests me least of all, Adam. My only wish is to get home with all decent haste, with my boy's body. Thomas knows my anxiety. The boy was murdered and somebody should be hanged, I suppose, but I have no interest in a manhunt."

"They say an Indian is guilty, they have somebody in custody. James was like a son to me, and I am grieved —shocked—but I don't want his death to be used as an excuse to satisfy a local prejudice. I know what these communities can be like. That's why I want to stay, at least for twenty-four hours, to satisfy myself on that score."

His sister would not be persuaded by such an expres-sion of concern—that ground had already been covered. He only smiled at the futility of trying to appeal to a sen-timent that was not among her qualities.

"How can you be concerned, at such a time? And

how can you expect to learn anything in twenty-four hours? You'll probably spend twenty-four days, and forget what we came to do, what Thomas and I came to do."

Having spoken her husband's name, she turned to him for support.

"Is it an unreasonable thing, my dear, that a mother should want to bury her dead, discreetly, and not involve herself in questions of social justice?"

Both men started to protest, but Adam gave way to his brother-in-law, who had moved away from the window and stood looking down on his wife, still leaning on his knobbed cane.

"That's what we call a leading question, in court. But we'd have to say, you're privileged. What you wish is, of course, what I also wish. Family comes first. Take our boy and our sorrow to ourselves. But Adam has a point. I don't like the scalawags down there in the street. I've been watching them—they all need shaves and a change of clothes. If Adam can make it plain to these people that we want an honest investigation, not just a hanging..."

"Oh, Thomas—" his wife flared, but the tone of her voice softened, and the pout was washed away at last. "If you insist on standing up all afternoon, you won't sleep tonight. You'll have such pain."

"Right, my dear," he eased himself into the other horsehair chair, his stiff and useless left leg sliding out across the frayed carpet.

Only Adam was left standing. He was always aware of his tallness and thinness, and of late years he was also aware of an increasing forward stoop. A solicitous tailor would not let it go unmentioned—until Adam offered one day to take the little tailor to the back room and bump his head against a door frame until ducking became for him an equally unconscious act. The undersized garment-maker thought he meant it and hastily removed the basting pins from his mouth.

He felt that he should seat himself to continue the conversation, but he also needed to pace, and this need was stronger. The truth was, his sister agitated him.

"Tell me, Gen. I know you don't like what I do; among other things, the museum, which incidentally now has one of the largest collections of Peruvian textiles and ceramics in the world. Tell me, how is it at home? Am I considered an ingrate and a boor because I spend my money to please myself and don't contribute to the Foreign Mission Society or donate a bandstand to City Park? Some kind soul occasionally sends me clippings from the old *Clarion* in which I am mentioned in a remote way—the 'erstwhile' or the 'sometime' this or that. Nothing flattering, or maybe the flattering ones, if any appear, are never sent. Tell me, is this the home sentiment? I don't expect to do anything about it, but I'm curious."

He watched her, his dear Geneva of the growing-up years. And watching her, he found himself remembering a question he had once put to her, in that long-forgotten time, and his blood quickened. He saw again the quiet place around the eyes, the half-parted lips, the play of innocence. The question involved a laughing-eyed girl for whom, at the time, he felt a wild attraction. Possibly the girl did not merit the extravagant sentiment, but at the time it seemed to be the decision of a lifetime. *The point was, dear Geneva, you told me a sordid and calculating lie, cheapening the girl, and I went away. A long time later, and too late, I discovered you had gaffed me—for what pleasure of your own, I could never grasp. It destroyed the innocence of our childhood, and for a long time I wished never to see you again.*

She touched tongue to lips, an old habit. "You stand and look at me, Adam, as if you were accusing, not asking. And I don't think I understand your question anyhow."

"Well, it wasn't direct, and it doesn't much matter. It's been a long time, years, but I haven't kept track. I suppose I can expect to be remembered, but will everyone have acquired from you a distaste for the career I made for myself, the interests I've developed?"

"How can you say such a thing!" Coloring had come to the usually toneless face. Her back had stiffened. "As your sister, I've followed your career with the greatest interest, and pride. Even though most of what I've learned has had to come from newspaper accounts. I will say, though, I've felt hurt, we've all felt hurt, that you seemed to cut yourself off from your friends, your very kinfolk. I remember a Christmas, years ago, just after you'd been named chairman of some board of directors—I can't remember those names. I was so happy at the time, thinking surely you'd come home at last, to share your triumph with us. But a day or so later another account said you'd sailed for South America to visit your Indian friends in some jungle. I had even made plans, called up old friends, and you can imagine what a ninny I felt when they called back afterward and laughed in my face —as if I weren't important enough to have anyone of your great stature for a holiday guest. No, brother, if anyone alienated the people at home, you did it yourself. I believe you despise us."

Thomas Cooke was visibly uncomfortable as he watched first one, then the other, and could think of no way to divert the conversation.

Adam was lost for a moment, then caught up again. The chairmanship, as best he could recall, was with Consolidated Forest Products, one of the first mergers he negotiated, just when trust-busting was entering into parlor discussions and finance houses were reluctant to identify themselves with consolidations.

"I have no jungle friends—or perhaps the news story did not mention "jungle," perhaps that was your interpretation. I was going to Peru that winter, the Andean highlands, to fulfill a promise I'd made years before. It's a long story, too long to go into now—and you might not care for it after I'd finished."

"Let's have it," the watchful Thomas interrupted. He sensed that Adam really wanted to talk about Peru, but mostly he wanted to steer the conversation away from these painful family recriminations. "The idea of Peru, just the idea, has always fascinated me. What was the promise?"

Adam smiled. He knew his brother-in-law was trying to play peace-maker. He remembered him, though not too clearly, as the son of the Episcopal minister who moved to New Brighton just as the Pell family was falling apart—a soft speaking young man who played tennis and rode a bicycle. How had such a man accommodated himself to the loss of a leg?

When Gen threw a quick, reproachful look in her husband's direction, Adam came to a decision. He was not one to indulge in stories about himself, since he never thought of his accomplishments as being in any way exceptional. The Sunday Supplement stories in metropolitan newspapers dramatizing the essentially shallow lives of business executives he found repugnant. So it was not with any thought of projecting himself that he talked at such length that day. Rather it was a nagging desire to answer something left unsaid in the exchange between himself and his sister. Perhaps it was the remark about jungle Indians, or perhaps it was only a matter of her attitude; something at any rate impelled him to break in upon her insularity; to explain why his interest in Indians deserved her respect.

He paused in his pacing, but only long enough to catch and hold her gaze. Then he moved into his story.

"It started in a brownstone house in the Murray Hill section, a few years after I arrived in New York. I'd rented the parlor and second floor of what had been a comfortable family house—high windows and lace curtains, carved marble mantles, all that. After I'd been in the house a year or so, I struck up a friendship with a Peruvian young man—not so young either—from a wealthy family, who was in the Harvard Graduate School studying marketing. I don't know how we met, and it doesn't matter, but I believe I first saw him in the Peruvian consul's office, where I was getting information about the production of mahogany. It turned out that Carlos's family was associated with this industry —later he sent me a pair of colonial-period cartwheels, fully five feet across, made from a crosscut of a mahogany log, one of which I had sanded and polished and made into a table for my study. I put a brass plate over the axle hole and engraved on it the story of the cart wheel —still have it.

"The more he told me about his country—I already

knew the pre-Columbian history—about its contemporary problems and what he wanted to do, the more fascinated I became. Of course I talked to him about my country, and I guess the satisfaction was mutual. He didn't unburden himself all at once; he was naturally reticent. After he came to share my bachelor quarters—I had four bedrooms and a housekeeper-cook—we had more time for talk, and that was when he confided in me his real purpose in coming to New York and studying our business methods.

"His family was mestizo—that is, at some time in the past a Spanish forebear had married a daughter of one of the accomplished tribes that made up the great Inca empire. Families of pure Spanish descent are relatively rare in the country; the great bulk of the population is still Indian, and most of the remainder is this mestizo mixture. They consider themselves Spanish, and will not only not admit but will deny the Indian heritage. Carlos's father, a wealthy landowner and military man, was especially sensitive about his ancestry, which he traced to the Conquest itself. He imported his household servants from Europe rather than employ Indians attached to his own plantations.

"I won't go into all the details Carlos told me about his life—schooling abroad, when he thought he might become a painter; but then he cut himself off from the old general, his father, and worked as an ordinary seaman; and at last he discovered the Indian history of his own country and suddenly found his mission. We had that in common, except it came earlier to me, and we pursued the interest in different ways. I became a collector, an archivist, an institution. He became concerned—I should say outraged—over the injury done his people. I won't stop to describe him, but he had a sadness in his face, around the eyes, and he looked quite Indian; darker, say, than a Mediterannean, and a blocky nose such as you see on a Maya glyph. He had in fact disavowed his father's claims to Spanish gentility and called himself Indian, only he said it hesitantly, as if he realized that the ragged and barefoot *Indios* of his own countryside might not acknowledge him. When he spoke of them, you felt the rage in his heart. They were the majority, yet they didn't exist, except when a new general needed strong young men to chase a rival general into the hills. They were like livestock on the land—without them the land was valueless, yet they had no voice in the nation and no court of review.

"I'll get to my point in a moment—just let me add that I knew the Peruvian Indians, the pre-Hispanic Indian of the highlands and the north coast, long before I met Carlos—knew them to be among the greatest artisans, builders, craftsmen, engineers the world has ever seen. I knew their monuments, their woven tapestries, their ceramics, their horticulture, their political accomplishments. And I knew that this had all passed away and I watched the descendants of those marvelous people walk like living dead on the very roads their ancestors engineered across desert and mountain.

"What I didn't know was that anyone in Peru cared about that past, until I met Carlos. When the general died—Carlos had a portrait of the old gentleman, a fierce glare and an enormous mustache—and before mama and his three sisters realized what was happening, Carlos had transformed one of the most fertile of the family holdings into a cooperative farm. The peons, who belonged to the land like livestock, were made joint proprietors. He brought trained agriculturists—made the contact through a harvest-machinery company representative—down from the States, and they introduced improved strains of wheat, barley, potatoes, and livestock—all familiar crops. But the greatest innovation was in modern soil tillage and chemical fertilizers. He set up a purchase plan by which they could pay for the land and their capital investments.

"And that was just the start. Next they took over some neighboring church lands, *cofradias*, which had operated in the same manner as private haciendas, with peons obliged to work without compensation certain days of the week, all proceeds going to the church society.

"These developments did not occur without arousing some noisy protests, as you may imagine. Carlos found himself under attack from all sides, especially from his own family and social circle. Even the church society, which benefited from the improved land-use contract and eventually sold the land outright to the community at a good price, was disturbed lest the peons, upon becoming free men, be led into sin.

"I don't mean to be tedious, but I want you to understand that these were not jungle Indians. When opportunity came to them they were quite capable of adopting new ideas.

"Government in Peru is a highly centralized affair, and local towns are governed out of a central district seat—it's as if one of our county seats controlled by appointment all the towns and villages within that county. The municipality of Cuno, where this all took place, was one such local town. Although it had been an important population center in Inca times, during the colonial period most of its outlying lands had been preempted by Spaniards. What was left to the Indians were parcels of community lands in and near the town, used jointly by all the Indians, who had their own *comunidad indígena*, or council, to control the use of the land and represent the Indian group. Cuno itself, although its population was largely Indian, was governed by a municipal council appointed by an absentee official, and these appointees were drawn from the minority mestizo population. Indians were not represented—perhaps they had no expectation or hope of ever having representation. The world was so ordained.

"The criticism directed at Carlos was of a social nature, and not always pleasant; there was gossip about his political ambitions and his presumed revolutionary connections, and social snubs. But all this was easily answered by the successes achieved. The people were instinctively conservative, and as money came into their hands they did not indulge in orgies. A few households bought sewing machines. Children began to wear shoes to church. Some houses were enlarged. But most of the money went to purchase extra livestock and farm tools. Money was pooled to buy a community tractor and a steam threshing machine. But the stroke which first began to turn local opinion to the favorable side was a considerable donation of funds and materials for the repair of the local church and parish house, most of which had been in ruins for years. A year later the Indian group voted to provide funds and volunteer labor to build a new school, and a petition was dispatched to the national government at Lima for additional teachers. The old school was so crowded and expensive that attendance was limited almost entirely to mestizo children. Very few of the Indians in the *comunidad indígena* at that time could write their names.

"And now, a real change came about. Responding to the obvious advances being made by the Indian population, and yielding to popular opinion, as officialdom sometimes will, an Indian was appointed to the municipal council of Cuno for the first time. This action met with such general approval, even among the mestizos, that by the following year half the council of ten members was Indian. Even the *alcalde,* or chief officer, was eventually an Indian—but that came later.

"That brings me finally to the point of my story— which was to tell you about the promise I felt compelled to keep, and why I could not come to Gen's Christmas party . . ."

Adam Pell had ceased pacing and had seated himself, hands under knees, on the wicker-and-cretonne sofa between the two horsehair chairs, facing the windows. Telling the story of Carlos Mendoza had quieted his first agitation, and he found that he could look at his sister and not really see her or feel her. And when he gave it thought, as he did in this reflective moment, he surprisingly realized that he had not neglected her. She and Tom had visited him in his New York house or at his summer place, in recent years at least. She never seemed to enjoy the visits, she had her mind so fixed on showing him off in Ohio. She could be quite frank and cross about it. Such things, he supposed, meant a great deal to a woman, but she seemed not to realize that the harder she pressed the matter with him, the more he would resist. He had never liked being on exhibition.

Before his reflections could carry him further, Tom was urging, "What was the next development? Peru! It has always fascinated me, ever since I read Prescott— many years ago now." Realizing that he was repeating himself, he broke off.

Mrs.Cooke did not comment, but neither was she pouting.

"Well, quickly, since we have decisions to make:

"It was then that Carlos came to New York, just as the first Indian was appointed to the municipal council at Cuno. He was in his early thirties and had been working with these people for almost ten years. Development was so fast and questions of methods and procedures were piling up at such a rate that he began to feel inadequate. He had come north to gain perspective, but it wasn't easy for him. He received a report at least once a week, and every time that report came he would have gloomy spells.

"Finally, after two years, he couldn't stand it any longer. The *comunidad indígena* was considering dissolving its separate existence and becoming one with the municipal council. It was a disturbing proposal, of course. It could mean that the Indian community was being captured by the more aggressive and more politically experienced mestizos—or it could mean, as was claimed, that the centuries-old traditional division between the two groups was being healed over and they were ready to work together. The immediate reason to consolidate forces was a proposal for the town to build a hydropower plant.

"Carlos was so agitated that he talked to me for half an hour in machine-gun Spanish before he realized that he had lost me after his first explosion.

"The upshot of it was that Carlos took passage on the next available sailing—and that was when the promise was given. He would return to Cuno, make a careful appraisal of the situation, and if everything was in order and the proposal to build the hydro plant was sound and practical, I was to come and take charge of design and construction. I agreed, feeling all the time that it was a most improbable brain wave from some mercurial

Spanish mind. Scarcely a town outside the larger Peruvian cities had electric power, and here was a mere hamlet proposing to go into the power business.

"I waited then for months without a word from Carlos, becoming convinced that nothing further would be heard, except perhaps an embarrassed apology in due course. And then, just as I was well into another job, the cable arrived asking me to come at once. It was just before Christmas, as you reminded me, but summer there in Peru.

"What I found in Cuno—a beautiful little town of white stone houses with red roofs nestled at the foot of high, brown hills and cut into segments by avenues of eucalyptus trees—was an extraordinary human community. After almost four centuries of conquest, which is to say of murder, pillage, rape, sacrilege—all those outrageous defilements of the conquered man—these people were discovering what it meant to be human. Nobody felt obliged to step aside to let another pass, though they might smile elaborately. Every man's house was open to any who wished to enter. In the meeting rooms was no separate seating for the high and the low. Juan Tomás of the half-hectare farm was free to speak directly to Don Carlos with his ten thousand hectares. These may seem like trifling observations, but considering the short time in which it had happened, it was extraordinary. I suppose if one traced the historical process at work, it wasn't all so sudden, but one had the impression of an overnight revolution. The dreadful outcome of a master-slave population, such as this had been for twenty generations, is the brutalization of both parties; the upper man loses his capacity for compassion, although he may live on a high plane of esthetic expression, while the bottom man must live without hope, and sinks himself instead in fatalistic religion, or alcohol, or wife beating. The Peruvian peasants had found their escape in coca chewing.

"When I reached Cuno, the town and the neighboring countryside had been mobilized. The old *comunidad indígena,* as a final act before dissolving and merging with the municipal council, had turned over its remaining treasury to the building fund for the light plant. The

148

municipal council matched these funds by levying a special assessment on all non-Indians—and this, too, was a final act of its kind: there would be no distinction in future between citizens on account of race or birth. The six church societies dug down into their treasuries and contributed from funds which for generations they had extracted from the faithful. In addition, each householder agreed to contribute a specified number, according to the size of his house, of dressed stones, adobe bricks, and roof tiles. All this was awaiting my arrival—which explained why Carlos had not cabled sooner.

"Construction of the plant was simple, although no one had had the least idea of what the machinery we would need would cost, and it turned out that their assessments and voluntary contributions were sadly inadequate and we had to negotiate a sizeable bank loan. Even this was no problem, after we made a hurried survey of the market potential. The Lima banker's eyes popped, but he came through when I informed him that my New York bank would consider it a privilege to make the investment.

"We built upon the foundation of an old mill dam, which had been solidly anchored in bedrock. A strong perennial stream bordered the town, and we simply raised the elevation and built a powerhouse. When the first lights were turned on, the town exploded with enthusiasm—firecrackers, church bells, a brass band, barking dogs, motor horns, bleating sheep, bellowing cows. I was made an honorary citizen and was embraced and given a medal by the mayor.

"I still hear regularly from Carlos. The bank loan has been paid off and the revolution goes on.

"Until I went to Cuno and lived with its problems for a while, I had never given much thought to the living Indians—our own, or those in South America. I had read their histories, but only because I needed to know the background of the materials I had started collecting as a youngster in Ohio, those boyhood excursions that annoyed you, dear Gen, because I would slip away without you and come home all grubby and bulging with bits of incised pottery and carved shell and even an occasional skull. Those I believe I kept from you sight. . ."

"No, Brother. I knew all about your pile of bones in the woodshed, and all the broken pots. I helped the junkman load them on his cart one day, but mother came at the wrong time and made me unload them again."

"Ah, yes." He looked at his sister briefly, and saw the faint tinge of embarrassment. Confession, even of a long-buried fault, did not come easily.

"Yes, I remember now. I spent a week sorting things out again and no one would explain what had happened. Bones and broken pots they were, to you and to every farmer in Ohio who tossed them out of the furrows they plowed. For a long time I saw only what the farmers saw —curios, they were called—and noticed that many farm-houses had little pieces stuck away on a kitchen shelf or in a corner whatnot, pieces that a museum today would pay handsomely to possess. They went to the junkman, and sometimes the junkman became rich.

"Cuno was the continuity for me, a bridge into the past. I saw faces in the street that matched perfectly the portrait jars and bowls fashioned a thousand years before—hunchbacks, toothless old dames, warts on a nose. And I realized in a rush of insight what sharper minds than mine had known for a long time, that the people who created those wonders were still with us. Only we had buried them in peonage or in something that in this country is called wardship. We were rushing into the future and had no place for the surviving artisans and creative minds; their artifacts, labeled relics or curios, could be stowed away in a museum and safely ignored.

"Well!" He sprang from the wicker sofa, which cracked and snapped from the sudden weight release. His stride took him all the way to the window, then he turned back.

"I've never talked about these things, it is true. They never seemed relevant when you visited in New York. Being here in Indian country—a different kind of Indian country, but maybe not so different—brings back some of this, the sense of encounter that I lived with for a time. Maybe I mean discovery. In a way I can't explain, not to your satisfaction, I am sure, I feel a kind of responsibility for what could happen here. Do you follow me?"

"I don't see—" his sister began, then found herself lost.

Thomas Cooke rose, pushing himself up with his stick and the arm of the upholstered chair, and what he said startled Adam Pell and confounded his wife.

"Murder is not an isolated occurrence. It has its roots, its certain logic. Justice has the task of discovering that logic.

"My dear, I'm going to arrange for a car to drive us out to this Indian headquarters, whatever its called. A day won't matter. I feel our boy would approve."

"Oh, Thomas!" The sound was drawn out, like a child's wail. "I knew you would side with him!"

That was how it started.

19

Rafferty knew immediately that Sid Grant had bad news to report and held back only because he found visitors in the office when he pushed the door open. He was, in fact, on the point of speaking out, when Rafferty interrupted him.

"Mrs. Cooke, I'd like to introduce the United States Marshal for this district, Mr. Sid Grant. He's been working on the case night and day—wouldn't you say, Marshal?"

Sid Grant pulled his hat from his head and half-swallowed an acknowledgement: "—to meet you, ma'am. As the superintendent says—"

"And this is Mr. Cooke, father of the young man. And maybe you know Mr. Adam Pell, who was out here, he tells me, several years ago."

By the time he had shaken hands and brought his deputy up to shake hands, the marshal's manner lost some of its brusqueness. He knew how to act before gentlefolk.

"Sure am glad to meet all of you. Yes, I most certainly remember this gentleman, Mr. Pell, though like as not he don't remember me. You was up here when they started the dam. Made a good speech, too."

Adam Pell looked surprised. "I did?" Since he never made speeches, he looked a second time at Sid Grant.

"Shall we sit down?" Rafferty suggested. "Bull should be here soon. My interpreter will bring him in as soon as he arrives. We're just visiting at the moment. Mr. Pell was telling us about his visit and about the dam in the canyon. I never appreciated before what an engineering accomplishment we have up there. . . ."

Rafferty's office was designed for staff conferences—that is, it had more space than was needed for a desk and chair. It ran to one long dimension and was well supplied with heavy oak chairs and even an upholstered sofa.

The sofa faced the outward window and a view of the thrusting mountains beyond. The Cookes had chosen the sofa. Adam Pell sat next to them, in one of the heavy chairs. His hand rested on the leather arm of the sofa, and at times he reached across and took his sister's hand in his. At the end, she had yielded gracefully and agreed to come—this further journey. The veil was drawn back over the round black hat, and her eyes, as she stared across into an unfamiliar world of mountains, were dark pools of brooding. Of the three, Thomas Cooke seemed least interested in the surroundings. His left leg was thrust forward in an awkward position, but he showed no concern about that. Other scenes, perhaps other inquiries into the logic of murder, seemed to be on his mind.

Rafferty could watch the three faces from his desk, which was farther down the room and placed at an angle to the sofa and chair. He sensed that husband and wife had not initiated this encounter, that the urging had come from the lean-faced, domineering Adam Pell. And Rafferty had not yet discerned the full range of his motive.

He regretted at first that he had mentioned the subject of the canyon dam. Pell took it up promptly and talked enthusiastically, and it seemed not to be an appropriate occasion for an engineering discourse. But when Sid Grant came thrusting forward, obviously anxious for attention, Rafferty decided to encourage the interrupted discourse.

"It was already in operation when I arrived and I have been up there only a few times. What do you mean when you call it a 'run-of-the-stream' operation?"

Adam Pell looked fleetingly at his sister, but her eyes did not meet his, so he continued in full course.

"Why, it just means you run the natural flow of the stream through a generating plant, without storing water behind your retaining wall. What we did up there was plug the lower end of a natural basin and raise the elevation some fifty feet, as I recall, enough to build up a good head. But we don't hold back any storage, don't need to since the stream is remarkably constant, flowing out of springs and deep ice fields in the high mountains. We spill some water down the old stream bed at the peak of the spring run-off, in order not to overload the canal. Otherwise the water after it clears the turbines is diverted through a canal to the north end of the valley, which is the high line, and there we empty it into a storage reservoir. Then it comes by gravity through feeder canals and laterals and irrigates the entire valley—fifty thousand acres. Beautifully simple."

Only an engineer would put all those things together, Rafferty thought—cement, turbines, diversion canals, contour lines—and call the assemblage beautiful. He dwelt on the man, the lean, angular frame, clothed casually in rough-spun tweeds and a stiff wing collar. Long, supple hands. Stooped shoulders. And keen gray eyes that fastened on things, penetrated, and moved away. An artist could inventory the environment in such a manner; he had not expected to find the gift in an engineer.

"Beautiful, you say. But why did the Indians object to the dam, as I understand they did?"

The sharp eyes turned on Rafferty, and lingered. Then Adam Pell smiled.

"Ah, there you have touched something. I want to talk about that. Later, shall we? I want to ask this lawman something."

He turned from Rafferty to Sid Grant, who was sitting with his deputy at the opposite end of the room, near the door. Rafferty knew that his strategy of ignoring Sid Grant had to fail sooner or later, still he groaned with an inward voice.

"Mr. Marshal. I understand you're ready to charge an Indian with this crime. Perhaps we should congratulate you for your good work—your deputy as well. Are you satisfied you can get an indictment?"

Sid Grant's eagerness had subsided and now he seemed reluctant to speak out. He turned the question around in his mind, as he turned the wide-brimmed ranger's hat around on his knee and smoothed the crushed crown. The question was sharper than he would have had it.

"Looks pretty good to me," he answered, without glancing up.

Adam Pell waited for some elaboration and frowned when nothing more was offered.

"You are satisfied. But you won't be the prosecutor. You won't be in the jury box, if the matter reaches there. What I want to know, and the boy's father and mother want to know, will your case ever get to a jury? Have you got a case—or don't you need to make a case when the defendant is an Indian?"

The questioning startled Rafferty, who looked at Adam Pell as if he had not met him until that moment. Sid Grant looked even more startled. His voice came like a growl.

"Being an Indian don't make no difference around here, spite of what you might hear. As for the case going to a jury . . ."

His gaze went to Rafferty, and the next words seemed to be addressed to him.

"It'll get there, all right. We've got the gun that killed the young man. Prosecutors like to have something like that—juries like it too."

Rafferty felt the full force of the marshal's steady gaze almost as a physical impact. He returned the gaze until Sid Grant at last turned to Adam Pell.

"That answer your question?"

"Just a minute," Rafferty's voice slid quietly into the pause. He had continued to watch Sid Grant even after the latter turned away.

"I'd like to learn more about that. When you and your deputy went up to Bull's camp, you couldn't find a thing, so you reported. Are you now saying that's where you found this gun, which you say was the killing gun?"

"That's what I'm saying."

"Tell us about it. How did you miss it the first time?" By then Rafferty was making pencil scrawls on a blank piece of paper, suggesting an air of mild interest.

Adam Pell caught the drift of Rafferty's tactic. It was, in fact, amazing how quickly he fitted himself into the mood of a conversation.

"Yes, Marshal. I seem to detect that the finding of

this gun required a display of ingenuity—and persistence. Tell us about it."

Sid Grant looked first at Pell, then at Rafferty, and his shoulders relaxed. He had moved into the center of the stage, where he felt he belonged.

"I admit they fooled us that first time. Of course, we couldn't give the camp a good going over the way it was. I was watching the men, not knowing who might make a break—and Amby, here, going through the tepees, had to watch that some squaw didn't sink a hatchet in his skull. So it was best to get them out, which we did. Mr. Rafferty here didn't quite like it, but it was the best way, as it turned out."

"I can't agree, but go ahead." Rafferty was still making scrawls.

"Well, so we went back up there yesterday, and found the women had all cleared out—went west, riding their horses right over the tracks we had followed in the day before. That itself looked mighty suspicious, since that wasn't the usual way of going, if they was just bent on going down into the valley, where I suspect they've taken cover with relatives. I was dead certain then we'd find the gun in that camp. I figured them squaws wouldn't risk carrying it out, in case they was stopped and searched.

"An old squaw was left behind, I couldn't figure how come. We found her sitting in her tepee by herself. We poked around a little bit, then I got an idea we might learn something if we just sat and watched. We rode off a piece and tied up our horses out of sight, then walked back where we could watch the camp without being seen."

The marshal again looked to his audience, out of an emerging smile. And Adam Pell paid the anticipated compliment. "I hope I never have you on my trail, Marshal. Go on, please."

"We sat there maybe a couple of hours. Then we saw the squaw leave her tepee and for a while she just stood in one place. She was looking, but she was also listening. You watch an Indian when he's out hunting. He don't just run around looking everywhere and likely scaring the game out of the country. Chances are he'll stand still and let all his senses work for him. If a squirrel breaks off its chattering, or a bird flies up—that's when Mr. Indian gets interested, begins to plan how he'll move. So we watched that squaw. After she stood there awhile, she made up her mind that nobody was watching her and she walked through some low brush until she came to an old pine snag that had been lightning struck and burned out. I was lying in a brush patch up a little hill with a pair of field glasses. It was a cache, and she went up there to get something. It told us what we needed to know, and as soon as she went back to her tepee we began a fresh search. We didn't find what we wanted in that particular cache—and I had a hunch we wouldn't. I figured that was her private safety vault. But we went around tapping trees, old stumps, fallen logs, and looking for stuff that might be tied in trees where there might be a thick growth of leafy branches. Well, we uncovered quite a collection of hidden goods—left it alone, of course.

"And then we found the gun, in a rotting log that was buried under old slashings. When you looked at the spot, you'd swear those slashings had been there for years and hadn't been touched. Dead grass and weeds grew up through the stuff and nothing had been crushed down or broken off. We walked past the log I don't know how many times before I decided to have a look. When I pushed the stuff aside and kicked at the old log, it practically fell apart—and there she was. In a buckskin scabbard, wrapped in an old blanket.

"When I came out of there, the old squaw was standing back of me, just looking. I don't know why she didn't axe me down—she had all the chance she needed before I even saw her."

Rafferty felt a numbness in his hands as he put his pencil aside.

"You're sure that's the gun? It checked out?"

"Oh, sure. I tried a cartridge in her and got the same markings on the casing."

Thomas Cooke, who had been silent since the introductions were made and seemed hardly to follow the conversation, shattered the marshal's mounting complacency.

"That still leaves a major question to be answered," he said, and looked past his brother-in-law to Sid Grant. "Two questions. Who owns the gun? And after that, you'll have to ask, Who fired it?"

Sid Grant didn't answer either question. Not just then.

The door had been pulled open, and when they turned to look, they saw Bull and his grandson and The Boy framed within the opening.

Rafferty, rising from his chair, realized that he had asked Bull to walk into a trap.

20

The first sound came from Geneva Cooke, a soft, indrawn "Oh, dear!" And for her the moment became real, immediate, and personal. The sound was audible only to her husband and to Adam Pell, but it had come from a deep consciousness.

She saw the man standing forth, just inside the threshold, and had the impression that his eyes uncovered her and burned her flesh. She was only barely aware of pressing her knees together and tugging at her skirt, already tightly drawn. This was no savage, as her mind might have registered in abstraction. The reality compelled her to see him as a man—unexpectedly.

He stood tall, muscular, rugged in feature, and obviously in control of the world in which he moved—that is, of himself. He wore a blanket over the left shoulder, the right arm free, with his left hand emerging to hold the folds of the blanket together over the right hip. It might have been the toga of a Roman senator out of her schoolbook reading. The impression was fleeting, and when it passed, Geneva Cooke felt herself shrinking into the background.

Adam Pell went forward with Rafferty to shake hands, and before the introductions were completed Thomas Cooke had pulled himself to his feet and joined the group in the middle of the room. Only Sid Grant and his deputy remained unsmiling, immobile.

When they were seated, Bull, at the left of Rafferty's desk, could look across to the three strangers who had come, it was said, from some far place across the mountains. They had come for their son, who had taken a bullet in his body and was gone. These white men would say what was to be done. He understood this, since it had been that way now for a long time. He looked across the room and could see nothing bad in the faces of these people. And that was the way it had been for a long time also.

The one whose leg didn't bend was turning into an old man, with graying hair and glass pieces before his eyes. He looked to be a strong man, with firm flesh, though one leg was gone. The moustache was also graying —the face was pleasant. When their eyes met, the man smiled, and Bull's gaze moved on. The woman did not look up, but he had already seen her. She was the mother, and inside she was crying, waiting for men to stop talking so she could be with her boy. And then she did look up when his eyes came to her, but she looked away again. The thin man was already watching when Bull met his gaze, and they held each other for a moment. One would have to watch him, listen carefully to what he said, and try to decide what manner of man he was. This one had sharp, clear eyes, the eyes of a man who could find his way. Bull looked at last to Rafferty, and he could tell that the government man had a cloud over his face. Perhaps he was angry, but he could not find the cause of it.

Bull was the first to talk. It was a leader's privilege, but the suddenness of it surprised those who did not understand the custom. He had let the blanket drop to his waist, where it was gathered together. His neat braids hung down over a clean white shirt, a white man's shirt. He turned to The Boy:

"Tell this woman I am sorry about her son. This is a bad time for a mother. Tell her I can feel this sorrow. She will look at me, and wonder how a man so ugly, all brown and wrinkled, can have these feelings, but tell her it is not like that inside. She has lost a son. Tell her I am a man who has lost all that went before, all that belonged to my father and my grandfather, back to the beginning. My people are lying like dead trees all around me and we are no longer a forest. And still I am sorry about her son."

When these words had been translated, Geneva Cooke and her husband looked in astonishment, first at each other, then at the large Indian across the room, who seemed so unaware of the troubled thoughts and the impulses and passions that surged in that room.

She managed, "That is very kind—of the—gentleman. Please thank him."

Thomas Cooke nodded vigorously. "Yes. Yes. We appreciate what—Mr. Bull—has said to us. His words will not be forgotten."

Bull heard the words translated, watching Thomas Cooke, and then he smiled.

He told The Boy: "These people are polite. Maybe in that country they come from they make a different kind of white people.

"Now, say to the government man that I came because he asked. My elder brother was still with me this morning, but I think he will not be here much longer. You heard him yesterday ask about Feather Boy bundle —but you answered just part way. If you can answer the rest of the way, I will carry it back. Maybe he will still be there.

"But first, the angry man is here, and I guess he will ask questions. Tell him it is all right. I am ready."

Rafferty knew that Sid Grant would pounce as soon as the way was open, although he sat back in his chair and appeared to be relaxed and disinterested.

Rafferty said: "Tell Bull that I appreciate his coming I wanted to explain what I know about the medicine bundle. It isn't very much, but I did not want to worry Henry Jim yesterday. He might think I haven't tried very hard. Well, it just takes a little time. But now, these people are here and they want to know what happened to their son and we want to tell them everything we can. We will have to take care of that first."

Leaning back in his chair, he rolled two pencils back and forth between outspread palms and the pencils made a clacking sound as they rolled over the heavy ring on his right hand. He neither heard the noise nor saw the turning pencils. He saw only Sid Grant straining at the delay.

And he went on: "Tell him that in white man's law, to have a suspicion about a man is not to make him guilty. When we talk hard at a man, it is not because we are condemning him. A man may try to hide something he knows, so we ask hard questions until he gives up. That is the way in our law. It is our way of finding out what happened."

Bull answered through The Boy: "This man is trying to make it easy for me. But tell him this. It is all right for white men to have this law among themselves. They grow up together and know what to expect. My people never made such a law. When I hurt somebody, his family knows about it. I have already talked about it in my own family. They know why I did it. Maybe I was angry and did it without thinking, or maybe he did something to me or to one of my kinsmen. Then the two families get together, or they call in somebody to listen to both sides. We settle it right there. Nobody has to talk hard, unless he is still angry. And then the others try to settle him down. I don't like your white man's law—it makes everybody angry, like that man over there. He came to my camp and shouted at us, the way we shout at dogs when they get to fighting and won't listen."

Sid Grant was leaning forward now, ready to take up where he had been interrupted, but Adam Pell moved in ahead of him.

"I am grateful," he said, "for Mr. Bull's statement. He has said something very true about our law, our white man's law, as he calls it. It is a contest, and sometimes in these contests we get so far away from the search for truth that we make a travesty—excuse the word—we make something bad out of our good intentions. Each side in these contests tries to read from more books than the other side—which is just another way of trying to shout louder than the other side. And too often it is done in anger, as Mr. Bull says."

Bull watched Adam Pell while The Boy was translating, and when it was finished, he said: "This man is also trying to make it easy for me. Are they afraid I might cry if they talk hard?"

The Boy did not translate the remark.

Sid Grant finally broke through and terminated the philosophical session. He introduced himself with a smile, but not a warming smile.

"I hope Bull don't get the idea that murder is not

serious business, to be settled in friendly neighbor talk. Just tell him, if you will, that the white man's law is what operates here. A man was murdered, a white man, though that don't matter. The crime took place inside an Indian reservation—that's what matters. The federal court is in charge, not some J.P., and I represent that federal court.

"Now, I want you to tell him that I have something in my possession, something that came from his camp, and I want him to look at it and tell me if he recognizes this object. Amby, go get the package."

The silent little deputy jumped from his chair and pushed the door with such violence that it swung back against the wall and rattled the frosted glass window.

"Oh, pardon!" he cried out, startled by his own show of strength.

"Amby gets excited," the marshal explained.

"Why can't he tear down your door instead of mine?" Rafferty was irritated by the little deputy, but irritated even more by the marshal's tactic of surprise and ambush. He thumped on his desk with the eraser end of a pencil.

Bull told The Boy: "If he has found something in my camp, he has sharper eyes than most white men. I'm afraid of this man. I think he will keep going until he finds my young kinsman. And it will be as I said in the beginning. They will hang him. One way or another, they will cut us down, and we will have to sit like this and watch them do it."

He turned to his grandson: "Toine, I don't know what will happen here. It may go bad for me or for your uncle. This man won't let go once he gets started. If it looks like they're going to find out about him, you must leave here. They won't stop you. They'll say he's just a boy, let him go. Go to your uncle and tell him to run. It will be his only chance." Antoine began to burn inside, that his grandfather should turn to him to help.

The Boy stared straight ahead, saying nothing.

The deputy returned then with two packages, both wrapped in heavy brown paper and tied with twine. One package was long and round, the other a shapeless bulge.

"Put them there, in the middle of the floor," Sid

Grant directed. Then he looked around the room, counting noses. When everyone had looked up, he turned to The Boy.

"I want you to tell the Chief something for me. He said I came to his camp and shouted at his people. Maybe I did. But just you tell him what it's like to be a lawman. You can talk from your own experience. The lawman, why he's the enemy, but only if you got something to hide. He has to go where he is told. If somebody has committed a crime, or there is a suspicion that he has, the lawman has to go in there and ask questions, make a search, maybe take somebody into custody. Sometimes he gets hurt, and sometimes he doesn't come out at all. Every man who works for the law sooner or later has some rough experiences. He learns to live with people who don't like him, and he learns to take care of himself as best he can.

"When I come to his camp that day, I am following a trail that leads straight from the spot where a man has been shot to death. The trail takes me to Bull's camp. And when I ride in, I know I am being watched. I think this boy here, or somebody his size, watched us from a ridge. Well, that's how it was. I'm expecting somebody to take a potshot at me just for the hell of it. And if I talked loud to his folks, why, you can say I was nervous."

He waited until The Boy finished translating, but he didn't pause beyond that. He wasn't waiting for comments. He told his deputy, "Just untie that small, lumpy package, and spread it out."

The paper parcel was quickly opened, and the deputy withdrew what appeared to be part of an old red blanket. When Ambrose Whiteside spread it out, they could see two narrow black bands parallel to one edge. The blanket was thin and faded, and apparently it had been torn in two at approximately the middle.

"Now, just hold it. I want you people to notice how the tear near the edge is even, like a knife cut started it, then the rest is ragged, like it was torn by hand."

Then he looked up, facing Bull. "Maybe you recognize this old blanket, Chief. We found it in your wife's lodge, the one they call Veronica. It was stuffed in an old rawhide bag along with other old stuff. What my woman calls a 'rag bag.'"

Bull looked, but said nothing.

"All right." Sid Grant continued. "He's not talking. Not yet. Open up the other package, Amby."

This took longer, as there were several knots, and a quantity of brown paper to fold back. And the deputy seemed not to hurry his movements.

Finally, he drew out an object wrapped in folded red material, also tied with twine. When these knots were unfastened and the material was removed—and the deputy unwound the material carefully he held up a rifle encased in a buckskin scabbard.

"Just hand me the gun for a minute. I want you to show them the red blanket first. Lay both pieces on the floor, torn parts together."

The pieces obviously matched.

Sid Grant made a sound in his throat that sounded like a laugh. "Your old woman is like mine. She didn't want to waste a whole blanket, even if it was going to pieces. So she saved half of it. And what did it get her?"

When this was translated, Bull ignored the rough-handed joke. He said: "You found somebody's gun, and you found a blanket. Maybe you put it there—or this little man." His lips pointed to the deputy.

Rafferty had moved from his chair behind the desk and was standing in front of the desk, staring at the ragged blanket halves. And when he looked up, he saw a shadow beyond the frosted light in his door. Someone from his staff probably wanted to see him, but that would have to wait.

He asked: "Is it conceivable that someone—whoever did the shooting—came through there, after you left with the men, and planted this stuff?"

Sid Grant gave this a cool thought, looking at Rafferty with the contempt the professional has for the amateur. "Conceivable, but not likely. The women were still there when I took the men in, and they didn't leave camp next morning until just before we got there. So whoever stuffed the half blanket away knew just which bag to choose. Like I said, it was kind of a rag bag."

He broke off there and turned to Thomas Cooke, who talked like he knew something about legal process. "You asked two questions, and now I'm going to give you the answers, far as I know them as of now. You asked, 'Who owns the gun?' and 'Who fired the gun?' I agree, that's what we have to know."

Again he looked around the room, making sure there were no stragglers.

"The first question really don't matter too much. I'm not even going to ask Bull whether this is his gun." He was holding the weapon across his lap, and patted it.

"Like as not, he'd just say no. When the time comes, I think we can prove it's his, all right. Leastwise, it belonged in that camp. It's that second question I'm looking at. 'Who fired 'er?' "

The Boy had been interpreting along the side as Sid Grant talked, and Bull interrupted.

"In my camp, when somebody wants to go hunting, he just picks up a gun. Nobody asks, 'Is this your gun?' Only my grandson has his own gun, a little one."

The marshal smiled vaguely. "Exactly, Chief."

Again Bull broke in. "Tell that man to stop calling me 'Chief.' We don't use that word any more. I'm just 'the talker' for my camp."

The vague smile became more definite after The Boy translated. "Whatta you know, seems like he knows at least one English word. They always let on they don't." Sid Grant turned back to the business at hand. "Whatever he says. I figured that ownership of the gun wouldn't tell us what we want to know. And now I'm going to say that whoever was up there at the dam and fired that shot, and threw out a cartridge shell which fits the markings made by this old .30/30 Winchester—it wasn't Bull. . . ."

When he paused at that point, Rafferty left his place in front of the desk and returned to his chair. For the first time he found it possible to look at Bull. He could even smile and go back to making pencil scrawls.

Thomas Cooke also smiled, as he began to appreciate the marshal's blunt manner.

In Adam Pell's mind, the design which began to form hours before was suddenly bright with promise.

And Geneva Cooke discovered she was pleased that she need not think of this man with abhorrence.

Of them all, Bull was the only one who did not seem to breathe easier or to relax into an easier sitting position. When he was told what had been said, he snapped, "It's a trick! This man still wants to hang somebody!"

"I may have to change my mind," the marshal continued, "when I get all the story together. But just now I got two reasons for saying Bull ain't my man. Just tell him this, that as of now I'm accepting the story he told me when we first brought him down here from his camp. He was madder'n a roused-up mother bear with a cub, but he told us, and you interpreted, that he returned to his camp just as it started to snow. If that story stands, it means he got back to camp before the shooting. It lets him out. Does he stick to that story?"

Bull answered through The Boy: "When I talk to a white man, what does it matter what I say? He will turn it around the way he wants to hear it. If he's going to say that somebody returned to my camp after the storm, I don't know what he's talking about."

The marshal looked hard for a moment, but did not comment. He continued instead with his own recital. "He hasn't answered my question, but let it go. The other reason would let him out anyway. The man who went up to the dam and fired that gun was wearing cowboy boots, with sharp heels. I've asked around, and nobody I've run into ever seen the old man wearing cowboy boots."

The marshal looked at Bull, and suddenly smiled. "Watching the old man walk, with his toes turned in slightly, he'd probably throw himself in high-heeled boots. That's just personal—you don't have to translate it."

On a common impulse, everyone looked down at Bull's smoothly moccasinned feet, which were tucked partway under his chair. He looked at his own feet then, and remarked: "If I walk in hard shoes, the ground won't reach me. Then I won't be Indian."

Sid Grant continued his pursuit.

"I'm ready to eliminate Bull as a suspect, but not his

camp. This is what I want you to tell him. The man who used this gun to kill the young man up at the dam came from Bull's camp. I want him to tell me who took this gun out of camp."

Bull raised his head when the question was explained. He stared at the marshal but said nothing. The set of his jaw made plain that he did not intend to say anything.

Antoine got to his feet and started toward the door, looking straight ahead. He had to pass close to Sid Grant's chair, and just as he was about to walk by the marshal thrust out his arm.

"What you up to, boy?" he asked abruptly.

Rafferty had been watching this by-play, and then he saw something else. The shadow that had appeared from time to time against the frosted door-light became sharper in outline, became more pronounced.

Then the door opened, and Pock Face stood framed against the outer office.

He was a tall, slender young man as he stood in cowboy boots, carrying a stockman's hat at his side. He had a smooth, dark face. He seemed to see each one in the room, yet his eyes held steady.

After a moment, he drew the door closed behind and walked toward Bull's chair. Antoine had pulled back to the place he had left, his eyes shining.

Pock Face spoke, in English, addressing Rafferty: "I stood outside. I listened. They said I couldn't come in. But I came anyhow."

Sid Grant exploded. "So! You *do* talk English! But I already found that out. I was coming to that—"

Pock Face had walked past the marshal, and now he turned to face him, cutting off his words. "You don't have to jump on my uncle. He had nothing to do with that shooting. I did that myself."

He turned to Rafferty next. "The old man out there just died . . . so I came right away to tell this. He wanted you to help bring back our Feather Boy medicine bundle. That was the last thing he talked about. I was afraid if you thought my uncle killed that man up there, maybe you wouldn't want to help. Now you know who did it—"

"But why!" The faltering cry pierced them all. And

Geneva Cooke sat forward, her small face pale and shattered. A deep furrow split her forehead. "Why? Did you know him? Did he do something to you?"

Pock Face seemed to lose his tallness and litheness. The arm carrying his stockman's hat drooped. He looked at the floor.

"He didn't do nothing. I never saw him before. He was there on the dam. They killed our water there. They took it away..."

Adam Pell, looking puzzled, asked gently: "I don't understand. Why did you shoot him for that?"

The reasons were remote and entangled in Pock Face's mind. No words came. After a moment, The Boy spoke.

"They feel it badly. They say the water ran there from the beginning and a man should not make the water stop. They say the white man killed the water. I guess he thought he was hitting the man who built the dam up there."

At that Adam Pell felt strangled. His staring eyes went from Pock Face, to The Boy, and finally to Rafferty. Then he said:

"You asked a while ago, Why did the Indians object? Now I realize I never knew. I thought maybe they objected to irrigating land owned by white men." He broke off. "We didn't stop the water or kill it—we put it out on the land, to make the land rich, Indian land as well as white man's..." The enormity of the misapprehension swept over his mind and silenced him.

For Antoine, it was a moment of dreadful expectation. The afternoon on the mountainside burst like a flame in his imagination. Here was the very man! The man who killed the water! He pulled back into himself, waiting for his grandfather's anger to explode, as it had that day. Surely his grandfather in anger was a power beyond the likes of men.

But Bull, when Adam Pell's words were translated, half rose in his chair. Then he subsided. His legs would not push him up. His elder brother had asked his help, and he must give it. He could not fight these men, if it meant losing Feather Boy. He was back in his chair, feeling that a great danger had passed.

Rafferty had watched, had seen the dark blood rise like angry water, and watched it ebb away, and he too sank in his chair, his hands inert and clasped together.

Sid Grant, without understanding what had passed before his eyes, decided that the time had come for him to resume his appointed role.

He stood up. "It seems to me, with the confession this young fellow has made—"

Before he could finish, Thomas Cooke had taken control, without rising from his chair. He seemed to do it naturally.

"Mr. Rafferty, I take it you are in charge of this meeting. If you'll allow me, I'd like to advise this young man. He seems to have come here and given us information, at great risk to himself—because, did he say, an old man just died and he wished to protect his uncle? A man who will take that responsibility deserves the full consideration of this court. Excuse me. I happen to be a judge in the small town where I live, a state circuit judge. Now it seems the young man is trying to make a confession, and I presume the marshal was about to have it taken down in writing. I suggest that the young man—it seems he understands English—that he make no statement, and that we in this room forget that he seemed to be on the point of making a statement, until he has had the benefit of counsel. Don't forget that he came here with some idea of protecting his uncle. So the story he was about to tell may be construed in that light. Yes, I would advise him to speak with a lawyer—a competent one, might I add. He will have a hard adversary."

Sid Grant would not have hesitated to arrest Pock Face at once if he had been challenged by a local law officer, but Thomas Cooke's unexpected intervention took him by surprise. He barked out "He's wearing them coyboy boots, ain't he?" But the remark seemed not to inspire action. The marshal had no desire to find himself wiped out by some smart city lawyer on a technicality. He needed time to think it over.

To Rafferty he said, "We'll be back. Just see this young feller don't run off."

He grabbed his hat. "Come on, Amby. Gather up

the stuff and let's get out of here." At the doorway he turned back. "A pleasure to meet you folks, I'm sure." But he did not sound pleased.

The marshal's departure was not acknowledged by anyone in the room. Adam Pell had not recovered from the shock of discovering that in some remote way— unbelievable, except that it happened—he had contributed to his nephew's death. "That bullet was meant for me, the boy just happened to be there," his mind kept saying. He avoided looking at his sister.

Thomas Cooke leaned forward, both hands resting on the knobbed end of his walking stick. He had not meant to rout the marshal, but the sudden retreat suggested that Sid Grant was not accustomed to having his methods challenged. The thought induced a discreet smile.

For Rafferty, the marshal's departure lifted a burden from his conscience. From the moment Bull had stepped into the room, to be confronted by an accusatory Sid Grant, Rafferty had been unhappy with himself, since he had asked Bull to come. But the relief was brief, for now he had to give the answer that Bull came to hear, and he had no answer. He turned to The Boy and spoke as if the matter were not on his mind.

"Explain to Bull that he can go home now. I think the marshal will not bother him any more. He will come back for Pock Face, like he said, but we will take care of that when it happens."

Bull would not have it. He remained seated and gazed steadily at Rafferty. He told The Boy: "This man who was going to help us. Why doesn't he tell me what we want to know?"

The Boy translated, then added: "Henry Jim said you would help, but Bull is not sure. He needs to be encouraged and then he will be your friend."

The problem was that Adam Pell and his party had come on short notice, just a phone call from Elk City, and there had been no time or occasion to ask about the medicine bundle. Until he could be sure the object was in Pell's museum, Rafferty felt that he had to continue a tactic of evasiveness, a tactic not likely to encourage friendship.

"I will tell you how it is," he said. "Henry Jim came to see me just a few days ago and talked about the medicine bundle. He gave it to Stephen Welles, and the missionary sent it to a museum back east. That much I found out. Tell Bull a museum is a big house with many rooms and many boxes where they put things to keep them safe. When I ask those people at the museum about the bundle they will have to look in all those boxes, all those rooms, before they can give me an answer. Tell him he will have to trust me to find out."

The translation took a long time and Rafferty guessed that The Boy was doing his best to be "encouraging" and secure the friendship. Bull, however, gave no sign of relaxing. He looked from Rafferty back to The Boy.

"I said it before, I don't know how to talk to these people. Grandson, Elder Brother has gone ahead and I have no message for him. But let's return to his camp."

When the words had been translated, Rafferty sensed that he had been dismissed like a boy making poor excuses. Bull had that force.

It was after Bull, Antoine, and Pock Face left the room that Adam Pell discovered the other dimension of his involvement. Rafferty gave a quick account of the situation, then commented: "When the missionary accepted that sacred object and sent it away, he became a party to a strife that split the tribe, literally brother against brother. He wasn't aware of that, I suppose, not that it would have mattered. Pagan customs were to be destroyed, in his view, regardless of how that twisted the lives of the people. Loved ones became enemies trying to hurt each other."

Adam showed only mild interest until Rafferty brought the story home to him.

"The sacred bundle is in your museum; at least it was sent to you, according to Stephen Welles, who doesn't want to see it returned. I haven't mentioned this to the people here. I didn't want to make it appear that you were party to Welles's theology, in case you were not in agreement with it."

"Oh, my!" Adam's head jerked backward, as from a

blow. "Oh, my! Am I culpable here also?" He was on his feet, feeling the need to pace the floor.

"Of course, I can't answer you, not here and now. A museum collects many items, and keeps most of them. But sometimes it trades with other museums, if it has too many objects of the same class. If we have this object, it will be in our catalog. I will check it and let you know."

He turned to his sister and caught the fleeting smile of a small triumph. But he spoke to Rafferty, not to Geneva. "We'll go out to Ohio to conclude this sad affair."

Then he brightened. "If I find this medicine bundle, I'd like to bring it back myself. Maybe I'll be forgiven, then, for killing the water. What an extraordinary idea!"

21

Even some of the "stiff collars" who happened to come
to Little Elk just then attended Henry Jim's funeral service,
at which the Reverend Stephen Welles officiated. It was
the daughter-in-law who went to fetch the missionary
priest, since no one else thought of it.

The visitors from Washington went about shaking
hands and lamenting that "such a great leader was lost
to the Little Elk Indians." When they asked how it happened that Henry's body was carried from a tepee instead of from his elegant house, Rafferty extemporized
an explanation. It was an ancient tradition, he suggested
in an assured tone. Doc Edwards verified this. The officials
were impressively silent. There were two of them,
wearing dark overcoats and hard city hats. They did not
offer to go up to the grave when they learned that it involved a long horseback trip into the mountains, and in
any case they were not invited to go along.

Stephen Welles did not go to the burial either. Only
a few did go, in fact. Rafferty and the doctor watched
the small party take off. The pine box containing the
body was roped down in an old wagon. And they saw
the big bay horse being led by Henry's son, Victor. The
body would be carried over the last hundred yards and
left in the rock-slide on the mountain where his wife had
been placed before him. The big bay horse, Red Son,
would be led to the rock-slide and shot in the center of
the forehead. The Boy went up with the burial party and
reported on it later, in scant detail.

"Why are they taking the horse along?" Stephen Welles
asked, as he stood in a little group off to one side of the
camp, which was beginning to break up. The wind blew
strong and cold across the valley, carrying streaking

snow and camp smoke. The horses had bunched, putting their rears to the wind.

Doc Edwards added a footnote to Little Elk ethnography. "Why, it's a custom they took over from the military. You know, in the army they lead the officer's favorite mount behind the caisson bearing the body. The horse is saddled, the gear is all polished, and the officer's boots are inserted in the stirrups, in reverse. The Indians didn't use saddles, of course, just the women did, so they lead the horse, bareback."

The missionary stared hard at Edwards, but made no challenge. "Odd, I never heard of it before." Then he turned to Rafferty. "I just learned this morning that Mr. Adam Pell was here, and left again. Sorry I did not get to meet him."

"You may have another chance," Rafferty answered. And because he still thought about the bleak conversation he had shared with the missionary, he added: "He has promised to return the medicine bundle."

Welles stood for a moment, tall and hollow-eyed, but all he said was, "Really? Oh, dear!" He turned into the wind, the tails of his overcoat flying out, and hurried away.

Edwards scarcely waited for the missionary to get beyond ear-reach. His gray eyes sparkled. "He'll do that? He promised?"

Rafferty scuffed at the hard ground, apparently putting great effort into dislodging an imbedded pebble.

"Well, he's not sure he still has the thing, but he promised to look. I saw no point in going into detail with the preacher."

He looked up from his ground-digging. "But I'm sure he means it. The Indians sounded like they might demand he tear down his dam. He'd rather return the bundle if he has it. He's proud of that dam."

And because Edward's excitement had chilled into a frown, Rafferty added: "You can't compare my small exaggeration with that bald-faced invention you gave the preacher."

The little doctor talked in the caustic way that came most naturally. "Long as he's been around here, he ought to know why they took that horse. I gave him a nice item to put in his memoirs. Someday he'll be quoted as an authority."

He looked up at Rafferty, who stood almost a head taller.

"I'm going to tell my wife about you. She's always saying 'That nice man' to me. You're getting to know too much."

Rafferty was conscious of being caught up in something never before experienced. When he reflected on the matter of the horse, it surprised him to realize that Henry Jim's request, and its fulfillment by his people, did not disturb him. Actually, it pleased him to know that an act of faith was still possible in a world turning away from faith.

He did not relate these feelings to Doc Edwards, as together they watched the camp for a while. Tepees and square tents were spread across the small hay meadow, and it appeared that some families had slept in or under their wagons. Horse blankets and odd pieces of canvas had been draped over wheels to form windbreaks. In the strong wind the drumbeat and song came to them only faintly. The people were reluctant to pack up. Henry Jim's body was on its way up the mountain, but he had left something behind that moved in the people's minds and had to be talked over in quiet language.

Rafferty could imagine how their talks might run. This too was part of the new consciousness he was experiencing. Quite suddenly, and effortlessly it now seemed, he had begun to get the feel of their perceptive world. It had something to do with motion, with the way they gestured, their facial movements, and the way they walked—he had glimpsed it for the first time the day he watched The Boy mending the fire, and only partially absorbed it. Later it grew large in his mind. But there seemed to be a still larger aspect, and this he did not yet understand. It had to do with their way of talking, and that followed habits bred in the senses themselves and made the world the way it is to a seeing and hearing and feeling man.

Anyhow, he thought he had a sense of how the talks

would run as the people sat together, sharing their one-ness. They had been falling apart, but Henry Jim, even as he was preparing himself to leave them, had pulled them back together.

To the doctor he said: "I think we're not needed here, you and I," and he gestured toward the encampment.

The doctor nodded. "We're from the other side of the moon."

For three years the Little Elk superintendent had worried because nothing happened. Nobody came to see him, nobody responded to his offers of help. They smiled when he talked, then went away and never came back. But now, as the winter wore along, men came to his office, unannounced, and sat down. First it was Jerome, then Frank Charley, then Iron Child—all the men who came that day "to speak" for Henry Jim.

It was Iron Child, the carefully braided, thick-chested one, the first talker that day, who divulged what all the others were trying to say.

"You didn't get mad at anybody when we took his horse up there and left it on the grave. Old Henry was afraid of that. He thought it might make you mad. Because it is an old custom which nobody wants to follow any more. White people get mad at us for doing that, but you didn't say no. Our people have been talking this over."

And then one day an Indian he had never seen before —a tall, long-faced, unsmiling elderly man with thin gray hair, calling himself Henry Two-Bits, "my English name," walked in noiselessly and sat down, as the others had, and placed his tall brown hat in his lap. He looked carefully everywhere, without moving his head, before he said a word.

Then: "I need a team. Don't have to be big horses, but strong workers. I need that."

Rafferty didn't ask what for, just made a notation on a piece of paper, after "Henry Two-Bits."

"I need pair of harness, too," he added after some moments of silence.

Rafferty made the further notation.

The man looked over at the paper, as if to make sure that words were written down.

"A wagon, too, I need that," he explained.

Rafferty was getting worried by then, thinking of the moment when he would have to explain that he did not have these things to give away. They would have to be paid for—a loan, repayments . . .

"I going to plant wheat this spring. So I need seed wheat—also plow and seeder machine." He paused. "I get somebody cut and trash my grain next fall, so don't need binder machine. Maybe next year."

Rafferty put his pencil down. "That's over a thousand dollars right there, maybe more . . ."

He looked more carefully at his visitor. Certainly he didn't look like a wheat farmer. His long, thin braids, uncalloused hands, and moccasins made it unlikely.

"You ever plant wheat, Mr. Two-Bits?"

The old man followed Rafferty's eyes. "This hair don't get in my way. I tie it under my hat—see!" He knotted the braids on top of his head and put on his hat. He stuck out one foot. "Moccasins work all right." He laughed. "Sure, I work white rancher's place. Too bossy, that man. My old woman tell me come home. I work another place. That man make me sleep next to pigs— I come home before I smelling bad."

"But you never planted wheat on your own place?"

The visitor paused then and studied the floor.

"My people used to say, 'Don't cut the ground.' They said, 'Leave the ground the way it was made.' When that old man, Henry Jim, cut up his ground like a white man, that sure made us mad. They said he would get sick. He would have bad luck. Looks like he lived a long time. Had good cattle. Good hay. Lots of wheat. And when he died, he said, 'You Indian people hold together. Help each other.' He didn't turn his back on us."

He looked up from the floor then, and his eyes caught Rafferty's gaze.

"Some are saying, 'It's all right now. You can plant wheat.' I guess they see it didn't hurt that old man after all. He stayed with his Indian people, too. Everybody talks about it."

After three years, Rafferty heard himself saying to a Little Elk Indian, "I guess we can make you a loan, Mr.

178

Two-Bits. First, we'll buy you the things you need. An agency farmer will go over it with you and make up a list. After we know how much it will cost, we'll write out a paper for you to sign—"

At that point the old man came up with a little buckskin sack, pulling it out of his shirt-front, and handed it over.

"You look. Maybe it's enough already."

Rafferty first felt foolish—amazement came later. When he picked up the little sack it was still warm. He loosened the drawstrings and began to pull out ten- and twenty-dollar bank notes, each little wad of ten or more notes tied together with a piece of grocer's twine. When he reckoned out two thousand dollars, he stopped.

He looked up, and saw that the old man was enjoying a smile that was almost at the point of laughter—he had fooled somebody, the government man himself! Without waiting to be asked, Henry Two-Bits began to explain.

"I got two boys. They work here and there—Spokane, Portland, Seattle. Good carpenters. They send money all the time; they tell us, 'Buy good grub.' But just me and old lady. We don't eat much. Our daughter, he married, got good man. We don't have to feed them, so we put the money in this sack.

"Now, I tell you something else. I see in your mind, you asking yourself how old man like me can plow and plant wheat and do all like that. It's like this. My two boys got mad at me when they grown up. They want to make farm, plant wheat. I tell them no, it's not the way for Indians. So they just pull out. They good boys, always stay together, still they don't like it here, just sitting around. When I send word, how I gonna make farm, they come back. You see."

It was like that all through the winter months—men coming to his office, sometimes to make plans for themselves or their children, sometimes just to sit, smoke a cigarette, and watch him work.

The Boy was now making frequent visits to Bull's camp, a new thing. They were not of the same group of related families, and so had no kinship ties. Also, he worked for the government. At first he went up there to report what had been heard from the United States marshal, the United States attorney, or other dimly visualized men of authority. But when there were no messages, Bull still said, "I have a place at my fire. Come and sit."

One day when they were alone in his tepee, the headman said: "It is a new thing now, a new way for me. In all these years I talked only in our own councils. When somebody had to go below to talk with the government man or some white man, we sent a talker for us. I didn't know how a white man talked, because I never went to listen. It might have made me mad, so I stayed away."

He studied it over, then:

"It is changed now. My brother put it in my hands. If the government man wants to talk, I will have to go myself. This I can't give to somebody to take care of for me. Maybe that man is different. I watched him. But I can't decide how it's going to be. Our old people always said, 'Don't listen to what a white man says—watch how he acts.' This man talked good, said he would help us. What does he want for his help?

"Every day now I think about this. What does that man want? Nobody in my camp or out there in the flats can answer it for me. Yet I will have to talk to him, talk for my people."

Finally he said what was already in his mind.

"You know our language, and you know this man's language. I want you to be the man who talks between us. Anybody else would mix everything up. You are now like my son and it will be that way between us."

After The Boy studied the fire for a while, he said, "It's good to have it that way."

22

Though Marie Louise scolded the other women because they had gone off and left her alone in camp, still she was pleased to have them come back. It was lonesome sitting there, just herself. Even the camp dogs had followed the other women, including the big brown dog and the little black-and-white one that belonged to her tepee. It was wrong to take her dogs away. Didn't they realize how lonesome she would be without her dogs!

She told how the marshal had come and poked into everything, then she went with the women to their food caches to make sure they couldn't say afterward that she had taken anything. When she described how the marshal looked at her with big eyes after he found Bull's gun, she beat her hands together and laughed.

"He was scared of big old me—I might shoot him in the tail. And I didn't even have a gun!"

So they came back to the camp. When the horses were unsaddled and turned loose, they shook themselves, raced into the mountain meadow, throwing their heels high and snorting at the ground. The dogs ran everywhere. They sniffed every bush where they had sniffed a thousand times before. They hurried after invisible tracks in and out of camp. They whined and howled. And only after they had drained themselves thoroughly did they come with flagging tongues to lie down by the new-built cooking fires.

Pock Face did not return at once, and the girl-wife, Lucelle, walked around with staring eyes and was of no help to anybody. Bull himself could not explain what happened, except that the government man said it would be all right but they would have to do things to please the man with a star to keep him quiet.

Though he did not speak of it in camp, Bull was troubled. Things were happening that never happened before and he could not understand what was yet to come. Veronica knew when her man was troubled. How many times had she seen it! But the way of showing it had changed. When they were young together and the quarrel with his brother was just starting, the days and nights were often filled with the noise of angry people. For a while he drank whiskey, and he would wake up shouting in the middle of the night and grab up an axe or a stick of wood and strike at tepee poles, at cooking pots, anything that his wild eyes could see, until the lodge was demolished. He never attacked a person, but perhaps only because those around him stayed out of his way and nobody tried to control him. Veronica kept the tepee stake pin loosened next to her pallet, and at the first sign of trouble she would slip outside, taking a child with her. He never tried to stop her and he never scolded her afterward for running away. When her people jumped on her for staying with "such a man," she brushed them away. "He won't hurt me, but he might hurt himself— and somebody will have to be there to take care of him."

His drinking years ended suddenly when he fell off his horse coming home one night and lay in the snow for some time—nobody knew for how long. When his horse came home they went out to look, and he was already stiff with frost. Ice crystals were on his feet when Veronica cut the frozen laces of his moccasins. She and one of the other women rubbed bear grease into his feet all that next day, until he could walk without collapsing.

The years were less violent after that, but the trouble was still there. She knew days when he pushed his food aside, and when he couldn't stand sitting and staring into the empty air, he would saddle his horse. She never knew where he would go or how long he would stay away. Sometimes he got other men to go with him, and they rode to a district of broken headlands and wandering canyons, where wild horses ranged. When she learned from others, not from Bull, of the hazards of racing down slopes of loose shale rock and leaping across deep, dry gulches in pursuit of an admired horse—and the possibly greater hazard of mounting a captured animal and riding it to exhaustion in a wasteland of shattered rocks and fire-killed tree snags—the whiskey-drinking days sometimes seemed less frightening. She would be waiting for the word to come, when she would be needed.

But when he came himself, solid and refreshed inside, his eyes danced and he would be full of teasing words. In the quiet of the sheltering night he would pour into her the urgent tenderness of his most naked need, and she would be made whole again.

So in the winter after the death of Henry Jim, she sat with him or watched him move around the camp, and her eyes were dark mirrors of remembrances. It was not his habit to speak of his troubles—the others talked, but he didn't always listen. Sometimes, when they paused, they realized that he was singing just under his breath and had heard nothing. She would watch him leave the group and go to young Catherine's lodge, where he would find the inner rest which once he found only with her.

She felt no anger, no jealousy about this. As the years had passed between them, it was no longer as it had been in his wild days. Now, in these later times, when he came back from a day's absence, or from a three-week hunting trip—time made no difference—he would put his hand on her head and ask for food. Nothing more. He rolled up in his own blanket and slept the night. A woman could draw within, could find ways to limit her needs. But a man was not made to draw within himself. He had to push outwardly, to prod, to discover, to capture. That was the only way he stayed a man. When she had come to that understanding, knowing that all within her had been explored and captured, she found a simple answer. She visited her sister, who lived in the upper end of the Little Elk country, and brought home her sister's first daughter, already turning into a woman and able to cook and tan good buckskin.

Because she had acted in that manner, Veronica could watch Bull go to Catherine's lodge and feel a kind of contentment. She was respected by the other women too: they looked to her strength and came to her when they were troubled. Her man had not brought a stranger, someone who might have been quarrelsome, into the camp.

Bull would not have Catherine as a wife at first. He considered her just another child come to visit who ought to be with the children, not sitting around the fire with the women. She barely reached to his chest, he thought —but later discovered that he was mistaken. He knew Veronica had arranged it, and why, and it embarrassed him. One day when he found his wife sitting alone just outside the entrance to her tepee, sewing moccasins, he faced her with it.

"This girl you brought to camp. Seems like she's been here a long time. Has she no family?"

Veronica had a peaked face, with a high, thin nose and cheekbones that pulled her face forward. The lips were thin and flexible and seemed to give sharpness to her voice.

"She comes of my family—or have you forgotten what I told you? She likes it here and I think she will stay, if she is liked. The women find her pleasant, she is always helping somebody."

He poured a cup of coffee and sat on his heels, and for a while he just watched his wife pushing her sharp needle through the soft skin.

"She should have a young man," he suggested.

The sewing dropped in her lap and she looked into distance and into times past.

"When a girl marries a young man, she can expect hard years ahead. If she marries a grown-up man, the years will be quieter. She won't be free to run like a colt in spring weather, but she will be treated gently. It is not an easy choice. But this girl I think has made her choice."

"It doesn't matter, young or old, a man does what he does for his woman. A young man has trouble finding out what his woman wants—or he can't decide he wants to do it the way she wants. If this girl already knows, her young man will find it easier."

"If she wanted just a young man, she could have stayed in her own camp."

"The only men who come here are old, coming to

tell me their troubles. Their eyes water or they can't hear well. Why should she want one of those?"

"Have I said she came for one of that sort?"

"You haven't said why she came. Such a girl needs time to find out what she wants."

Veronica resumed her sewing. "I think you better take a close look at her. But don't wait too long—don't hurt her feelings."

"I haven't pushed you away."

"Well, I haven't pushed you away!"

He was annoyed in the beginning because the girl seemed to ask nothing of him. If he hurt her, she was silent. If he neglected her, she never pouted. If he tried to ignore her, she just waited. He wanted to feel contempt for her for being so weak and yielding, but he never reached that point, partly because of the way others accepted her. She was respected in the camp. She did her share of work. When she sat with a group, laughter and good feeling made the air seem light—and when she walked away, to look after a child or a cooking pot, their eyes followed her. After a while he realized that he alone made her seem timid and unsure of herself. His manner toward her became easier. He began to use teasing words. He would even hold her chin while he looked at her, and she seemed to grow into a woman all at once.

After a year, she had her first child, but it died within hours of birth.

Sometimes when he stepped inside her tepee, he just stood, while his senses tried to define the ways in which her living space was different. His eyes immediately saw orderliness and neatness—the canvas ground-cover always swept, the mountain goat skins freshly aired, bags and boxes placed out of the way. In the daytime her bed was rolled back against the inner wall. When she tended a fire, the ashes were closely contained and a small supply of wood was stacked near the entrance. The pail for fresh water stood on a low bench and was covered with a cloth. His nose discovered a blended odor of sage and cedar and sweet grass. But when he had identified these immediate sensations, and could name them, his mind still searched for the indefinable substance which was there around him. It always escaped him, yet it was the very innerness of the girl, different from all the others. So it was in that winter of troubled thought. When talk tired him, he walked away from it and sought quiet. Catherine watched his approach that day from her place near the fire. She motioned to the goat skin near her, and still her eyes watched, deciding what he would need.

He settled himself at her side, bending slowly, as if moving without awareness, and took her hand, as often he would when they were alone. And when he began to talk, he rushed on, as if he might never get to say all the things that had to be said. The winter sun went early behind the mountains, and the stars wheeled up and the clear sky showered frost crystals earthward. He talked right on, hardly pausing when Catherine asked if he would eat, and then eating without noticing what he put to his mouth.

What he said to Catherine, but to himself first of all —and he said it in many ways, and repeatedly—seemed at first to be a very simple thing: "We have been ourselves all these years, behind these mountains. When Henry Jim left our camp and went below to follow the white man, it looked like that might be the end. Our people would all go the same way. Instead, they stayed together. Our camps did not break up. Then my elder brother got ready to die. He called us together and told how it had been a mistake to act the way he did. He moved out to his old tepee so he would not die in a white man's house. That made us happy. It seemed to make us stronger than ever. But see what is happening now! The people are changing in their hearts. They are saying: 'Henry Jim was not wrong after all. He plowed the ground and planted wheat, and still he lived to be an old man and had lots of cattle and horses.' Now everybody will plant wheat. Henry Jim turned back to us at the end, became one of us as in the beginning. How many of these others will turn back once they go away? Just when it began to look good for us, it has all changed."

What had started out as a simple matter to think about had become baffling and complex.

"That man from the East took the water from the mountains and spread it over the land, and some of our people will say it was a good thing. Maybe he is a good man—I watched him, and that is what I think—and yet he will destroy us."

"Talk it over with the old man, Two Sleeps. Tell him to take it to the mountains and pray for a word," Catherine murmured. It was the first time she had ever tried to tell him what to do; the words just came out. She was kneeling behind him, brushing and fresh braiding his hair, when her warm voice moved him out of his brooding dream.

He looked up. "Yes," he said, "I will ask the old man to go to the mountains."

And he slept that night as if a good answer had already come back.

23

It was a winter of heavy traveling, and every time Adam Pell returned to New York he wanted to know what information had been assembled during his absence. Not that he spent much time with the folders and documents that were accumulating on his desk.

"I'll get to it—just keep the stuff coming," he would tell Miss Mason, his long-time secretary, as another flying trip called him to Canada or Mexico or the West Coast.

Miss Mason knew the pattern. She had worked with it, and around it, and in spite of it, for twenty-odd years. When he had an idea stirring around in his mind, he seemed to put off coming to a decision and was satisfied to have staff members crowd his desk and his office with impedimenta, which once included a number of pickled specimens in tall glass jars that gave off a bad odor. If the idea failed to survive this trial by inertia, Miss Mason knew it when he exclaimed, coming fresh from a trip:

"For God's sake, Miss Mason! What is this junk all over the place? Get rid of it!"

She dressed properly: dark skirt and white shirtwaist closed at the throat with a pink cameo or silver brooch. But in the inner office where she performed prodigious feats with typewriter and filing cabinets, she often swore colorfully and at length and smoked cigarettes in a blue haze. Adam never entered her domain, though he had once come to the threshold and had staggered away at the sight of her pounding the typewriter keys, her skirt pulled above her knees, and a cigarette hanging from her lower lip.

A letter from A. T. Rafferty, Superintendent and S.D.A., managed to go unanswered, in spite of Miss Mason's usual vigilance about such matters. It simply dropped out of sight among accumulating documents.

"I have in mind," the letter ran, "your offer to look for the medicine bundle and the possibility that you might return it in person, when you locate it. Needless to say, the Indians here set great store by the object. It seems to represent a kind of controlling force in their universe—if that is the proper way of expressing it. I trust we may have a report soon. The Indians seem to think I can do something about retrieving this lost treasure."

While the letter did not immediately stimulate the search that had been promised, it did encourage an inquiry of a different, though not unrelated, sort.

Adam's office, one of several through which he moved, occupied a large second-floor corner suite of his museum, The Americana Institute, which sat on a gentle knoll overlooking an uptown park. The building was a great quadrangle of limestone and marble occupying most of a city block, with a glass-sheltered Mexican garden of banana palms and shrieking parrots filling the hollow center. And here, soon after his return from the West, he began at first to browse and presently to dig avidly through the accumulation of reports, Congressional hearings, surveys, and a miscellany of public and private petitions and protests borrowed from various libraries across the country. Miss Mason was content to see him thus occupied. It meant that her labor and the labor of other staff members in assembling the material would not be wasted.

And browsing and digging, he began to discover a history of events that shocked him. He would call out from his desk: "Great jumping Lucifer! How can such things be? Miss Mason! Get me the senator on the phone!" And he meant the senior senator from New York State with whom he had been associated as client and friend for many years.

And later: "This is monstrous! Get me the judge. Ask him to have dinner with me, if he's free." The judge, a member of the appellate court, was another close associate from his first years in the East.

All he obtained from these students of the law, and from others, including finally the solicitor for the Department of the Interior, was confirmation of what he found in the public record and had rejected as unworthy. The conversations left him feeling exposed and naked, and considerably embarrassed. He had rushed into these discussions with some confidence, expecting his good friends, lawyers all, to click their tongues and nod their heads in agreement. He had not permitted his mind to wander in the mystic realms of legal remedy, realizing that the events, however fresh and strong the stench, were ex post facto—events of fifteen, twenty, even fifty years past. But at least he had been sure of sharing a common sense of outrage. The past might not be remedied, perhaps never could be, he thought, but ways might be found to devise a present equity.

What denuded him was the discovery that his sentiments were *not* shared, that what he expressed, however indignantly he said it, was just a personal sentiment. With kindly hands, they led him through the jungle of the law: to John Marshall: *By common accord, the nations of the world recognized the right of each to chew off what it could, and to keep what it could hold;* to Vattel: *The nation with superior skill could appropriate to its own use the domain of a less accomplished people.* They even led him to the Christian Bible: *Multiply, and make the earth bear fruit.*

These were not sentiments, these were principles of international politics—and how was it that he, a businessman of the world, should be raising such questions?

Indian lands had been taken because they would be put to a higher order of use, because they would contribute to the advancement of a higher order of society —and the law had legitimized such taking. The law was in society and society was in the law. Could he imagine what it would be like otherwise? Whose law, whose society, were irrelevant and immaterial questions.

Adam had not placed his query at such sublime heights, but the judge, Judge Carruthers, liked to elevate simple legal questions to levels of abstraction which discouraged argument over particulars. Moreover, their talks took place in the decorous air of the Harvard Club, usually at a remote dinner table for two, where the speaking voice was instinctively modulated. The judge preferred the Harvard Club over the Yale Club, of which he was also a member, because of a tendency at the latter for gentlemen to shout to one another across the dining room. And he knew that Adam had a tendency to get up and stride around when his mind was exercised —an activity not encouraged at the Harvard, in either the dining room or the lounge.

So Adam sat aghast, but helpless, while the judge exposed him as a romanticist without, of course, resorting to that word.

"A great nation, one of the powers of the modern world, has been built on this continent. Should we have left it in virgin forest where the red man chased his dinner through the undergrowth?"

Adam's fading blond hair looked especially ashen in the lamplight. His very long upper body, clothed in tweed, yielded only slightly to the necessity of bending forward to the table—and be-damned if he would yield in any degree to the judge's chauvinism. That's what it was, but Adam was equally considerate and did not utter the word aloud.

"I'm not talking against progress. That's how I make my living," he said in a voice as mild as the lamplight. "But these people should also share in that progress, which is not going to happen if they are robbed of their resources and chased off into the desert.

"I'm not trying to argue legal principles with you, I know my limitations. I'm against thievery, and that's what happened out there. The law was clear—and I'm not raising the question whether such a law should have been passed. It was on the books, and it said clearly that the President, at his discretion, could divide up an Indian reservation held in common ownership and give each man, woman, and child a piece of that common property. The President didn't have to ask the Indians whether they wanted it that way, and even if they opposed it to a man, he could still do it. The law was clear. He could go further, consulting only his political advantage. He could invite white men to come into that reservation—though it might be protected by treaty against alienation—and take up homesteads on any lands left after each Indian had been given a little piece of his own earth.

"All right. That was in the law and it was very clear. But now I'm talking about what happened at the Little Elk Reservation. After the land was divided among the Indians and white men were invited—exhorted, really, with literature advertising the rare qualities of soil and climate and mountain wealth—a grave miscalculation was discovered. The land was really too arid and parched to make a crop oftener than once every four or five years. It needed to be irrigated. While this conclusion was being verified by expert studies and discussions were going on about what to do, the first homesteaders began to go broke and everybody set up a great outcry. So Congress authorized the construction of an irrigation system.

"The law didn't authorize the President to divide up the water as well as the land, but Congress—our Congress, you and I—decided to do just that. There were several perennial streams that came out of mountain snowpacks and flowed out of the valley to join a river flowing through an adjoining valley. The mountains were still owned by the Indians—no white man wanted to homestead a mountain peak—and the water flowing out of them was certainly their property.

"So Congress said, 'Build dams, collect the water, and put it on the land.' I built one of those dams—or rather, a construction company in which I am involved built it. The last of a series of dams, the largest, and I believe the best. I had no knowledge of this background when I went out there. It was just a job of construction and my company built a good dam.

"Now, two things emerge. One: Very few Indians had taken pieces of land in the open valley when the reservation was divided up. They knew about the hot, dry summers, the treeless, unsheltered flats. They made their selections in the foothills, in the timber country, along forested streams. Consequently, when their main perennial streams were blocked off and diverted out to the dry valley, only the white homesteaders benefited.

No compensation went to the Indians for this appropriation of their property.

"Two: The Indians had received money for the land which had been taken over by the homesteaders—at a dollar and a quarter an acre, I believe. This was not a negotiated price. The government, our government, you and I, just said, 'That's what we'll pay, in order to encourage strangers to come and take your land.' This revenue was deposited in the United States Treasury as it was paid to the government. And would you believe it, these funds which, like the land itself, were held in common ownership for the Little Elk Indians—this money was used by the government to pay for surveys, soil studies, engineering estimates and all manner of preliminary work that went into the development of the irrigation project, to benefit the government-invited homesteaders. I haven't yet found out whether any of this diverted money has been replaced.

"The latest thing I've discovered, and I haven't reached the bottom of the pile yet, is that the reservoir sites—these are areas containing thousands of acres in which the mountain water is impounded, the ownership of which is still in the tribe—these sites were taken without agreement or compensation of any kind, as far as I can determine, and again, without benefit to the Indians.

"Now, Judge," and Adam's voice finally began to climb to a level just noticeably above the modulated tone of the room, "will you tell me that such conduct is what makes a nation great? The Indians say we killed the water, and damned if they aren't right!"

"But Adam," the judge said, advancing his white head as if to convey a very private thought, "you know as well as I that political action is often hasty and not well considered."

Adam pulled away from the confidential tête-à-tête. "The actions I've been describing occurred over a twenty-year period. One could hardly say they were taken in haste. I would say they were well and ingeniously considered as devices to exploit the Indians."

He broke off, then veered the direction of his thought. "I'm too old to be making these discoveries. A younger man would feel he could do something about it—like Carlos, when he set out to remake the world at Cuno."

The judge looked puzzled. "Cuno? Never heard of it."

"Well, it's too long a story for now. Carlos had this advantage at the beginning—he had something to give, he could show good faith—"

At that point he smacked the table with the flat of his hand. The clapping sound went through the murmuring shadows like a pistol shot. Dishes jumped and faces turned toward the judge's table.

Adam excused himself as gracefully as he could. "Maybe I do have something to give! Maybe I do!" He left the club, trailing the topcoat he retrieved from the cloakroom.

His first act when he reached his desk the next morning was to call for Rafferty's letter, and for the first time he gave it a careful reading.

What followed after that, or what failed to follow, involved Adam in the final disaster at Little Elk.

24

"Ah, my kinsmen! My journey has been long since I left camp two days ago. A long journey. Almost to the end. But, you see, I came back!"

Two Sleeps would say no more. Not then. He needed to sit by himself, smoking his long-stemmed pipe. He huddled close to Veronica's morning fire, his stubby old feet pushed toward the warm ashes. He knew the camp waited to hear what he would say, but he would not talk about it. He let his pipe go cold and drop from his hands, and he seemed to sleep.

It had been, as he said, a long journey. Behind his closed eyes, shutting the others out, he traveled again out of the camp, as he had traveled two days before. If he could follow it out, just as it happened, if he could see everything again, he might escape the fear. It might then be that he could talk about it.

It had been afternoon when he left camp. Snow lay deep and quiet under the pine trees, and a fresh storm was moving darkly against the mountains. Weather made no difference for what he had to do. He wrapped his old legs in strips of woolen blanket; a robe made from a winter-killed buffalo calf weighed upon his body, and his white head was swathed in otter fur. He toiled up the trail like a slow-footed bear after eating heavily.

The winter night came quickly, the storm bringing it on, but he moved even so. Old men who have lived a long time with their own thoughts know how to be at ease with the night. And storms are filled with the voices they wish to hear.

So he moved up a trail that was not there, and when the wind paused and seemed to listen, his own voice sang steadily on, as if to encourage the wind.

"My friend, the storm, I am still with you," he chanted. His voice was like laughter.

He moved in what he saw as a shower of light, a mantle that spread from him and moved with him in the night—but only darkness encompassed him. The ice crystals which formed on his lashes refracted the bright-lying snow and tricked his faltering eyes.

He remembered another such night of cold-blowing wind and snow, at a time so distant now that it was scarcely more than a feeling of fear, the pictures were so dim and ragged. He was with his own people then, a people who lived east of the mountains, far out in the prairie along a big river. He had been with a hunting party following a buffalo herd which moved upstream toward the mountains. Another hunting party was also there—waiting. A heavy snowstorm came during the night, and in the morning while the snow still fell and muffled all sound, the waiting mountain people charged the camp, and red blood streaked the white snow. He was then a young man, and a young wife waited for him on the bank of the big river. For two days he lay as dead from a skull blow. The small hunter's tepee had been knocked over during the attack and the raiders missed him when they gathered up their prizes and rode away.

When he came from the dead and crawled into daylight, he didn't know where he was or where he came from, and he didn't know which way to go. And he was alone, without a horse or a weapon. He walked into the mountains, following a snow-buried stream. He saw game, but could not reach it. He chewed twigs and ate snow. One day, from a ridge, he watched a great herd of buffalo in a sheltering valley—but by then he was too weak to go down to it.

That night, when he knew he had reached the end, he saw a small fire throwing a pale glow against pine trees. He stood up tall, singing his death song—and that was when he joined the people, of which Enemy Horse, Bull's father, was then headman.

Now it was another night of cold-blowing wind and whipping snow. It might be the night to finish off what did not end the first time. But a man learned much in a lifetime, including one special thing. Above all else, a man learned to be strong in support of his kinsmen. A man by himself was nothing, a shout in the wind. But men together, each acting for each other and as one— even a strong wind from an enemy sky had to respect their power.

This night he was acting for those who took him in as a kinsman—nothing else would prevail, not even death.

He emerged from the heavy timber and skirted an open face of the mountain, where a sharp-edged wind swept fiercely up from the black depths of the valley and lashed the snow into a fury of whirling ice clouds. He slowed, wavered. He crawled on all fours for a while, a dark creature pushing its way into a nameless and forbidding world.

When he could get to his feet again and his breath returned, he still sang: "My friend, the storm, I am here with you! My brother, the storm wind, stay here with me!"

The wind came roaring again, turned shrill, and exploded against a barrier of thrusting rock.

The frost reached his blood and his face turned to stone, but he crawled ahead. The fire within his body would keep him going awhile longer. And then he would dream. The dreams that come just this side of death were the strongest of all, but only a strong man dared go that far. Only the very strong came back.

It was becoming difficult to hold his thoughts together. They flew up and away from him and it was necessary to hold on to them. He had to work out what it was like to be in the world, to have an understanding. If death was to come, he wanted to be full of understanding. Even to be smiling at what he understood.

To be born was not enough. To live in the world was not enough. How was it, then? He stood there, swaying slightly, trying to hold it in his mind. When he moved again, he was following his thought once more, but it was getting dim. One had to reach. That was what a man had to do. It pulled him along. He had to reach with his mind into all things, the things that grew from small beginnings and the things that stayed firmly placed and enduring. He had to know more and more, until he himself dissolved and became part of everything else— and then he would know certainly. Reaching with his mind was part of that, a kind of dissolving into the mist that was at once the small seed from which the pine tree would grow and the mountain that endured forever. And a man was there, in the middle, reaching to become part of it. That was something of what it was like to be in the world.

And yet, there was more—if he could hold fast to it.

By the time he had crossed the mountain's face and was again in a sheltering grove, his strength was leaving his quaking body. Breath came in fast and shallow gasps. Numbness began to seal off all feeling. While he still knew what he was about, he crawled under the spreading arms of a spruce tree, where he dug a hole in the quiet snow. There he rolled himself into a ball within his buffalo robe.

And there he dreamed.

25

During winter days and nights when snow and cold discouraged travel and no one went out so long as food was plentiful, the camp drew in upon itself. It was a time for story telling, for remembering what the old people used to say, and for playing jokes or evening old scores. It was a time when people laughed a lot and felt their closeness. Even one given to bitter talk like Louis would sing old songs that no one else knew, and his harsh speaking-voice had a surprising softness when he sang. Everyone would listen and urge him on.

But this was a different winter. It would be remembered as the winter when the elder brother was carried to the rock-slide on the mountain, and the thin man came from the East; the winter when Two Sleeps went to the mountain to pray and returned like a man coming back from the dead. Days would go by before the old one could sit up, he was so torn with pain and weakened by fever, and the people were troubled. They watched unobtrusively and worried when he did not eat all the food set before him. At night someone went to his cabin, two and three times if necessary, to keep a fire going in his iron stove.

Bull was especially watchful. He sat with the others, without being one of them. Someone would be telling a story but he would be singing quietly, just under his breath, unaware of his own inattentiveness.

To be watchful was to wait, and for Bull it was a winter of waiting. Something had happened on the mountain, but talk about it could not be hurried. It was that way with dreams. That much was understood, but as the days passed and the old one stayed behind his closed eyes, the silence began to speak for itself. The mountain had given no answer, or the answer was something the old one found too disturbing to report.

The winter was different for another reason. No one talked about it since it was a family affair, but it could be felt. It was Antoine's first winter at home after his return from the government school, and his presence in the camp brought back something that had been missing. When the people saw Bull and his grandson walking in the woods or riding their horses side by side, large man and growing boy, they realized that it had been a long time coming. When Bull put his hand on the boy's shoulder at the midsummer dance, a bad time ended.

What was unpleasant to remember was that, until the incident at the midsummer dance, Bull had ignored his grandson. No one ever saw him playing with the child, or talking to him, or mentioning him to others, and that was not the way for a grandfather to act. No one would interfere however deeply they were troubled.

It had been that way since the boy's birth and it seemed likely to continue. Bull was a strong man and no one expected his manner to change. Even Veronica, strong in her own way, could only wait for the trouble to work itself out.

The working out was not a simple matter and could not have been predicted, certainly not from the way it began.

The camp, in effect, had been invaded and Antoine taken away to school. That incident and the anguish it caused, in time worked a healing change. The incident occurred in the fall, two years before Rafferty came to Little Elk and the "reform" administration put an end to the practice of kidnapping children to fill a school quota.

Bull and the men from the camp had gone hunting in the mountain country behind the Little Elk range. They were gone two weeks, and when they came back, their packhorses staggering under mounds of dressed meat, the boy was gone.

The men rode into camp at nightfall and found the cooking fires cold. While they sat their horses and studied the situation, the annoyance of their first discovery ebbed away. All the women were in Veronica's lodge. All were wailing. The men, hearing this, thought surely there had been a death. They unloaded in silence, each man trying to answer his own questions.

Veronica came out first, and the others followed, some holding their shawls over their faces. Antoine's mother, Celeste, hardly more than a girl in build and manner, came, leaning on Veronica. Her eyes were staring wildly.

"They took the boy," Veronica explained. "He is gone. They came early this morning. Nobody saw them coming until they were right here. You will have to bring him back."

Bull raked aside the cold ashes and started a fresh fire. When it was going, he said: "Now, tell me. Who came for the boy? Where did they take him? Where am I to look?"

He asked these questions so the women would stop wailing and give heed. He suspected what the answers might be, since it had happened to others, but he wanted the women to talk and turn their minds away from grief. And after they had talked awhile they began doing the things necessary to make a meal.

He watched Celeste all the while and a deepening worry troubled his mind. Most of the time she only stared. Even when great sobs wracked her, she seemed not to be aware of any feeling.

She was the first child Veronica bore, and Bull had always felt a close attachment to her. She would hold his fingers when he walked out to where the horses were pastured, and when he caught his horse he would seat her on it and carefully bring her back to camp. When he was counseling with other men, she would enter the lodge and tumble over the seated men until she reached his place, and he would hold her in his lap until the heavy talk put her to sleep. The men said: "He will make her a chief."

It was a sorrowful thing that she grew so fast, grew beyond his reach. When a swaggering young man came to camp, she ran after him, arms outreaching, as if he had just come to bring the morning sun. He got her with child, then went out and had his neck broken riding a wild horse that threw him and fell on him.

And so Antoine came into the world—and Bull would not cross from his tepee to look at the child. The hurt was too great.

But coming back from the hunt that day, and looking at Celeste, his own first child, the deep feeling came rushing back. He went to her, drew her away from Veronica's arms, walked her to the tepee. Inside, he sat down and pulled her to his lap. He cradled her head, and for a while her body shook with rending sobs in the way of a young child. And holding her, he knew the deep and helpless feeling of not being able to carry his child away from a time of trouble to let her start over again.

Then it happened. She rose first to her knees, then leaped away from him. Her face was twisted and full of pain. She screamed: "You! You! You hated my boy! You told them to come and take him away! You sent him away! Because you hated his father! You sent him away! I have nothing!"

She ran out, screaming. The women tried to catch her, but she tore at them, scratched and kicked, broke away and ran into the woods.

She never came back to her senses, and was more animal than human until she died. And Antoine came home from school.

What should have been a winter of story telling was, instead, a winter of uncertainty, of waiting. But the winter thinned and they were waiting for the spring to come. By then, Two Sleeps was eating well and complaining that young people no longer knew how to behave and telling how it used to be when boys got up early to run the sleep out of their eyes and girls knew how to cook. It cheered the people to hear the old one scolding again.

Then Bull's manner changed and he surprised everybody by joining the storytellers. Many of his stories had come to him from Enemy Horse, his father, and he enjoyed remembering them. He laughed with the others when he heard about Basil, who got up early one morning and stole the rabbits from the snares that Louis had set. Louis tracked him right to his tepee, and found the rabbits being roasted. It was reported that Basil said: "Oh! I didn't invite you, but you are welcome to share my rabbit!" Everybody knew Basil was too lazy to set his own snares—but he was even too lazy to cover his tracks.

In his storytelling, Bull turned to his grandson, as if pulling the boy to himself. Others would be in his lodge, but he would start out, "Now, Grandson, someday you will need to know where our people came from and what it was like in the beginning. Perhaps your own son will ask about it, and it will shame you if you can't tell him."

A small fire in a tepee throws a big light, as flame and glowing embers are reflected back from sloping walls. Antoine watched the listening faces and he heard an occasional affirming "Yes, that's how it was" as the story unfolded. But he did not miss what was behind the talking voices and the listening faces. He felt the tension that no one talked about.

When his grandfather and the others told stories, they were saying all the time, "What is to happen to us?" He watched their eyes, and saw the question come and go. It stood in front of their vision. He watched when they went outside, when they thought they were alone. They just stood and listened. It was a camp of watchers and listeners, as he had been aware all through the winter. There had been nights at the government's school when he lay in bed holding his knees and listening to his heart pound, knowing that trouble in some indefinable form would come.

A boy knew these things, but could not talk about them. When his grandfather leaned toward him, Antoine knew something was being said that did not come out in words. He wanted to say "You can tell me, grandfather. I can understand." But he never said it, and Bull never reached across to span the years. The distance between them was close, and yet it was an entire lifetime.

Deep within, Bull still carried the remembrance of the boy's mother, of the hurt that came to her. He would start to explain to the boy how such a thing could happen and how the people could no longer protect themselves or their own children, then he would stop short. A boy should not grow up feeling that his life would be worthless. Bad times would come soon enough, of their own accord, without a grandfather telling how nothing good could be expected. A people needed young ones who would put the sun back in the sky. It was better to tell Enemy Horse's old stories and to laugh about the roasting rabbits.

That's the way it was when Bull began to talk about Feather Boy.

"It's a holy story, all right. But don't try to tell it to a white man. He'll just laugh at you. There are things we don't even talk about among ourselves. If you talk about these things, after a while they can't help you. A man tried to keep his strength inside himself: the things that lie in his mind; the songs and stories he knows; the dreams that come; the words that make pictures.

"I will tell you this, because I want you to have it to carry with you and be part of you. It will keep you strong.

"Yes, the story of Feather Boy is the great story of our people. That's why we keep it to ourselves.

"There will be a day in summer when you look up to a clear sky. It will be all clear, except for one cloud streak—not really a cloud—a breath that comes from somewhere and floats by. You can see through it, it is that thin, and the edges move and disappear. You look away from it, and when you look again, it has all disappeared. That's when I think of Feather Boy. I think that's how he appeared, when he came to visit our people long ago—a breath in the sky.

"It happened so long ago we don't know when it was. The people were living then in a country where there was just one high mountain. It stood all by itself, surrounded by a flat country of timber and open meadow. But I don't know where this was. Some say it was east of here, others say south, and some say west. Or maybe it was in the north.

"Well, you can see this was a long time ago. It was a time when animals still talked like men. There's another story that tells how animals lost this power, but I'll tell that story another time.

"This is the only story we have that tells about the Thunderbird. Maybe the people knew more stories about him long ago, but they have been forgotten. The ones who knew them died out and didn't pass them on.

"Thunderbird had great power. He could cover the entire sky with his wings and make it dark. The lightning from his eyes was a terrible thing. His voice was the thunder, the way you hear it when it rolls in the mountains. But he could use his power in different ways. When he wanted to, he could make himself no bigger than a louse, or he could float on the wind and not be seen at all. People never knew when he might show up.

"One day, when he was in the house of his father, the Sun, he said, 'I want to go down there and visit the earth people. Maybe they need my help.' His father didn't think well of it. 'They can get along all right. I need you here to carry my shield and my arrows. let those earth things go their own way.' Every day Thunderbird would say, 'I think I'll just go look at those earth people. Maybe they're sick and need my help.' And his father would make the same answer: 'I need you here to keep my shield bright and my arrows sharp. Let the earth things go their own way.'

"Four times they said these things, and finally Thunderbird just went by himself, and that day Sun had to turn around and go home. Right in the middle of the day he found that his shield and his arrows were missing and he was angry. It was the first time his own son had disobeyed him and it made him feel bad.

"But Thunderbird flew down to the place where he had seen the earth people, and when he got there he flew all around, taking a good look. And sure enough, he could see that the people could hardly move. They were hungry and sick and just dragging themselves over the earth.

" 'Now,' he thought, 'If I fly down there among them maybe they'll just drop dead out of fright. I'll have to think of a way to do it so I won't scare them.' Then he made his plan.

"He flew high above the camp and changed himself into a feather—a downy feather, such as an eagle will sometimes shake loose from under its tail. He floated down, spinning a little bit. He made the wind stay away from there so he wouldn't drift too far. Finally he came right over the smoke vent of a tepee. The fire was cold and no smoke was rising. Inside, a young girl had just gone to sleep, and she had loosened the tent peg next to her bed, because she was expecting her lover to visit her after the camp was dark.

"Well, the feather floated down and drifted around until it found the right place—and next morning the girl thought her lover had been with her.

"That's the way it happened, just like that. In a little while—for in those days it didn't take long for things to happen—in just a little while, the girl was carrying a child, and very soon after that a boy was born.

"Well, the boy grew very fast too, because that was in the plan from the beginning. In a day or two the boy was big enough to go around talking to people, and you can guess how this frightened them. They knew it wasn't natural and they talked about driving the boy and his mother out of camp. The girl's own parents, an old man and an old woman, were too frightened to talk either to the boy or to their own daughter. They sat in their tepee expecting, I guess, to be clubbed to death at any minute. The boy was so big.

"The only one he could talk to was his own mother, which wasn't the way Thunderbird planned it, and it almost spoiled everything. He asked her what her people needed most of all, what would help them to be strong and brave and have a good life. The girl had never thought about such things, and when he asked her that question she would say, 'Just let me think!' Every day he asked the same thing, and always got the same answer. Then her own mother heard them talking together, heard the question, and the answer, and she forgot all about being afraid. She spoke right up: "You foolish girl. Anybody can see what we need is food to eat. We never have enough and our bellies are always squeezed tight. Just tell that creature to get us food and we will be satisfied. Then he can go away and leave us alone. The people are already blaming us because we let this happen to you.'

"Feather Boy—for that was what he told his mother to call him, but he really was Thunderbird all the time—

didn't like that answer. Why should he help these earth people, when they thought only of their bellies and were mean to each other? That was what he thought, but he knew what he was supposed to do. And he knew that if he told his father, the Sun, how the people acted, he might throw his arrows at them and wipe them all out.

"So he told the scolding old woman, 'Just wait right here.' He went alone into the tepee and the people heard a loud clapping sound, as the thunder will sound when it comes sometimes out of an almost clear sky, and afterward the clouds rush in on high winds and the water just pours on the earth. The people were stunned and just stood as if planted in holes. For the first time they realized that the strange boy was Thunderbird himself. And they were more frightened than ever.

"Well, he went up through the smoke vent and flew away, but nobody saw him. He flew a long time, always heading south. After a while he came to the place where food of all kinds just grows everywhere—on trees, in the fields, in the water, everywhere. He came down there and began to gather up seeds. He gathered about everything, I guess—corn, beans, potatoes, squash, melons, all the things that Indians like to eat. And the last thing he gathered was tobacco. He put them all in a sack and started back.

" 'The people can plant these things,' he said, 'and they will never be hungry again.'

"But as he was flying along, he got to thinking: 'Why should I bring all these things? After all, they think too much about eating, and they are mean. It will be better if they don't have too much.' So when he thought that, he reached in his sack and threw away the melon seeds. Then he flew on, and after a while he thought, 'Why give them all these things? Let them be a little bit hungry.' So he reached in and threw away the squash seeds. It went that way all the way home. He threw away the potato seeds, then the beans, then the corn. Finally, he had only the tobacco, and he kept that. But they say that Indians south of us, where the climate is warm, plant all those crops. It's just what I hear.

"When he got back, as you can guess, those foolish

people were not happy. They thought he was going to bring food, but all he had was tobacco, which the people had never seen.

"So he scolded them: 'I brought you the most powerful present of all. The smoke which will come from the dry leaves will make my father, the Sun, very happy with you. It will rise upward like your breath, like a prayer. If you have this smoke, you won't need those other plants. In time, they will all come to you. The buffalo and all game animals will come to you. If you need rain to make your crops grow, just let this smoke rise from your pipe and it will come to you. If your enemies are preparing to attack, smoke the pipe and they will drop their weapons and run away.

" 'Come. I will show you.' Then he filled a pipe and offered it first to the East, then to the South, then to the West, then to the North, and finally he sent the smoke upward to the Sun. It was the first pipe ceremony.

" 'Look!' he told them. And there, just beyond the camp, a field of tobacco was just coming into bloom. It was the first tobacco our old people ever knew.

"Then he went into the tepee again, and when he came out, he was carrying a bundle, wrapped in white buckskin and tied with rawhide thongs. He gave this to his mother, who had never been angry with him.

" 'Keep this,' he told her. 'All the good things of life are inside. Never let it get away from your people. So long as you have this holy bundle, your people will be strong and brave and life will be good to them. My own body is in this forever.'

"Then lightning came from the sky, lightning without thunder, and the people knew then the Sun had sent one of his own arrows.

"Thunderbird's wings swept a strong wind across the faces of the people, blinding them, and he was gone.

"So ends my story," Bull said, and he looked over and saw his grandson's eyes shining with wonder.

26

The next letter from A. T. Rafferty, Superintendent and S.D.A. was like the small stone high on a mountainside, which shaken loose by some odd chance begins to slide and roll and leap, dislodging larger stones and rock ledges, and becoming at last part of a roaring crash into the void.

Not that the letter was in any way ominous. It was intended as a reminder that the previous letter had not been acknowledged, but without referring to the oversight. The pertinent part read: "It seems the old man who died while you were here told the people the medicine bundle would come back and the good days would return with it. I gather his words are taken as prophecy—and the people put great store in prophetic utterances."

It was the concluding remark that put Adam Pell's thoughts in a spin. Rafferty's letter continued: "Needless to say, I have not identified you with the bundle, but it becomes increasingly difficult to abstain from giving at least a hint of encouragement to a people who have so little left of the world that was once complete, and all theirs. I hope we hear from you soon, with good news."

The phrase lingered: *so little left of the world that was once complete.* His reading of the documentary history of Little Elk permitted him to understand the phrasing, and to react to it.

Adam tore his museum apart—and made the final discovery. The medicine bundle had effectively disappeared, although not absolutely. It had been tossed into a lumber room, still bearing its identification tag, along with broken furniture, battered steel cabinets, abandoned exhibits, including stuffed birds and animals too mangy to be refurbished. But someone had failed to take it out of inventory and it showed up as a registered item. The unending battle museums wage against rats, moths, organic decay, and an assortment of molds, mites, and enterprising worms had caught up with the medicine bundle. Mice had eaten their way through the buckskin covering and had bred and reared countless generations, each generation chewing away at hide and the inner contents, whatever that might have been. The only remains consisted of a few pebbles and the shafts of some feathers. Other objects may have dropped out, but no one had bothered to gather them up in disposing of the bundle. What was left of the hide and binding thongs were tattered and profaned, devoid of holy mystery.

It was a monstrous discovery.

The notion that the dam in the mountains, with which he was now identified, had killed the water had troubled him. An irrational conceit, but the minds that conceived the notion were the minds of rational men. They worked with different data and a different order of reality. An urbanized man arrived at other conclusions only because he had a wider range of information and theory. What at first seemed bizarre became on reflection a valid ordering of experience. The dam was an unnatural disruption of a functioning universe, a kind of crime against life.

He had reached that point in his thinking before he discovered the missing sacred bundle; and with that discovery his involvement was compounded. He felt too chagrined to reply at once to Rafferty's letter, but he did come to a decision. He would return to Little Elk.

"How am I to show good faith?" To his surprise, the question was verbalized aloud. He was sitting at his desk, an empty expanse at the moment, and Miss Mason, on the point of leaving the room turned back, questioning:

"Beg pardon?"

"How am I to account for this loss? We were the custodians, but we didn't do our job."

"You can't be held responsible . . ."

Obviously he was not listening, but continuing a dialogue with himself. "Carlos had this advantage. He could give something that had been denied his people, and the gift could make them a whole people. Not just the land, though that was essential, but the power to decide things for themselves, to be in control of their lives. That was his gift."

Miss Mason, quite lost, sat down, one hand holding her note pad in her lap, the other hand fingering the pink cameo. She knew Adam expected her to listen, whether or not she understood.

"If I could have returned, bringing this bundle with me, we could have talked together. They shot that young man, my nephew, because nobody tried to talk to them, not in their terms. I suppose somebody said something about the economy. The young man who fired the gun—I met him, he was a strong young man—believed that he was acting for his people. His people will certainly agree that he did the right thing and they will conclude he is being persecuted. I can't imagine what may come of that. My meeting with them was kind of hectic, stressful I guess is the word, and it gave no clue. They are a solemn people, and solemn people are likely to be unpredictable."

Miss Mason was able to unravel something of what he said. It seemed to her that he was searching for an answer, some way to appease some Indians whose existence she could not visualize. She was an excellent secretary and organizer of work schedules, but the museum and its collections remained a place of strange objects and stranger obsessions. That was why she could suggest what she did and feel no temerity.

"If you want to give them something, why not that little gold thing, that figurine? It certainly cost enough to make most people feel happy."

It was some seconds before Adam heard what she said. Meantime, he stared at her until in reflex action Miss Mason flipped open her note pad and scribbled in shorthand.

The outrageous suggestion shifted his thinking in an entirely new direction, but when he spoke his voice showed no strain: "That's all for now, Miss Mason. I'll call you if I need anything."

That "little gold thing" had been pursued by him for at least fifteen years, and the pursuit had involved him, or his agents, in some absurd encounters. On one occasion he had allowed himself to be taken muleback to a remote village in the Peruvian Andes, the last few miles blindfolded, to meet a notorious *bandido;* a little journey from which he returned with an empty wallet and nothing to show for his foolhardiness.

"Ah, yes. The little Virgin," the smiling highwayman had exclaimed. "Yes, we had her, even in this little village. But as you see, we are a poor people. We had to part with her. A man came and paid us well. He didn't say who he was or where he came from and we did not ask—only we knew before he came he was not from the *policia.*" The smile flashed again, showing white teeth under a black moustache. "We had the same word about you."

"Quite. And you advised me to come alone."

"Ah, yes, señor. We live by staying alive."

When for a second and third time the point was made about "my poor people, my starving little ones, as you see all around you," Adam emptied his wallet— purposely he had not carried a large amount—and climbed back on the mule. The faces he saw looked remarkably knife-scarred and menacing, but well fed.

"Well," Carlos had said when Adam was back in Cuno, "it will show up somewhere, sometime."

The "Virgin of the Andes," the little gold sculpture, had been a rumor, a tantalizing legend, word of which had passed among collectors for years.

In the first days of the Conquest, literally thousands of gold objects—plaques, breastplates, masks, intricate headdresses, molded figures, embossed and cast forms— had been melted down and shipped to Spain as bullion. But occasionally in later years, in some remote tomb or under the ruins of a demolished temple, great stores of a vanished art could still be recovered by plundering *vaqueros,* and the museums and private collectors of the world tripped over each other in their eagerness to grab what they could. The Peruvian law prohibiting the exportation of "national" treasures was rarely invoked— many collectors were not aware of its existence, and those that were would bribe if necessary, and count it as part of the cost of acquisition.

Adam was prepared to negotiate with the Peruvian museum officials for the release of the figurine, offering a suitable item from his own collection in exchange, but the occasion for negotiation never occurred. The object had been smuggled out of the country long before he began his search, although he did not discover that until he had spent some years following false leads. When he finally located the little Virgin he had only to make a leisurely boat trip to England and bid for her at Christie's. A collector does not count cost if he gets what he wants. He gave her a private showing restricted to his board of directors and their immediate families, and after that placed the figurine in a velvet-lined walnut case and locked her in a vault.

He liked to look at the figurine in daylight, when the golden surface came alive, and he would turn the object over and over in his hands, catching overtones in the diffused light coming from a high window. No characterizing style or technique gave a clue as to a possible place of origin. Speculation had it that the piece came originally from one of the population centers in the central highlands, and perhaps late in the pre-Inca period. It had been torn from its sociocultural setting, as a jewel might be pried loose from its mounting, and its only present value was as a piece of merchandise. The piece, about nine inches high, had been cast in a lost-wax mold, and its fairly thick walls gave it surprising weight.

The modeling of the nude figure was skillful, combining accurate proportioning with expressive detail. The adolescent body was clearly portrayed—breasts just swelling, hips just emerging, the vaginal cleft slightly mounded, childish plumpness forming into rounded curves—but above the torso was the face of a mature woman, staring calmly out of almond-shaped eyes.

That was the "little gold thing" Miss Mason suggested he substitute for the Little Elk medicine bundle.

It was an impossible equation. How could he, successful engineer, businessman, museum director, arrive at a rational decision when the factors were the intangibles of sentiment, personal choice, folkways verging on the irrational? What he was looking for, he told himself, was a scale of values by which he could act responsibly, and he found himself quite alone. Any number of scholars, museum collectors, and probably even pawn-shop brokers around the world could put a price on the Virgin of the Andes. He respected their avarice by keeping his possession in a vault and withholding it from public display. What he could not determine, and no one could help him here, was the value the Little Elk Indians would perceive in an object conceived in an alien mind and fashioned by hands they had never seen. But coming at the puzzle in another way, he arrived at a different kind of dilemma. It became a question of trying to determine what the Little Elk Indians had lost, and how they valued the loss. They had this notion that their water had been killed, but that, he felt, could be rationalized; they might even be brought to see it as a benefit. The medicine bundle was another matter, an area of human experience where he had never traveled.

Rafferty's remark, *so little left,* implied more than it stated. How far would they go, what price would they pay, to have this totem or fetish restored? More pointedly, how deeply would they grieve when they learned it would never be recovered? These were not the kinds of equations an engineer ordinarily computed.

This searching and questioning occurred at one level of awareness. At another level, but never remote in his consciousness, was the knowledge he had gained earlier from official documents telling how the Little Elk Indians had fared at the hands of their guardian, the federal government. The anger and sense of humiliation he experienced when he first read through the record came back in flashes at odd moments, as when shaving, or reflecting after a meal, or dictating his correspondence. "By damn!" he would call out, mid-course in a sentence, and Miss Mason would look up expectantly, but no explanation followed. Her impulse to puff on a cigarette came strong at such times.

He then came full circle, realizing that his original impulse to make amends by returning property he had no moral right to possess had come to nothing. He had entered into partnership with the government in taking what was not his, without compensating its proper owners. And now, as in the taking of the land, it was ex post facto. Sorry. My deep regrets. But nothing can be done.... "The nations of the world" could keep what they could hold. The pundit spoke, and the world accepted.

Somewhere at this point, as the bright green leaves of spring appeared, he returned to Rafferty's latest letter. The reply he now dictated was in part an apology for his long silence, "not a carelessness on my part," he assured, "but a reluctance to report a misfortune."

In the course of composing that letter he came to his decision. He would return to Little Elk, and he would carry with him the Virgin of the Andes, wrapped in black velvet, secure in a walnut case. His reply made no reference to the loss of the medicine bundle or to the little statue, since that would require more explanation than he cared to put in a letter. In his own mind, however, he saw clearly what he must do, and why.

27

The Boy brought the message to Bull's camp. He tied his horse to the little fir tree between the corral and the first of the tepees, where visitors always tied up. The ground around the tree smelled strongly of horses, and horse-flies kept the animals occupied.

The camp had been located at the same spot for some years, though it had occupied other sites at different times in the past. When the women complained of the distance they had to go for firewood, or when the refuse piles moved in on them, the camp would move, always upstream. When the present camp was set up, Two Sleeps built himself a log cabin. He brought from somewhere an old army cot and an iron stove and told everybody he would never move again. So the camp ceased its wanderings.

"They want to have a talk." The Boy drank coffee and smoked a cigarette before he delivered the message. He let the words hang in the air for a while, then added: "The thin man from the east came yesterday. He wanted to come up here himself, but the government man told me to come and ask what you want to do. He doesn't like to be hurried, that one."

Bull did not turn his head, just stared at the quiet fire. "Is that all?" The remark was a kind of politeness, not a question.

"Yes. There is another thing."

By then others had come to Bull's lodge to sit around the small fire in front. The spring air carried the warmth of the young sun and the fire was not needed, but it was good to have a fire. Louis of the bitter mouth still wore his lumberman's wool jacket of red-black plaid, as if the winter had not passed. Basil, the emaciated one, was also dressed for winter, wearing rubber overshoes over his moccasins and wrapping himself in a blanket.

Pock Face and Theobold had joined men from other camps to hunt up stray horses. Pock Face had been arrested by Sid Grant, as expected, then released when Rafferty agreed to have him in court for trial. During the late winter, horses that were not used regularly wandered off in search of the first spring grass, and sometimes the men spent more than a week gathering up the strays; if mares were in the group there would also be a colt or two, walking on stilts. Two Sleeps was also missing, but no one went to find him. He would come when he heard voices.

Bull asked, "What is this other thing?"

The Boy seemed to hesitate, perhaps not sure how his words would be taken. "It's like this. The thin man brought another man, a lawyer, he says. He wants Pock Face to come with you so this lawyer can talk to him." He used the English word, since his language had only the word for "talker" and that was not the same. The people had no lawyers so they did not need such a word. The Boy explained, "This lawyer will talk for Pock Face if he has to go to court."

Antoine, sitting near his grandfather, could feel the shift in the air. Bull pulled his back straight and really looked at The Boy. But before he could speak, Louis jumped ahead.

"Why do they want my boy? I don't like this thin man. Who is he? Is he going to make trouble?"

Bull put out his hand to stop the questions. "Let Son Child tell us more. Tell us if the government man agrees to this. Pock Face is not here, as you see."

"He said it is all right. The lawyer man talks nice. He will tell Pock Face what to do."

That was enough to stir Louis into more words. "They want my boy. That's why they ask him to go down there. They want to hang him." He stopped short, having said that. It was as if his own words might reach out and strike the boy.

He rose to his feet. He was not a strong man, but he

217

had a hard face. In his younger days he had been like his son, Pock Face, quick to anger and quick to act.

"He did it for us, my boy. He knew we were angry about the water, but we were old men and we did nothing. He shot that man to make us feel good. Now they want to hang him, and we sit here, old men. Me, I am going to find my son. I will take him to the mountains."

Even when they agreed, Bull was often annoyed by his brother. They had shared the same camp all through the years, and Louis was loyal, but he had a way of talking that caused Bull to stare at the ground. Rarely would he express what he thought, for he knew Louis's story and he did not care to push him down.

Now he spoke quietly. "Just sit with us until we talk this over. Maybe Son Child hasn't told us everything yet. Then if we decide that way, I will ride with you to find your boy. First I want to find out more about those men down there."

It turned out that The Boy had not told everything. "The thin man told me this. He has a gift for the Little Elk people. That's what he said. The government man was silent about that. I guess he wanted the other one to be the one to tell about it. But that's all he said."

No one was ready to speak, and Louis even sat down. Everyone looked at The Boy, as if they expected him to tell of other startling events. A message is never told all at once, especially if the listeners are talking and asking questions. He was sitting on his heels, and now he spread his hands out flat, indicating he had said it all.

Bull put his hand on Antoine's knee. "Grandson, go and see if the old one has finished his sleep. I want him to sit with us. Just tell him the coffee is hot and he will come."

Two Sleeps was already standing in the doorway of his cabin, waiting there until his eyes would accept the bright daylight. Every day some of his flesh seemed to leave him—his legs thinned, his arms shriveled, his cheeks were deeper hollows. The winter had been hard on him. When Antoine held out his hand, the old man paid no attention, just grasped his staff with both hands and stepped away from the doorway.

"You are a good boy, Grandson, but these legs will carry me where I have to go." His steps grew stronger as he walked.

Louis gibed: "Just watch this old man. He'll play a trick on you. We know him."

Bull ignored the remark and waited for Two Sleeps to lower himself to a spread-out blanket near the fire. "I was sleeping inside," the old man said, "when I heard Bitter Mouth singing like a bluebird. I decided I would have to see for myself."

He drank the coffee Antoine handed him.

Bull watched the old man carefully, without looking directly at him. Ever since he had spent the night in the mountains he would sit with others, as now, but his voice came from a distance. When the women brought an extra shawl for his shoulders, or a bowl of soup, he would not tease them, and his face was so wrinkled they could not tell whether he even smiled. The winter passed in that manner; nobody pressed him to speak, yet everybody waited.

Bull repeated the message brought from Little Elk Agency, mentioning the man from the East and the lawyer, and Pock Face. After he explained that it worried them to let Pock Face go down there, he gave the rest of the message.

"Son Child tells us the man from the East brought a gift. We can't understand why he would bring a gift. When a white man gives something, he expects to be paid. It is their way. You see many things, Grandfather. Maybe you can help us to see what this man has in his mind."

While they waited for him to speak, the old man surprised everyone by putting one hand over his eyes. Then they realized he was weeping, silently, like a child in grief.

Antoine, watching this, felt his own eyes turn to water, and daylight became a blur of many colors. He had never seen an old man cry, and the world shattered into many pieces as he watched. What was especially wounding was knowing that he could not reach out his hand, could not speak his sorrow.

The men sitting around the fire—Bull, Basil, Louis,

The Boy, and some of the women who had left their own fires, were profoundly silent. If Two Sleeps had dropped dead at their feet, they could not have been more astonished.

It passed. Two Sleeps removed his hand and brushed his eyes. "I know you have to do this," he pointed to Bull with his lips. "You have to go down there. Our brother asked you to take his place and put yourself and your people in the hands of these men from the outside. When we lived by ourselves in these mountains, our grandfathers before us and all the children born among us, our only troubles we made for ourselves. We didn't have to ask outside people to come and make trouble for us. The sun was ours, the mountains, the trees; we had water when we needed it. Now, when an outsider comes among us, we have to ask, What does he want? What will he do?"

He broke off there, and perhaps traveled backward in his thought. Next they heard him singing: "My friend, the storm, I am here with you! My brother, the storm wind, stay with me!"

The bodies bending forward to catch the words felt chilled, though the spring air stayed warm.

He said only one other thing: "I wanted to know everything, to be inside of everything—I thought. But my brothers, that is a terrible thing to want. My heart is already dead."

They could not understand him and waited for more words to come. When it became clear that he would not speak, they were troubled. Bull was now certain that the old one, as they called him, knew something, or had seen something, and did not want to talk about it. The question put to him had not been answered. Bull glanced skyward, looking for the black clouds that brought a storm. The air felt like that.

It was Louis who spoke his troubled thoughts and broke the spell for all of them.

"The outside is closing in on us and I am growing small. They took our land. Next it was our water. Now they want to take my boy. When will they take our women, this grandchild? Me, I am getting ready to run. The mountains can still hide us."

Bull spoke again, this time with some hardness in his voice, to quiet Louis. "This touches all of us, not just you and your boy. It is not our way for any one to decide when all are involved. If you take your boy away, that will only make it hard for the rest of us. It doesn't matter for myself, but I don't want that hard talker to come here again and tear up the camp, scaring the women, and bothering this old man. No. This is something we must talk over among ourselves. Our kinsmen are down by the big river gathering up the horses. We will join them down there and together we will decide what is best for all of us."

Louis knew this was the proper way, but he could not hold back the hard words. "If they take my boy, I will shoot somebody. Just remember I said it."

Bull gave him a sharp look, but said nothing to him.

"Son Child," he said, "go to the government man. Tell him we have to find our horses first. Then we will come, maybe in a day, maybe two. The man from the East waited all winter. He can wait some more."

Antoine, listening, bright-eyed, felt tightness in his belly when Louis seemed ready to speak further in anger. But the moment passed without a word, and the tightness went away.

Later at the corral, as they were saddling their horses, Louis came from his tepee carrying his rifle in the crook of his arm.

Bull paused in pulling on the cinch strap, but before he could say what was passing in his mind, Louis spoke up.

"The boys have been chasing horses. Maybe they are hungry. Maybe they will want fresh meat."

That was all he said, and again Bull held back, not wanting to prolong the quarrel. He finished his saddling.

28

The old people could remember when the Little Elk valley, like the sky above it, had been free and open—a country of low rolling hills, wooded stream courses, meandering wagon roads, and game trails leading to watering places. Then surveying parties came and drove wooden stakes in the ground. After that, strangers from across the mountains came. And after that, wire was stretched between posts and the open country was gone. Now the soft rolling hills and gentle swales were cut into squares, and the traveler could only go where roads or lanes allowed passage between fence lines.

The coming of the fences puzzled, then angered those who stayed with the old style. They rarely came down from the foothill country which, because it was rough and timbered and unfit for farming, had not attracted the fence-builders. When they did come down from the hills, as when they rode out to gather up stray livestock, they were reminded all over again that the country was no longer their own. The anger was not as sharp as it had been. Now it was more an annoyance to have to ride miles in one direction, then miles in another direction, following section lines, in order to arrive where they wanted to go.

When livestock strayed from home pastures, whether cattle or horses, they too followed the section lines, feeding as they traveled along, but they always headed westward, where the big river gathered up stream water coming down from the mountains and carried it off to the ocean a thousand miles away. The big river country was, like the mountains, rough country, cut up by tree-choked canyons and rim-rock ledges, unfit for farming, and therefore unfenced. Grazing animals had a sure instinct for this open range and the hidden meadows scattered among groves of jack pine, cottonwood, and willows.

The riders from Bull's camp knew approximately where they would find the horse hunters, and they caught up with them just at sundown. The strays had been driven into a narrow box canyon which was closed by tying ropes between trees. The men were planning to spend the night there before starting for home in the morning. Among them were the men who sang for Henry Jim and who rode together to talk for him at Little Elk Agency. All were related by blood or marriage. In previous times they had lined up against each other, some standing up for Henry Jim, some taking Bull's side. Now that the quarrel was covered over, they could sit at the same fire and everything seemed natural.

The men had killed fresh meat, as Bull knew they would have, but he did not ask Louis what he would now do with his rifle.

After they had eaten and sat at the low fire, Bull explained that the government man wanted to talk and the man from the East had sent word about a gift. No one knew what kind of a gift, or what it was for.

"It is a troublesome thing to know what to do. My elder brother had talks with the government man and he had a good feeling about him. He said he was not like those who came before and he would help us. No one says anything bad about this one. Just the same, he never told me he is going to help. All I know is he wants us to plant wheat, just what all the others before wanted. They say Henry Two-Bits is already plowing his ground. We never wanted that. Will I have to knock down my trees and put my little ponies in harness?

"That is not all. A talker [lawyer] is down there with the government man and the man from the East. Son Child told us they want us to bring Pock Face to the government place so they can talk to him. Louis is afraid of that. It may be a trap. They did not put Pock Face in jail, but they made out a paper and maybe the paper is no good any longer. Louis wants his boy to run to the mountains. I am troubled by that. If the boy runs now, they will go after him, maybe shoot him just for running.

That hard-faced man with a star would like to shoot his gun. I think it is best to talk, then decide what to do."

He did not ask the others to tell their thoughts, but the way was open for any who wished to speak. Even Louis held back, out of respect for his kinsmen.

Iron Child, the big man who had supported Bull against Henry Jim in the time of trouble, reminded them of the night when Henry Jim slept in his lodge and heard the voices come up from the grass. His rough voice was gentled by the remembrance. "Some of you were there that night. He told us the quarrel was healed, and we were glad to hear that. He said the new government man would help us. And after that we went to Little Elk and talked to the man. It is true he did not say he would help us, but he listened to all of us in a polite way. He didn't ask us to hurry up. It made me feel good.

"I agree with my kinsman. We should go there and find out. After that, if the boy wants to run, I will help him."

Then he turned to Pock Face, who sat back of the older men, away from the fire.

"But it is up to my young relative. I think he should tell us what he wants to do."

Pock Face was already a family man and entitled to speak among men, but he was still awkward at it. And because he felt young, he rose to his feet. "I think it is all right. I am not afraid. I stood in that room and I told them I shot the man at the dam. The government man did not get excited. Only the U.S. marshal [he used the English term] made a big noise. And when I said I killed that man because he killed our water, that man from the East, the thin one, was surprised, I guess, but he didn't get angry. There was another man there and a woman. I guess they were the father and mother of the man at the dam. The father had a stiff leg, he wasn't very large. He told the U.S. marshal not to write down what I said. He said a lawyer would speak for me. I guess this is the lawyer he talked about. I think it will be all right to go there."

Pock Face sat down, lost again in shadow.

Perhaps Louis knew that was the right way, but he could not say so. Too many dark places in his mind had

224

yet to be crossed, and that made him an angry man.

"My brothers, what we are saying here is foolish. We learned a long time ago that when we talk to the strangers from across the mountains, we lose something —our land, our water, sometimes a daughter. You know that a white man carried my little girl into the woods, and afterward he shot her. When we found her, some wild dogs were already there, tearing her apart. They didn't even look for that man. We looked, but I guess he left the country."

They knew the story, especially those in Bull's camp, where it had many tellings. In the first years after the happening, Louis lived with voices, some that called to him in the night, and some that rode with every storm, sending him with flying hair into driving rain or snow. "She was calling me. She called 'Father,' " he would say, when Bull or someone else in camp caught him and brought him back to a fire. Even after many years his voice shattered when he told the story, and those who listened waited until the wild look went from his eyes.

Now he continued.

"Son Child came to our camp and told us the man from the East brought a gift. I don't want his gift. Don't forget what our elder brother told us. He said the government man would find out what happened to our Feather Boy bundle and would help to get it back. I haven't heard a word about that. That is the only help I want. I don't want to plant wheat. I say we should send our grandson to the agency. They won't touch him. And he can find out what the government man wants to talk about. We can stay here in this rough country until we know what they want."

Antoine, sitting just back of Bull, felt heat go through his body. He looked to his grandfather.

Bull spoke gently. He was always careful with his words when he talked to Louis. "I cannot do that. When Henry Jim came to our camp that night, he said he would start the talk, but I would have to finish it for him. Maybe this will be the end. Maybe this will knock us down for good. But I have to do what my brother asked. The rest of you can stay if that is better for you, but I have to go, and my grandson will ride with me. He can sing a warrior song to keep me brave."

Louis was not pleased, but all he said was, "My gun will speak for all of us."

The remark went unnoticed, or rather it was brushed aside by Iron Child, who had a sudden prenotion.

"We know the dog-faced man sent our Feather Boy bundle away. It has been said he put it on the train going east. The government man told our elder brother he would find out where it went. My brothers, I think that has happened. The thin man from the East has our bundle, and our government man has pulled him back here and told him to give it back. That is the gift. Why else would the thin man be here? We are nothing to him. It must be that our government man found out about it, and now we will have our life again, the way it was."

When Iron Child stopped, perhaps amazed by his own words, Pock Face rose and came forward into the light. His words came fast: "I think it will be like that! The government man said Feather Boy had been sent to a big house with many rooms and he would ask the people in that big house to look. Maybe the thin man comes from that big house. Maybe he looked . . ."

Now it was Antoine who rose to speak among men. In his excitement he forgot to be shy. "Yes! I heard the government man say that. He would ask the people in that big house to look. He told that to my grandfather."

No one spoke again, not right away, but they looked at each other, or at their hands, or into the fire. In the silence they could hear the horses moving about in the dark, cropping grass, blowing through their nostrils. Dogs got up from their sleep, circled, and lay down again. Someone pushed a blackened log into the dying fire and sparks spiraled upward.

Before they slept they agreed what they would do. Bull would take his grandson, Jerome, Iron Child, Frank Charley, Pock Face, Theobold, Basil the eater, and Louis, who surprised the others by insisting on going.

Then they sang an old song, one it was said that Feather Boy sang for the people before he left them.

29

Ordinarily, Adam Pell was intolerant of delay. He would walk away from a business conference if the principals were late in arriving. It was not a materialistic interest in time, but a matter of courtesy, he would say, if anyone commented on his behavior. But of course his associates did not comment; they learned to keep appointments on schedule.

Thus it was quite out of character for him to accept calmly the word that the Little Elk leaders were going to look for some horses before coming in for a meeting. Instead of striding around the room, he stretched out his long legs in Rafferty's office and prepared to visit.

"They have a high regard for their horses," Rafferty explained. "Folks like Bull don't cut much hay and that means they can't feed their stock through the winter. But the stock out here is a pretty tough breed, not large animals, and they can take care of themselves in open range country. The Indians seem to prefer them sort of half wild."

After a moment, Rafferty continued. "I guess they feel that way about themselves. I didn't understand that at first. My job, of course, is to settle them down, but that's kind of ridiculous when you think about it. Some individuals will make that choice for themselves, and that's all right. I'm prepared to help Mr. Henry Two-Bits and others like him, if they come along. But if every one of our two thousand adults decided to go in for serious farming, why, hell, they'd be in a fix. There isn't enough good-quality land to go around. The homesteaders took most of it, at Uncle Sam's invitation, and left the Indians out in the woods. I guess they prefer that, but in fact they haven't any choice in the matter. They hunt and fish and run a few head of cattle, and manage to keep from starving. That saves the rest of us from embarrassment. All this I am just finding out, and it bothers the hell out of me."

Without realizing it, Rafferty was touching responsive chords in Adam Pell, who pulled in his legs and came to an upright position on the office couch.

"My God, man!" Adam finally exploded. "That clears the air! I wondered how I could talk about these matters with you. A guest owes a certain civility to his host, but I had to wonder if you were familiar with past government policy, and whether you approved of it. Last winter I began to read the record, the whole bloody documented history, And it mortified me to discover that I had been part of the fraud against these people. That dam in the mountains had its place in the pattern of exploitation promoted by government policy. You were not involved, since it was authorized before you came here, and I don't know how you look at it. I hope I am not embarrassing you?"

Rafferty's "Fire away!" was intended to convey agreement and appreciation of the tactful query.

"Anyhow, what I had seen as economic development, Bull and his people saw as disaster. It was a shocker, and more. I could not ignore the ugly fact that I was responsible for the death of my own nephew, a very dear boy. I believe you can understand that I am not being sentimental. Just troubled."

As they talked through that afternoon, the day after Adam arrived at Little Elk, the two men found a liking for each other. Rafferty had not associated with businessmen during his years as an East Side New York settlement-house worker. He knew downtown decision-makers only as donors—through their wives, of course—of used clothing and perhaps a Thanksgiving basket. The kind of people he associated with belonged to a different order of society, a sort of twilight, where pieces did not fit together and nothing came out as it should.

Now, watching Adam Pell, his long, bony hands gesturing, Rafferty had an unexpected sense of communication. He could talk to the man, and yet felt no pressure to make conversation. Words came at a natural pace, reaching always toward substance. And it was obvious that the troubled state he spoke of was genuinely felt. On his side, Rafferty felt an urging toward openness and respect.

Next day they traveled out over the reservation, with The Boy driving the agency car and Doc Edwards sharing the rear seat with Rafferty. They put Adam in front and enjoyed his frustration as he tried to maneuver The Boy into conversation, with The Boy answering, "Mebbe so," "It look that way," and other noncommitals.

Before they had been driving for very long, Adam began to get a clearer view of what he had read in the documents. When the road climbed to the crest of a low hill, Adam asked The Boy to stop, and when he got out the others followed. From the vantage point of the hilltop it was possible to see a large expanse of valley, all of it cut into squares and rectangles by fence lines. Only the irrigation canals had a way of their own and followed contour lines without regard for geometrical symmetry.

Adam gestured at the landscape. "I read about this, but I had to see it to understand it. The idea of the grid survey is peculiarly American and it comes late in our history. Earlier methods of measuring land surface in metes and bounds had a kind of affinity for the earth, going by surface features, stream meanders, and the like. Settlement of the Great Plains was responsible for the monstrous custom of applying straight lines and right angles to the earth—but I guess it was the only thing to do when you set up your transit and aimed it at an infinity of grass. It simply doesn't lend itself to a pleasant mountain valley like this one. Look at those fences! More than all the documents I read last winter about dividing up the common tribal land and giving each man, woman, and child a limited piece of his inheritance, this view is the most shattering. Let's get out of here, it makes me sick."

When they were back in the car returning to the agency, Adam told The Boy: "When we meet Mr. Bull tomorrow, or whenever, tell him I don't like what I saw today."

The Boy glanced sideways, trying to put together

the feelings he had about the thin man, whose long legs were jackknifed between the front seat and the cowl. "I tell him you gonna tear down fences." The quick smile implied the joke.

"I wish we could. I wish we could."

Doc Edwards was enjoying himself, hearing echoes of thoughts that often thundered in his own head. "The land had its own way of striking back," he said. "Most of the farms you see along these roads, with their unpainted houses, dead fruit trees, ramshackle barns, and ragged children, have changed hands at least twice, some of them three times. Farming out here has been a trap, a sure way to break your back and then find you were working for the bank all the time. The homesteads were too small, the returns too uncertain. The Indians were robbed, but the ones who came to rob took a beating in the pocketbook, the kind of hurt they could feel. The real loser was the country itself, the land. It had already changed when I arrived here twenty years or so ago, but before that, as I understand, when it was all open, the Indians ran cattle. There were no fences, and the families divided up the range according to their needs. The leaders of that time acted as judges, in case of disputes over a given piece of range land. No courts, no lawsuits, just a neighborly squabble, until the pieces got sorted out. Someday, somebody with enough money will come in here and buy out all these shirt-tail operators and turn it back into open grazing country, the way it was, except one man or one outfit will have it for himself and the Indians will still be out in the woods."

Edwards subsided into his corner of the rear seat, then bounced forward again. "What I started out to say was, the country was fat, the streams carried water out of the mountains, and the grass was waist-high, the old people say. The land was the loser, but of course the Indians were part of the land." He subsided again.

It was The Boy, finally, who turned their thoughts toward the subject matter that had been avoided until then. Rafferty had avoided it because he did not wish to importune, and Adam for reasons of his own. The Boy said: "The people say what brought the bad times was when they lost the medicine bundle, Feather Boy bundle. They say it would be all right again, they wouldn't care about the fenced-up land and the hard times if they had Feather Boy. That's what they talk about now." The statement seemed to hang in the air, inviting a response.

Adam's normally ruddy color paled slightly. His comment was just audible. "Yes, that was the question I asked myself. Now I understand."

No one quite followed his remark, and no one queried him. The drive was completed in silence, with questions waiting to be asked.

That evening Doc's wife, Nellie, a stocky woman, with a round smiling face and bright eyes, prepared dinner, helped by a silent Indian girl whose long black hair hung in a single thick braid down her back. The young lawyer, John Davis, joined them at dinner. Adam had recruited the young man in the law office of a Chicago business associate, with the assurance that he was a "crackerjack" in the courtroom. He was quiet, well-mannered, and obviously aware he was in unfamiliar territory. His eyes followed the Indian girl as she moved about the table.

After they had eaten and moved to the living room to smoke, Adam gave way to the tension that had been building up since the afternoon ride. The little walnut chest that he brought from the East was sitting on a small end-table near his chair, but he made no reference to it. Near the center of the room a larger table held a collection of magazines and a parlor lamp shaded by panels of stained glass. The panels threw a mixture of colors across the room, picking up the coils of smoke from Doc's pipe.

Adam was casual as he described the misfortune at the museum, how his staff tore the place apart, and what they finally discovered. He could not help interjecting: "A museum is not careless in its custodianship. We regard ourselves as trustees of the past. We have a corps of experts working full time repairing and refurbishing and monitoring things like heat and humidity. When something like this happens, it upsets us. So much for that. I don't mean to dwell on museum problems, only to suggest to you that this could have happened at any established museum, no matter what precautions were observed.

"Anyhow, gentlemen," his casual tone still held, "the object is gone, destroyed. There was nothing left to restore."

Rafferty could not believe what he was hearing. He stared at Adam, at first expecting him to explain away what had happened—perhaps a matter of error in identifying the object. But before the recital was ended, the small hope vanished. A chilled silence fell upon the room. He continued to look at Adam, but his attention shifted. He saw the same man—tall, angular, gray-eyed, with tufted eyebrows, emphatic in speech, a slight shoulder stoop—but he was not the man who rode into the countryside and spoke with feeling about fences and land losses. His senses were alive then; now he seemed remote, untouched. Professional, perhaps, was the word. Maybe it was his way of speaking, but somehow he had removed himself from communication.

Rafferty probed, still grasping for understanding. "Why didn't you tell us this in advance? I don't know what might have been done, but we could have prepared for it. What happens now won't be elegant. I suppose you thought about that?"

"Yes, a lot of thought," Adam answered, but he said it tentatively, as if he wondered whether he had really thought about it.

Then, more affirmatively, "You see, I was damned impressed by that young man, when he said we destroyed the water. It didn't make sense in any rational way, but then it was a question of whose rationality was under scrutiny. It made sense to those people, who had lived with that water a long time. When I reached that point, I began to consider what action, what strategy, might make it easier for them to accept what had happened. Obviously it was useless to talk about progress; that was just another question of whose rationality was being invoked. So that brought me to the medicine bundle. That seemed to be the answer: restore the medicine bundle and, in a way, restore something of the world they knew.

Maybe then it would be easier to accept the water thing. That was when I went to look for the bundle.

"Yes," he broke off. "I gave it a lot of thought."

He reached for the little walnut chest, turned it around in his hands. For a while he merely stared at it, as if it had become an unfamiliar object.

"I hope the answer is here." Again he was tentative. He looked up and found Rafferty's eyes, blue and remote, studying him.

With apparent assurance he took a small key from a waistcoat pocket and inserted it in the keyhole of the walnut chest. The lid came open, and from the black velvet lining he removed the gold statuette and placed it on the table of multicolored lights.

"It grows on you, just study it." Adam's voice was a disembodied sound hanging in the air, and no one acknowledged it.

Doc Edwards was the first to react, after a silence. "What is it? And what do you have in mind?" He left his chair and went to a table, picking up the statuette. "Christopher! Feel the weight of that thing!" He handed it to Rafferty. "Is that gold?"

The doctor often embarrassed his wife by asking rude questions.

"Pure gold. Cast in what is called a lost-wax mold. But the walls are thick and that gives it weight."

Rafferty rubbed a hand over the surface, studied the planes of light reflected from it, then passed it to the young attorney.

"I go along with the doc. What's the story?"

Adam was affirmative again. He had been sitting back in his chair, almost slumped. Now he roused himself up.

"It's a long story, and not important now. What you have there is a Peruvian piece, probably pre-Inca, possibly a thousand years old. I can say the art collectors of the world scrambled after it for a good many years. I was the fortunate one who ran it down and was successful in bidding for it. I would be embarrassed to tell you what I have been offered for it, once word got around that I had it. The insurance I carry on it is considerable."

He retrieved the piece from the young attorney, and for a moment he turned it in his hands, studied it by long habit.

"That is not the important consideration. The craftsman was an Indian. It is one of the relatively few larger pieces that the Spanish invaders failed to discover and melt down for bullion. But above all that, it tells something about the quality of the people who lived in this land long before white men blundered into it. This particular craftsman happened to be a village dweller in the Andes, but his was not an accidental talent. There were thousands like him in South America, in Guatemala, in Mexico. Had been for centuries. As a boy in Ohio I came across astonishing pieces of stone and shell carving, and what I found were fragments. The good intact pieces had already found their way into museums. I now own some of those pieces, as well as splendid California basketry, polychrome pottery from our Southwest, Eskimo ivory carvings. Add the great ceremonial dances one finds everywhere, the great chanting voices—"

He broke off there, conscious of the questioning faces around him.

"All right. You ask what I have in mind. The answer is simple. I want to give it to the Little Elk Indians, as a way of restoring something of what they lost through my carelessness—but also for my part in transforming their world into an alien land of fences and diverted water courses. I have to add that I prize this little piece above all the rare, even priceless, objects in my collection. And in that sense I suppose it might be comparable to the priceless thing they lost. Though I admit there is no scale of values to measure such things."

He placed the statuette on the table, where the colored lights molded it into new forms.

"But this is nonsense," Rafferty heard himself murmur, and having expressed himself he felt dismayed by his own rudeness. It shattered at once the easy, open relationship that had been growing between them. The words, though just audible, rumbled like thunder in the small room. Mrs. Edwards, who had just come from the kitchen and had seated herself away from the light, put her hands to her cheeks in disbelief.

Rafferty was thinking of that day in the late fall, the air smelling of decay, when he set out on the mission for Henry Jim, and confronted the Reverend Stephen Welles.

"Then these people have come to the end of the road. After what you tell us, it would be better if you told them nothing. That's what I mean when I say it is nonsense. This gift will not give back what they lost. It will only expose them to a terrible truth, destroy hope. Whatever nasty things we did to them in the past, this will be the most devastating. I am sorry."

Adam gave thought for only a moment. "But you see, that was my reason for coming here. I had offered to make an attorney available for that young man, but John would have come at my asking; it wasn't necessary that I accompany him. No, I have no choice but to tell them I am at fault. I would have no peace if I kept silent."

Doc Edwards searched for a compromise. "Wouldn't it ease your mind if you just offered this, this handsome little statue and said nothing about the bundle? As Mr. Rafferty mentioned, if they don't know, they can still hope."

Then his thoughts leaped ahead. "One thing bothers me a little. You see, these people are very modest about the body. I always find them reluctant, the men much as the women, when I try to uncover them for examination. I don't know what one of those men might do if I attempted a routine digital probe for prostate enlargement. I've never tried it. This lady, I notice, is very nude. That might give them a start."

Such comments were usually shushed by Mrs. Edwards, but in this situation she was too embarrassed to let her presence become known and so said nothing.

"I'm afraid that wouldn't do," Adam answered, still attentive to his conscience. "I have to admit my fault and try to make up for it by this gift."

He turned to Doc Edwards, not sure how seriously he was to be taken. "Are you saying they might be offended? The figure is really that of a child, you know. I intend to tell them about the Indians of the Andes, the great craftsmen, the great engineers and builders. I want them to realize they are of the same race, the same genius. Gold was fairly common in their country, and so they used it. If they had been northern Indians, they would have created form and design out of skins, feathers, quills, beads; and if the Little Elk Indians had been Andeans, no doubt they would have worked in gold. I hope they will understand the brotherhood."

Rafferty pursued his own brooding self-examination. He had been aware that day of Henry Jim's eyes under the hat brim, now hidden, now quietly watching. He had sensed that he was being weighed and tested and it amused him not to reveal his awareness. The request for help had been gently stated, and yet the note of urgency was unmistakable. His own response, as he remembered it, was prudent, not bravely affirmative, and for that he felt no elation. It was the rough intolerance of Stephen Welles that nettled him to decision, not the soft persuasion of Henry Jim. He might have made it up and come square with himself, if he could have been the means of restoring the sacred bundle. He could then think of the old man and his big bay horse in the rock-slide and know a kind of contentment. But that was over, finished, buried in museum dust and trash. His mind was so overwhelmed that he scarcely heard Adam Pell, and anger flushed his cheeks.

Adam realized at last that something had gone wrong and he turned to Rafferty, a look of concern pulling his thick eyebrows together. "Do you really think I should say nothing? You think it might make matters worse? But that's not my way! I must be honest!"

Rafferty cut in. "This is not a question of your preference, of what might save your feelings. It wasn't just a museum curio, a display piece you destroyed, and you can't make it up with a substitute. Your pretty piece belongs in a museum, since the people who produced it no longer have their lives tied up in it. They are gone. When you tell Bull what happened, he will be gone too. I say forget it. Give him the few more years he has to live."

John Davis, the young attorney, seemed to decide that he could be useful. His starched shirt and creased trousers contrasted with the country dress of everyone else in the room, even with Adam Pell's field boots and whipcord trousers.

"You need not say anything about those, ah, objects, you know. You asked me to look into that killing affair, and prepare the defense of the young man involved, if requested. For all they need know, that is the only reason you are here, to vouch for me, you might say. That should do it." His eager young face looked freshly washed.

Adam stared at the young man, as if he had just become aware of his presence. But he did not acknowledge the interjection.

Doc Edwards delivered the final blow. "These people already know that you killed the water. If you tell them that you also killed Feather Boy, that will do it. Of course, you'll be gone. They may burn your coattails, but you'll make it to the train all right. That will leave us here, to explain that the white man never does anything bad, except by mistake. Never otherwise, You get the picture?"

Adam knew, then, how grossly he had miscalculated, but he still expected to find a solution.

30

They rode three abreast: Bull in the center, the grandson on his left, and Iron Child, singing quietly, on his right. Next came Louis in the center, Basil on his left, and Pock Face on his right. And in another row, Jerome in the center, Theobold on his left, and Frank Charley on his right. The horses trotted easily, and two camp dogs full of morning freshness chased gophers until their tongues hung limp.

The sun rode alone in a cloudless sky.

For Antoine the solemnity of riding at his grandfather's side had not abated. Soon it would be a full year since the day they had walked together into the mountains, but it seemed much longer. The days pass slowly in a boy's mind, since so little is anticipated; ends are never seen in beginnings. But his mind still burned with the flaming image of his grandfather's face when he fired his gun at the wall of rock holding back the water. *What did you see today? What did you learn?* Like the images, those words were still there, reminding him of how a man should conduct himself.

They had started a journey that day in the mountains, and now, perhaps, they were coming to the end. Antoine felt a burning in his body, but it was a warmth, a quickened breath, reaching to him from his grandfather. The boy watched from under his eyelids and saw that the old man's lips had softened, at the point of smiling. A great thing would happen! They all felt it. Stories would be told into the night in days and years to come, and the people in camp would move about as if the world had been renewed and must not be bruised by careless acts or harsh words.

The men riding three in a row spoke little; occasionally a light remark broke into laughter. One would sing, then another, always softly, as if thoughts could not keep a song for long. The low rumble of hoofbeats on soft earth came up like a drum calling for dancers.

Bull was pleased that it would end this way. Though he looked straight ahead as they rode along, he was aware of his grandson and of Iron Child. He heard the voices behind him, the easy laughter, shreds of song, and these added to the good feeling. It had troubled him that his grandson would never know that his people had once been strong, had lived well, and had owned their own country. That time would not come back, the past never returned, but the people could be proud again. He thought about this many times, especially after that day in the canyon, when the dam made him a small man. He had seen pain in the boy's eyes that day. A boy had to have a good feeling about himself and about his people, or the fire would go out of his life. Bull rode easily, only vaguely aware of the horse moving under him. For the first time he was not worried about Two Sleeps, the old one, who would not talk about the dream he had had in the mountains. It was good to be lifted out of fear.

At a moment when all were silent and only the soft drumming of hoofbeats was heard, Louis began to sing, a far-off sound at first, then coming closer. It was always a surprise when he sang; the harsh voice that everyone knew became as gentle as a woman's, and as warm. Now he sang of the warm earth, of the sun standing above, of morning freshness, of evening shadow. The song was not in words so much as in the rising and falling sounds, like wind among pine trees. It contented the men to hear him sing; they knew he was not troubled.

When they were nearing Little Elk Agency, the men reined up. No one suggested the stop, the idea just seemed to come spontaneously. They put their horses in a small circle and leaned forward, resting on their saddle horns. The camp dogs running in advance trotted back and flopped on the ground, their eyes questioning and their tongues hanging out.

Bull was the first to speak. "I want to thank my brother for coming to my camp that night. I wanted to throw him out, but he just sat down and talked, as if he did that every day. I didn't want to believe him, as you know. He said the new government man would help us, but that was too much. How could one believe such a thing! But my brother did not give up. He just kept on talking. Then he said he would not last much longer, and that was when my quarrel ended. I agreed to speak for him. Today, I'm glad it went that way. I think he is riding with us, and he will be with us when we meet the government man and that other one. That's what I am thinking."

A murmur went through the circle. "Yes. That's how it is. He is still one of us, and we thank him."

Iron Child, his heavy face gentled by a smile, turned to Antoine. "Our grandson will remember this day. When we are gone and he is the leader of our people, he can tell his children that he put the sun back where it belongs and made the stars come out at night. The people will say, 'Hoh! We have a great leader! Hoh! We are a great people!' Our grandson will thank everybody and then he will go home and his wife will scold him for believing everything people tell him. You be careful, grandson. Pick a wife who doesn't talk too much."

It was good to be teased by a man like Iron Child. His powerful voice could always be heard above all others when people sat in council, but when he wanted to tease, his voice became a song full of laughter. Antoine ran his fingers through his horse's mane and tried to cover a smile under his big hat.

Louis made everybody sober again. "Our brother said the government man will help us. But I haven't seen any help yet. We know he talked some people into planting wheat. What kind of help is that? He asked us to bring my boy. Why would he ask that unless he wants to put him in jail? Is that some kind of help? Me, I don't know why we are doing this. Just remember, I asked you that."

Bull looked at Louis, and from him to the others. But instead of answering, he began to sing:

Hanay—haa-nay, hanay—haa-nay
Here I walk, here I walk,

On rolling clouds I walk.
Hanay—haa-nay, hanay—haa-nay,
Here I walk, here I walk,
In morning blue I walk.
Hanay—haa-nay, hanay—haa-nay,
Here I walk, here I walk,
In evening yellow I walk.
Hanay—haa-nay, hanay—haa-nay
Here I walk, here I walk,
To the end of the world I walk,
And I will walk this way again.
Hunuy—huu-nuy, hunuy—huu-nuy.

The others took up the refrain, softly, then in fuller voice.

It was the song Feather Boy had sung for them in the beginning.

They turned their horses around and rode out, in three rows, three abreast, still singing.

241

31

The old one stood in his cabin door just as the sky over
the eastern mountain opened to the light and the first
bird called. He stood there, leaning on his staff, listening
to the tumult of shrieking wind and wailing voices that
lay beyond the quiet of the morning. His eyes saw the
quiet, but his ears held the roaring of the storm.

Standing there in the open doorway, the old one
waited for strength. He knew what he was called upon to
do and now it was up to his legs to carry him there. He
could not wait long either, or the women would be
stirring around, and next thing they would be asking
questions.

As he stepped away from the doorway, balancing
on his long staff, an old female dog moved out of the
shadow and came to sniff at his hand. He touched the
dog's head and she whimpered softly. Then she followed
at his side, a black-and-white bundle of fur clinging to a
moving shadow. The old man and the dog went down
the trail where the trees still held the night.

His eyes were not blind to the trail, but all else was
obscured. He was enshrouded in a dream, in a womb of
days, from which outward sensation was closed off, and
he wandered alone in the immensity of self.

Something was there beyond his reach, yet he must
reach to come even. It had been that way during the
night of storm in the mountain—a reaching and a falling
back. A man could not live long enough to get beyond
his place of beginning. Moving within a dream, in a
womb of days, the sharp edges of denial were softened,
but the storm wind was still there and he was still denied.
He reached for understanding, but what he grasped was
his own howling emptiness. Yet he had a thing to do,

and he must hurry the doing or he would sleep again, and forever.

When the old one emerged from tree shadow, morning light lay upon a long meadow, and by now his legs were stronger and he began a kind of shuffling trot. The black-and-white dog whimpered again, holding back, then caught up and stayed at his heels.

He was well down the trail when Veronica went to his cabin to call him to eat. She went back to her fire, thinking that he was somewhere in camp or nearby. He often took little walks into the woods when, as he said, "the screaming women make my ears ache." After a while, when he still did not appear, she went to Catherine's lodge and together they made the rounds of the camp. No one had seen the old man. Even Marie Louise, who often was cross with him, showed alarm.

"He's so old, poor thing; maybe he fell in the woods and broke something."

All the women scoured the woods then, only to return without seeing anything. Soon it was full daylight and Veronica, following the trail out of camp, came upon the tracks of man and dog, and at the same time Marie Louise discovered that her black-and-white dog, her Two Spot, was missing. She broke out in her usual way of speaking, "That old man stole my dog!" The others frowned and turned away, and Marie Louise softened again. "Still, she is a good watchdog, that one. She will take care of the old man."

At first they all wanted to go after Two Sleeps, but Veronica was cautious. "You know that old man. He has a hard head. If he sees the women all coming after him, he won't budge and we'll all be screaming and scolding and he'll just make faces at us. I will go alone and speak like a sister. But first I will saddle a horse because he may be tired when I catch up."

She meant to take two horses, but when they went to the corral only Marie Louise's pink-eyed horse was there with its nose buried in some old hay. The other horses were scattered in a larger pasture, and kept a distance between themselves and the women with their ropes.

So Veronica rode out alone, in full skirts, a red kerchief knotted around her head, and the pink-eyed horse flattened its ears back and tried walking sideways, until she smacked it with a quirt.

The old man had already traveled several miles when Veronica caught up with him, and then he would not stop to talk. She would stop the horse and ask a question, but he would go on walking, and she would have to catch up again. Finally, she dismounted and walked alongside, leading her horse by the bridle.

Then, of course, he would not say where he was going and what he was going to do. "Would I be out here if I wasn't going someplace?" Or he would say, "A bird called me and I have to find that bird."

His unbound white hair bristled in the morning sun and his eyes were but slits in the wrinkled brown skin. He seemed so frail, and yet he walked steadily, with quick, short steps. Veronica was sure he was tiring, but she did not suggest it.

She had an idea all along of what was in his mind, and finally she brought it out. "You want to be with Bull and the others, but you don't even know where to look. You might wander like this for a week—who will feed you? The nights are still cold, where will you sleep?"

He stopped then, as if the questions startled him. And for what seemed a long time he stared at Veronica, his hands clinging to his staff.

She persisted. "You should have some warm food, some coffee. Back in camp we can talk about it. Maybe the grandson will bring us a message and tell us what to do. I brought the horse for you to ride, if you want to."

He turned from her, moving his feet until he was pointing down the trail again.

"My son went away before I could tell him what I saw in the storm. He is down there some place and he doesn't know the danger. I have to find him. Help me, sister. You are the only one who can give me strength."

"What is the danger, old one? Maybe I can carry the word, after I take you back to camp and fix some food."

She knew then she could not turn him back and would have to stay with him.

244

"All right. Then you have to ride the horse. He has crazy ideas sometimes, this horse, and he might take it into his head to turn around and go home. So I will lead him for you."

As she expected, he insisted that his legs would carry him, and he refused to mount the horse. So they walked and exchanged reproachful remarks for some time. After a while she noticed that he really was tiring and began to stumble. She did a simple thing, then. She picked him up in her arms—he was no heavier than a young child—and sat him in the saddle.

He should have said something insulting, which was what she expected, but instead his face became more wrinkled and Veronica made out that he was smiling.

"Why didn't you think of that sooner," he complained. "Now my legs can rest."

So they set out, Veronica leading the pink-eyed horse and carrying the staff, Two Sleeps riding the horse and looking like a bundle of old rags, and the black-and-white dog staying at Veronica's heels.

They came out of the woods covering the flank of the mountain into a different world, where fences contained the road and an irrigation ditch made a green path across a field of brown stubble. The sun was now at his high point and, away from the trees, the heat came up from the ground and made the air heavy.

At last they reached the low sandhills that stood away from Little Elk Agency. At the top of the rise they looked down at the white buildings placed among greening trees. They saw men standing near one of the buildings, not quite in a circle, but close together.

Veronica, watching the men, saw a small puff of white smoke, like breath in frosty air, followed by a second puff. Then, in quick succession, the flat sound of two gunshots.

She turned to the old man on the horse, her eyes flashing alarm. And she missed the third puff of white smoke that hung in the air some seconds before the splat of gunfire was heard.

The old one's dimming sight evidently did not catch the smoke puffs, or his mind was already overwhelmed by a different calamity. His voice was remote, coming from a dream.

"We are too late, sister. My kinsmen are already talking to the government man. Soon they will know the truth. Feather Boy is dead. I saw it on the mountain, in the storm, but I did not tell my son. I did not want him to feel bad. Now I fear the days of anger will come back, as when he rode wild horses and we waited to see who would be hurt. Something bad will happen and the fault is mine. Yes, that was a mistake, Sister. He will hear it from a stranger. And he will know what I knew. This is where we end. All our days are here together at last.

"Sister, let us go down there. We can sing the death song together."

So they came down from the sandhill—a woman wearing a red kerchief around her head; an old bundle of rags looking like a man on a horse; a little black-and-white dog trotting at the woman's heels.

32

Rafferty was standing at his office window when he saw the men come riding up, their high-domed hats rising and falling, a faint dust cloud moving along with them. He had been expecting them, but now he realized he was not ready for them. He turned away from the window, as if to postpone the encounter that was to come.

He had been at Little Elk four years now, and just at the point of becoming useful to the people, or what he thought would be useful. They had dropped some of their first suspicion. They no longer avoided him or his office, and sometimes they joked with him. He had learned something of the rhythm of their speech, the flow of their gestures, the ease of manner between individuals. In The Boy, he had found a man who could be loyal without betraying himself or his people, a man who handled himself with style. In Bull, a man who could hold a world together.

But for all his four years, nothing would remain. The thought had not left him since Adam Pell had pulled the sky down on all of them.

They ate breakfast together at Mrs. Edward's table, but it could not be said they shared the meal. The doctor, in his irrepressible style, tried to make conversation, but Rafferty was not attentive, while Adam and the young lawyer discussed the legal hazards of representing a reluctant client. Local courts were likely to be unfriendly toward an outside attorney, John Davis observed, and he wanted assurance from somewhere that he would have cooperation. Adam understood the problem, but at the moment it seemed of secondary importance.

Mrs. Edwards, looking round and jolly and crisply starched, pressed bacon and eggs on everybody, but only managed to pour more coffee. She chided that it was not a good way to start the day.

When Mrs. Edwards left the room for fresh coffee, Rafferty confronted Adam bluntly: "I could ask you to leave, but I won't. But I will ask you to respect my concern. I want no mention of the medicine bundle. That's out. If Bull or his people ask about it, put them off. If you want to offer the gift you brought, go ahead. You did send word you have a gift. It won't change their minds about the water, but you can give it a try. On the other matter, I have to insist. If you tell what happened to that sacred object, you will break that man's heart. I won't have it. Understood?"

Adam did not protest. Indeed, he seemed depressed. "My bags are packed. I can leave anytime, preferably before they come."

Rafferty looked at him, waiting for heat to go out of his voice. "Bull is coming here because we asked him to come. He probably has his horses by now and he'll expect to meet you. You owe him that courtesy."

Nothing more was said and Rafferty left for his office. And then the men arrived in a thin dust cloud and were tying their horses at the hitching rack just outside the gate.

Looking from his window, Rafferty saw the agency car in front of the office. The Boy had brought the car around to drive Adam Pell to the railroad station, but now he left the car and walked toward the men at the gate.

Rafferty turned from the window to Doc Edwards, who had followed him from breakfast.

"What do you think? Was I too rough on our long-legged friend?"

"He's a determined man, accustomed to calling the shots. You may have set him straight, but I wouldn't bank on it. He gave in too easily."

Rafferty puzzled. "I don't know how to take him. I thought I understood him yesterday, when he talked about fences and exploitation of Indian land. But something happened after that."

Edwards nodded encouragingly.

"At first it was all very agreeable, as we rode in the country. He seemed to be aware of what had happened out here, and he was concerned. Now I don't know how much he understood, or whether he really cared. It was kind of a good-will tour for him.

"I guess I'm still annoyed with him for letting us down. Why didn't he tell us sooner what had happened and give us a chance to prepare these people for the bad news! Now we have to make excuses for something we didn't do and try to save his neck by sticking out ours."

Rafferty was aware as he talked that time was running out and he would have to face Bull and the eloquent men in the tall hats—and perhaps that was why he talked.

"Because of his place in the world, his success, he assumed that he could restore a lost world by a simple substitution of symbols. Hell, that's what an Indian superintendent is supposed to do, to supply substitute symbols. I know it can't be done, and I'm just a bureaucrat!"

He looked at Edwards then, a long reflective look. "I took the people seriously, as you suggested a long time ago. And the response was as you suggested it would be. I became something less than a stranger to them, I think. But that's as far as it will go. When this is over and those men go home empty-handed, the chance we had to become part of their community will be gone, and probably will never come again."

He broke off, then added, "Our talks have been one of the good things to come out of these years. I hope you know that."

The expression of sentiment was swept away by his brusque, "Well, let's get out of here. This room will be too crowded for all of us. I'll have some benches set up outside. I've noticed that those old fellows feel more at home outside. When they come to my office, they become very formal, make long speeches."

So that was how it came about.

By the time Rafferty and Doc Edwards reached the narrow porch that ran across the front of the office building, Bull and his kinsmen, led by The Boy, had reached the agency car. Also at the car were Adam Pell and the young attorney, John Davis. Adam had just put his bags in the back seat and would have withdrawn, except that The Boy began at once to introduce him to

Bull and the others. Adam stood tall and thin in the group and moved gravely, shaking hands with each one. To each he said, "It is a pleasure." His pale hair seemed especially pale in the nooning sun.

After he finished shaking hands, Adam turned back to Bull. "It was suggested when I was here before that a good lawyer be asked to defend your young man in court. I have brought such a lawyer, Mr. Davis."

Bull's massive face remained fixed, and only his sharp eyes seemed to heed the speaker. Adam checked himself and turned to The Boy. "I forgot, of course. Please tell him Mr. Davis is here to help, if they wish it."

By then Rafferty had joined the group and the hand-shaking was repeated. As he went among them, with The Boy at his side, Rafferty sensed an air of expectancy in the men; it was in their eyes, in the warmth of their voices. It surprised him.

To Iron Child he said: "I am glad you came to talk. You gave a strong talk for Henry Jim that day. I remember it very well."

Iron Child smiled his appreciation. "We talked for our elder brother that day. It was what he wanted. Just now we were saying it would be good if he could be with us today." Rafferty wondered what Iron Child meant, but he did not ask.

He moved on. He told Louis: "The young lawyer will help your son, if you wish it. I think it will go all right. The lawyer will protect his rights."

Louis was wearing a blanket over one shoulder, with his right hand holding it together at the waist. To shake hands he had to let go of the blanket, and Rafferty thought he saw a flash of metal. He did not look closer.

Then he was standing next to Bull. "I hope you found your horses, and I appreciate your coming here today. They are fixing some food for us at the school, but it isn't ready yet. So we can talk until they call us to eat."

Bull told The Boy: "This man is polite, as everybody says. But he still has to learn something. An Indian always eats before he talks. But tell him it is all right this time since the food has to cook."

The other men recognized it as a joking remark and

they laughed softly. It pleased them that Bull was being polite. They wanted this meeting to go well.

The laughter surprised Bull, however, and he asked The Boy sharply: "What are we going to talk about? Why did he send for us?"

By that time a bench had been placed in the thin shade of a young tree and Rafferty invited Bull to join him on the bench. The others sat on the ground in a circle in front of the bench, their faces obscured under their domed hats. Only Louis did not sit with the others. "I'll just stay in the shade," he said, and stood with his back against the tree, slightly behind the two sitting on the bench. He still wore the blanket slung over his left shoulder.

Rafferty proceeded cautiously. "When we met here last fall, Sid Grant wanted to put your young man in jail. But we got the district judge to release Pock Face in my custody. Do you understand? That means I'm responsible for getting him to court when his trial is held. The trial will come pretty soon, now, and I want everybody to understand how it will be. We don't want any hard feelings when the boy has to come in for the trial. If you have questions, now is the time to bring them out."

When The Boy interpreted Rafferty's words, a kind of busy silence followed. The men shifted their sitting, they looked at each other. Louis took a step way from the tree, then stepped back. It was not the kind of talk they had been expecting, but no one seemed ready to say so.

Rafferty saw the uncertainty, and added, "Mr. Pell asked the young lawyer to come here to answer questions and explain things."

Louis told The Boy, "I don't like this talk about my boy. Why doesn't the thin man say something? That's what we came to hear."

Bull seemed to ignore Louis. He said, "Tell the government man we came here today because our elder brother told us we would get help from him. But the only one who has offered help is that thin one. He wants to give us something. We are waiting to hear what the government man will do."

The Boy added what Bull did not say: "They want to

know what Mr. Pell brought. They think maybe it has something to do with the medicine bundle. They don't like to bring it up, in case it isn't true."

Rafferty had had many occasions to appreciate the skill with which his police officer-interpreter played the role of the friend at court, representing his people without overreaching them, but managing to get full consideration for their expectations. And this was such an occasion. Rafferty knew he could not divert the discussion.

He turned to Adam Pell who, with Doc Edwards and the young attorney, was standing off to one side, not part of the meeting circle.

"I think the time has come for you to explain how you feel about the water," he told Adam, "and about the gift, if you like. I wouldn't go beyond that, if I were you."

Perhaps the tone was more peremptory than was intended, or possibly Adam Pell had never entirely acquiesced in the demand made of him. He was not usually in the position of taking orders from other men, and in this matter his veracity was at issue. In any case, the reasons were ample for his decision.

Adam took several steps forward, until he was just at the seated circle. He addressed himself to Bull, only this time he remembered to talk directly to the interpreter, and The Boy rose from his squatting position to stand at his side.

"When I sent the message the other day, I told you I had a gift for your people. And it is true I have it here. But I am bound to tell you that it is not the gift I intended for you. Mr. Rafferty asked me not to tell you this, because of the hurt it would cause you. But I feel bound to tell the whole story. Otherwise you will never know what happened, or you may learn part of the story and then you will think of me as the man who lied to you."

Rafferty half-raised a hand, signaling his alarm. But Adam was hurrying on and would not be stopped.

Adam could not have known how his words would affect the listening men, but even if he had known, or had suspected, it might not have mattered, so great was his concentration on what was expected of him, what he expected of himself.

"I must tell you that your medicine bundle, your

Feather Boy, came to me. That is, it came to my museum. The missionary here, Reverend Welles, obtained it in some fashion. That much you knew—only you didn't know what he did with it. Well, he gave it to us, in return for a small contribution to his mission. That was some years ago. He assured us that he was in proper possession of the bundle, and we did not question his word. We have dozens of such objects, from different tribes in different parts of the country. Usually a museum will display only one or two examples of a class of objects, and put the others in storage. Feather Boy was put in storage, in a bin, along with others of the same class."

Here The Boy interrupted, anticipating what he knew the men would ask. "We don't know why you are telling all this. Did you bring Feather Boy with you? That is what they want to know."

Adam followed his own impulse. "I am coming to that. Last fall when I came here in connection with the death of my nephew, I learned for the first time that you wanted this bundle returned because you had never agreed to give it away, and it was precious to you. I also learned that you had a bad feeling about the way your water was diverted. Your young man said the water was killed. And I was the man responsible for that."

By the time this was interpreted, Bull was standing up and all the seated men were on their feet. They looked at Adam with growing astonishment. Louis had come away from the tree and joined the others. No one spoke yet, but questions were in their eyes. Antoine moved closer to Bull, his eyes bright with excitement.

Rafferty saw the fatal error of encouraging Adam to speak. But he knew he could not stop him. He left the circle of men and joined Doc Edwards off to one side. Their glances crossed but they said nothing.

At about this time the old man, Two Sleeps, and Veronica reached the crest of the low sandhill and looked down.

"I have to tell you that I admire you people, the great Indian race. Ever since my boyhood I have tried to learn about you, your great leaders, your skilled craftsmen—"

The men began to murmur among themselves. Louis

said: "This man is hiding something. Why doesn't he tell us what we want to know?" Even Iron Child began to shift his feet in a nervous way. "I think we made a mistake about this man. There is no gift." The Boy did not translate what the men were saying, but Adam should have detected their growing impatience. They were no longer waiting to hear him speak.

Finally, Bull stepped in to settle things. "Son Child," he said, "this man is talking for himself. He wants to show he is a great man, a great friend of my people. He can save his talk for other white men; it is wasted here. Tell him, if he brought Feather Boy, we will thank him. If he does not have the medicine bundle, then he should stop talking and go away."

Before The Boy could translate, Bull added, "the government man has gone to stand with the cranky one. I think they know something is wrong and they don't want to get mixed up in it. Now, make this man talk."

Rafferty did not have to understand Bull's words to sense their angry import. And he saw Doc Edwards looking worried, his mouth tight and his brow puckered.

The Boy told Adam: "You better tell these men what they want to know. They think you are hiding something. Tell them if you brought Feather Boy."

Adam looked across to Rafferty, then took the plunge. "I was coming to that. No, I don't have the medicine bundle. There was an accident at the museum. It was destroyed. The medicine bundle is gone."

Before he translated, The Boy asked: "This is the truth? You destroyed it? Threw it away?" His voice rose sharply, in confused disbelief.

Adam tried to explain. "No. No. I didn't destroy it. There was an accident—"

The Boy ignored the explanation and began to tell the men what they wanted to hear.

Rafferty felt obliged to speak in Adam's behalf, even as he recognized that the damage was done and could not be repaired.

He said: "This thing happened before Mr. Pell knew about it. He feels very bad and you should not put the blame on him. Nobody wanted this to happen—"

The Boy did not even try to translate, since no one was listening. Astonishment was quickly giving way to anger, and strong voices were speaking out.

Iron Child seemed on the point of weeping. "I don't understand," he lamented. "We felt so good when we rode up just now. We were coming here for Henry Jim. All the bad days would be gone. But it was a trick. They always trick us."

The usually placid Basil was agitated. "Our brother told us the new man would help us. But now we find he is just like the others. My kinsmen, this is the end for us."

Adam appealed to The Boy. "I don't know what they are saying, but they sound unhappy. Tell them I brought a gift to take the place of their medicine bundle. Tell them—"

At that point all talking stopped. Louis had dropped the blanket from his shoulders and they saw that he held a rifle. He stood slightly apart from the others.

"I told all of you my gun would speak for me and I think the time has come. It is no good talking to these men. This is all they understand." He patted the butt of the rifle.

Bull was several strides away, but in a single leap he reached Louis and seized the rifle.

"Brother! I have waited for this—don't take it away!" As he spoke, he worked the lever of the repeating rifle, throwing a cartridge into the chamber.

Antoine saw his grandfather's face in the same instant, and recognized the look of wild despair. He knew that the thing he had imagined would finally happen. Black blood would spill on the ground. His grandfather would feel strong again, and the boy was proud for him.

Bull's voice came in great gasps, half strangled by the air he sucked into his lungs. "Just see, Grandson! He is no monster! He is a man like the rest of us! He can die like the rest of us! Now let them walk over our heads! We won't have to care anymore!"

Bull's words were never translated. With the rifle held hip high, he shot Adam Pell through the chest and saw him fall backward. The startled look in Adam's eyes dulled quickly.

Rafferty could not believe it was happening. Even as Bull turned the gun on Adam, he had thought it to be no more than a quick flare of anger.

After the shot, Rafferty leaped forward and at the same time called to The Boy, "Stop him! Grab the gun!"

Bull saw the movement. He swung the gun as Rafferty lunged forward, and fired, hitting him high in the forehead, just below the receding hairline.

By then The Boy had pulled his service revolver from its holster, after fumbling with the snap closure. He shouted, "Brother! I have to do this!"

Bull turned, knowing it was to come, and received The Boy's bullet point-blank to the heart. He had not tried to lift the rifle.

Now the old one, riding the pink-eyed horse led by Veronica, the little black-and-white dog at her heels, was coming down the near sandhill. He had already started the death song, and the wind bore it along, as from an enemy sky.

That day, the cry of the plover was heard everywhere . . . Ke-ree, ke-ree, ke-ree. No meadowlarks sang, and the world fell apart.

Afterword

Louis Owens

In *Wind from an Enemy Sky*, Toby Rafferty, the reform-minded agent to the Little Elk Indians, muses upon the systematic failure of Indian-white relations: "The problem is communication," he thinks. "The answer, obviously, is that we do not speak to each other—and language is only part of it. Perhaps it is intention, purpose, the map of the mind we follow." D'Arcy McNickle spent a lifetime exploring this "map of the mind." In the end, as *Wind from an Enemy Sky* amply suggests, for D'Arcy McNickle the two maps of the mind—Indian and white—simply do not correspond. The roads divide, compass orientations fail, signs point toward different destinies. For McNickle, an adopted member of the Flathead Tribe (officially the Confederated Salish-Kutenai) in Montana, himself of Metis or mixed-blood Cree ancestry who could pass as white and lived in both worlds, the implications of Toby Rafferty's words are enormous.

D'Arcy McNickle died on October 15, 1977. *Wind from an Enemy Sky* was published the following year as part of Harper & Row's Native American Publishing Program, more than three decades after the author began work on this third and final novel. During those years, McNickle had come to be a respected novelist and anthropologist, a founder of the National Congress of American Indians, and an active participant in the formation of Indian policy in the U.S. From the young creative writing student at the University of Montana who gave no indication of his Indian ancestry, McNickle had become one of the most prominent Native American spokesmen in America. For his adult life, D'Arcy McNickle lived in the white world as a representative of American Indians; within McNickle himself, as his fiction suggests, two maps of the mind struggled.

In a letter to Douglas H. Latimer, an editor at Harper & Row, McNickle explained something of his motivation in *Wind from an Enemy Sky:* "I guess the most general thing I can say is that I wanted to write about the Indian experience as objectively as possible; not just the usual story of the wronged Indian, but the greater tragedy of two cultures trying to accommodate each other." And, in the same letter, McNickle went on to explain, "I would like the reader to see the Little Elk episode not as an isolated tragedy, about which one need not get too concerned, but as a critical statement about the quality of human behavior when people of different cultures meet."[1] About the doomed but well-intentioned agent, Rafferty, McNickle declared:

> Most critics of government policy in Indian affairs seem unaware of their own involvement in support of the very morality which informs that policy; and this is part of the argument of the book. The incidents in the chapter [chapter 23 of manuscript] describe what actually happened on the Flathead reservation in western Montana.[2]

Wind from an Enemy Sky picks up themes introduced in McNickle's first novel, *The Surrounded*, in 1936. In that work, set on the Flathead Reservation in western Montana, we follow McNickle's half-blood protagonist, Archilde, on a rapid and seemingly inexorable arc toward misunderstanding and tragedy. Within Archilde two realities contend. Meditating upon Archilde's future, a Catholic priest in *The Surrounded* tells Archilde's father: "It was inevitable that a new age would come. It is beginning now. And your boy is standing where the road divides. He belongs to a new time."[3] Where the road divides in *The Surrounded* is at the point of contact between Indian and white worlds. Apparently there can be no merger of paths; the maps point in different directions and a choice must be made. Archilde opts ultimately for the Indian road and tragic consequences.

Whereas McNickle set his second novel, *Runner in the Sun* (1954), in pre-Columbian times and veiled his political message of self-determination for Indian people within a simple-seeming quest fable, in *Wind from an Enemy Sky* the author once again writes of a people very much like the Salish (Flathead) people he knows best. And again, McNickle gives us a dark picture of mistrust, misunderstanding, and death.

In the opening pages of the novel, the schism between Indian and white worlds is emphasized as Bull, Chief of the Little Elk people, looks down from his mountain retreat to "the open valley far below, a white man's world. A world he sometimes passed through but never visited." Bull, a man "who 'lives inside,'" has kept his people apart from the whites, isolated in the mountain camp, while his older brother, Henry Jim, has chosen the white man's way and a farm in the valley. The brothers and the Little Elk people have been split for thirty years (approximately the number of years McNickle devoted to this novel), neither communicating nor understanding one another.

McNickle develops the theme of misunderstanding in *Wind from an Enemy Sky* in the barrier of silence between Indian brothers, in the miscommunication between Indian and white, and in the seeming impossibility of dialogue between all men.

Early in this novel, we learn that Antoine, Bull's young grandson, has, much as had Archilde in *The Surrounded*, recently returned home from Oregon where he has attended the government Indian school. Soon after the novel begins, Bull takes Antoine to see a dam the government has constructed in a meadow sacred to the Little Elk Indians, a "place of power." When Bull realizes that the whites have indeed "killed the water," he shoots at the dam: "He raised the gun waist-high and fired into the concrete dam. Once. Twice. Nothing moved. . . . Not even a flash of a splinter. If the lead-nose bullet smacked against the structure, no one heard it. The sound of whining machinery and the thunder of water even smothered the bark of the gun. " In Bull's gesture, McNickle symbolizes the futility of Indian resistance to the white world of machinery and power, and foreshadows the novel's disastrous conclusion when Bull will once again fire into the impenetrable wall of white machinery. In the end, however, the machinery will be represented by two men, Adam Pell and Rafferty, the Indian agent.

While *The Surrounded* draws heavily upon McNickle's own experiences on the Flathead Reservation and reflects very directly the history of Flathead-white relations, in *Wind from an Enemy Sky* the author draws upon his knowledge of the Salish people to create a fictional tribe in a fictionalized setting. It is likely, however, that in the central story of the lost Feather Boy bundle, McNickle has in mind in this novel the experiences of the Hidatsa, or Gros Ventre Tribe of North Dakota. In 1938, about the time McNickle began planning what would finally become *Wind*, members of the Water Buster Clan of Gros Ventre journeyed to Washington, D.C. and New York to reclaim their clan's prized Sacred Bundle of the Water Busters. In exchange for the sacred bundle, the tribe presented the Museum of the American Indian with a Sacred Buffalo Medicine Horn, also invaluable and centuries old. With the return of the Water Busters' Sacred Bundle, the threat of drought was removed from tribal lands. As a government representative, McNickle participated in the 1937–38 negotiations for the return of the medicine bundle.

The Sacred Bundle of the Water Busters Clan, thought to have contained two skulls of Thunderbird deities who had come to earth many generations before, had fallen into neglect during the late nineteenth century when pressures from missionaries and the federal government were brought to bear upon Indian religious practices. Finally, the medicine bundle was sold to a Presbyterian minister who in turn sold it to New York City's Museum of the American Indian.

Inspired by the return of the medicine bundle, McNickle initially wrote a novel entitled "The Flight of Featherboy," which was submitted to a publisher in 1944 and promptly rejected. McNickle was to spend the next three decades returning fitfully to this manuscript, revising it until it would finally become *Wind from an Enemy Sky*. In turning the Hidatsa into the Salish-like Little Elk band, fictionalizing both tribe and place, and in changing the story as he did, McNickle ultimately made this a universal story of Indian-white relations rather than an isolated event in the very troubled history of Indian relations with the white power structure.

In spite of the greater objectivity achieved by means of a fictionalized tribe and place, and in spite of a more polished and sophisticated style in this third novel, McNickle's theme in *Wind from an Enemy Sky* is precisely what it was in *The Surrounded*: the difficulty, verging on impossibility, of communication, and the tragic consequences this entails. And, as in *The Surrounded*, while communication is particularly difficult between worlds—Indian and white—it is a problem common to all characters. Not only do the Indian brothers Bull and Henry Jim refuse to talk to one another for thirty years, even Featherboy, the incarnation of powerful Thunderbird, cannot talk to the Indian people he has come to help, because they fear him: "The only one he could talk to was his own mother, which wasn't the way Thunderbird planned it, and it almost spoiled everything." Bull admits early in the novel, "I never learned how to talk to the white man," a statement he will echo many times, later confessing, "I didn't know how a white man talked, because I never went to listen." When he is forced to talk to the agent, Rafferty, Bull says, "When I talk to a white man, what does it matter what I say?" Louis, Bull's brother, declares even more bitterly, "We learned a long time ago that when we talk to the strangers from across the mountains, we lose something. . . ."

Henry Jim has alienated his people not only by turning to the white man's road, but even more so by attempting to turn his people from the old ways by giving away Featherboy, the most powerful of the tribe's medicine bundles. The government has built a fine house and farm for Henry Jim but in the end Henry Jim rejects the white world whose "prize" Indian he has been. Henry Jim's final rejection of the white world is underscored by the fact that before he dies he has forgotten the English language he adopted. In the beginning, we are told, Henry Jim had tried "to discover what the white men were saying, and what they meant beyond the words they used," and he remembers that "The words were a marvel of obscurity, but in the days of telling they seemed important."

"How to translate from one man's life to another's," McNickle writes, "—that is difficult. It is more difficult than translating a man's name into another man's language." In the character of The Boy, the tribal policeman, McNickle illustrates this point. The Boy's Indian name is Sun Child, a name signifying respect and power, but as he is translated from one world to another, this man of great tact, understanding, and courage is diminished, "loses something" as Louis would put it, and becomes The Boy, an implement manipulated by the machinery of the white government.

Language not only defies translation in this novel, it also defines character. Antoine, approaching the Indian agency with trepidation, thinks of the government people he has known: "They had loud voices," he remembers. The terrified Eskimo girl Antoine recalls at the government boarding school had become mute in the face of the white world: "Antoine never heard her speak a word." The Indians initially approve of Rafferty because he doesn't insist on "talking at once" when someone comes to see him, and The Boy praises Rafferty by saying, "I guess he's all right. He talks good."

To talk good in this novel is to listen and to understand. As Henry Jim prepares to tell Rafferty the history of the medicine bundle, Henry Jim thinks, "Today talks in yesterday's voice." Henry Jim adds, "It was so important this time—so much depended upon a good understanding." In drawing nearer to the Indians, Rafferty is learning to hear "yesterday's voice," admitting to himself, "Maybe I wasn't listening before." Later, as he is gaining the confidence of the Little Elk people, Rafferty thinks nonetheless that "there seemed to be still a larger aspect, and this he did not yet understand. It had to do with their way of talking."

Adam Pell, the man who has designed the dam, is also director of the Americana Institute to which Feather Boy was given. And in Adam—a name suggestive of the mythic American Adam so prominent in American literature and so deadly to Indian culture—McNickle presents his most stark example of the consequences of misunderstanding. As the name of the "Americana" Institute implies, Adam, like many whites who would purport to "help" Native Americans, has "made a hobby of Indians." Adam has even gone to Peru to help descendants of the Incas (among history's greatest engineers) build their own hydroelectric project. Although Adam's sister says, "He may even be planning to talk to those Indians—he's always talking to Indians," it is apparent that while Adam may talk to Indians he has never learned to listen to them. Adam makes the fatal mistake of generalizing about Indians, perhaps the most common error in the history of Indian-white relations.

Bull's nephew, Pock Face, shoots Adam Pell's nephew who happens to be working on the offending dam. A young, angry Indian, Pock Face is caught between two worlds. He wears cowboy boots and can "talk about horses like a white man." He listens to what the elders of the tribe say, but he fails to understand the voice of the past. Pock Face tells his sidekick Theobold that he has been to the dam before but he didn't understand the significance of the place: "Somebody said the old-timers used to go there all the time. But I didn't know why that was."

Adam's nephew dies because of a lack of understanding on both Indian and white sides, and when Adam learns why his nephew has been shot, he recognizes his own culpability: "The enormity of his mis-apprehension swept over his mind and silenced him." The shock awakens Adam to a new understanding of the Indians. He realizes that "They worked with different data and a different order of reality," and he thinks, "They shot that young man, my nephew, because nobody tried to talk to them in their terms." But Adam's understanding is short-lived and insufficient, and Adam, good man that he is, brings about the final tragedy through the enormity of his mis-apprehension of the Indian world. Earlier, Bull had predicted this end: "Maybe he is a good man . . . and yet he will destroy us."

The enormous gulf between cultures in this novel is underscored by the "dog-faced man," the minister who has taken the Feather Boy bundle and given it to the museum where it has been destroyed through indifference and neglect. Summing up his view of the barrier between Indian and white worlds, the "dog-faced man" tells Rafferty:

> The Indian people start from origins about which we speculate but know next to nothing. We do know they are a people unlike us—in attitude, in outlook, and in destination, unless we change that destination. . . . Regardless of what we white men have attempted, the Indian has always remained beyond our reach. . . . He's always slipping away into the distance.

Ironically, it is communication that fails repeatedly and inevitably in D'Arcy McNickle's novels, and it is communication that McNickle devoted his life to realizing. No one—Indian or white—has contributed more to understanding between the two worlds than McNickle with his novels and such nonfiction works as *They Came Here First*, *Indians and Other Americans*, and *Native American Tribalism*.

Wind from an Enemy Sky ends with the line, "No meadowlarks sang, and the world fell apart." Published posthumously, these are D'Arcy McNickle's last words. For this great figure in American Indian literature and politics, the world he had spent his lifetime trying to make whole—the Indian-white world of America and the mixed-blood world within himself—fell finally and, it seems, inexorably apart.

Notes

1. D'Arcy McNickle, letter to Douglas H. Latimer, 6 July 1976, D'Arcy McNickle Papers, Newberry Library, Chicago.
2. D'Arcy McNickle letter to Douglas H. Latimer, 23 March 1977, D'Arcy McNickle Papers, Newberry Library, Chicago.
3. *The Surrounded* (1936; rpt. Albuquerque: University of New Mexico Press, 1978), p. 108.